RENTED GRAVE

RENTED GRAVE

AN INSPECTOR LOK NOVEL

CHARLES PHILIPP MARTIN

For Catherine

Praise for Rented Grave

"An atmospheric crime story savvily blending the sleek modernity of Hong Kong with China's tumultuous past."—*Kirkus Reviews*

"Charles Philipp Martin places you in the psychological heart of Hong Kong and China with this lean and masterfully written account of how past crimes and filial piety shape the lives of his characters. I was transported to a ruthless world where truth is manipulated and you can't trust anyone, a place where revealing secrets is dangerous. This book pulls you in and won't let go."—Carl Vonderau, award-winning author of *Murderabilia* and *Saving Myles*

"Rented Grave is a beautifully-crafted, relentlessly-paced crime story studded with edge-of-your-seat thrills. Never for a moment does it stop bubbling with tension and danger."— Ron McMillan, author of *Yin Yang Tattoo* and *Bangkok Cowboy*

"An as-authentic-as-you're-likely-to-get insider's view of Hong Kong police work…Martin pulls the reader through a twisty international thriller that ultimately satisfies while leaving us ready for the next installment. Exactly what you want in a thriller."— Bobby Mathews, Anthony-nominated author of *Magic City Blues, Living the Gimmick*, and *Negative Tilt*

"The criminal back alleys of Charles Philipp Martin's Hong Kong simmer with sumptuous corruption."— Gerald Elias, author of the Daniel Jacobus mysteries

"In noir, nothing goes according to plan. In Charles Philipp Martin's *Rented Grave*, we have a crime, done in a different culture, against an alien political backdrop. Everything is different to Western eyes, from corruption to police procedure, women, and justice. It is told in a crisp, vivid and relentless style that keeps the story moving forward and the mindset and values of a foreign city and its people at the fingertips, yet out of reach. Martin delivers noir in the darkest of shades."—Gabriel Valjan, Agatha, Anthony, and Shamus-nominated author of the Shane Cleary series

Author's Note

All of the Western first names given to Chinese characters in this book are true names, having been borrowed from real Hong Kong people.

There are approximately eight Hong Kong dollars to one U.S. Dollar.

A few Cantonese terms:
Gweilo—Westerner (literally "ghost guy")
Gweipoh—Western woman (literally "ghost woman")
Lan jai—Crook
Sin-sahng—Mister
Tai-tai—Mrs.

Cast of Characters

- Detective Inspector Herman Lok
- Ears (Detective Constable)
- Million Man (Detective Constable)
- Old Ko (Detective Constable Ko Man-man)
- Big Pang (Detective Constable)
- Airport (WPC Carrion Kwok)
- K.K. Kwan, Assistant District Commander
- Chief Superintendent Koon, District Commander, Shatin District
- Dora, Lok's wife
- Lai-ping, Lok's friend

- Horace Yang, accountant at Great Fortune Property Management
- Winnie Chan, Horace's wife
- Doby Yang, their son
- Kenny Yang, their son

- Mo Tun, entrepreneur
- Ivan Mo, Mo Tun's son
- Sylvie Mo, physician and Ivan's wife
- Bonitus Mo, their son
- Eunice Kwan, physician and Sylvie's friend

- Dollar Ten, jade seller
- Soddy Leung, chickenmonger

Undesirable Characters

"All men must die, but death can vary in its significance."
—Chairman Mao Zedong
Time: 2003, six years after the handover.

Chapter One

Yau Ma Tei District, Hong Kong, Friday, 7:31 p.m.

I t was not supposed to be like this.

Again the words come back to Horace Yang, persistent as the cat he kicks in the alley by his home, that wretched bag of fur that returns nightly to beg for what Horace doesn't have.

The words come back, like the blotch on his toe, a mustard-colored rot that vanishes with a touch of rice vinegar, only to bloom again when it dries.

He banishes the words from his mind, but they return.

It was not supposed to be like this.

They return when he awakens in his flat, which seems to shrink by the year, and again when he takes the day's work orders and prepares for the day's disappointments.

It was not supposed to be like this. It was supposed to be different.

The words remain after other words are forgotten. They remain after he answers a question from his son, a boy without guile and without future. At night they keep him company in bed while he counts the ways that life has thwarted him. And now they return in full voice as he clutches a knife bought in haste to kill a man.

There should have been time to plan, time to choose the weapon and the place, perhaps even a minute to tell Mo what he thought of him first. That would have felt good, might have eased the stress. That was how it was supposed to be.

But for Horace, things are never as they're supposed to be.

It should be dark, but darkness, like silence, is alien to Mongkok. A faint glow washes in from lamps on Temple Street. Filthy and forgotten windows at the back of the restaurant shed their anemic light on crates full of rotting *choi sum*.

Horace approaches the dormant limousine, adding a few inches to his stride to speed things up.

Given more time, he could have taken control and not had to sneak around. Why is it that people like him, who have the best minds and the keenest ambition, are the ones who can never get control?

One last look around. Except for Horace, the alley is empty. No one is passing on Temple Street behind him or on Woosung Street at the far end. If it's to happen, it must happen now.

Horace grabs the handle and throws the door wide open to reveal a small figure in the glint of the dome light.

"Who…?" The man stares up in confusion.

He drives the knife into the man's chest. They both gasp.

Up to this moment, Horace has thought only of himself: his own need for cover, for speed, for getting the thing done and getting away. And, of course, his resentment at how things have turned out.

Now, the deed done, he pauses to look at the man.

The wrong man. Not Mo Tun.

A stranger lies on the seat, eyes rigid in horror and pain. And then Horace sees what he hasn't allowed himself to see till now.

Next to the dead man, another pair of eyes.

* * *

Doby is waiting at the curb. Horace wrenches open the van door and shoves a young boy through, then scrambles in behind him. The boy, maybe ten or eleven, is wearing a blue sweater over a white shirt and gray flannel trousers. He clutches a blue nylon backpack.

"Let me go!" the boy shouts, bucking against Horace's grip.

"Drive!" says Horace.

Doby stares at the boy, whose spectacles have been knocked askew by Horace's shove.

"Who's that?" says Doby.

"Don't ask questions. Just drive!" Doby starts the engine and gets rolling.

The plan, such as it is, entails easing into the Kowloon night rush, drawing as little attention as possible to the nondescript commercial van.

The boy leaps up from the seat and grips Doby's shoulder.

"Stop here. I'm getting out!"

Startled, Doby slams on the brakes. A pedestrian glances at their van.

"Ignore the boy!" shouts Horace. Then, in a softer voice: "Just drive. But be careful."

This is bad. A passenger did not figure in the escape plan. And why are the brakes so damn loud? The van turns a corner, and for a moment Horace relishes the feel of being on the move, away from where it happened. The feeling lasts nine seconds, at which time his cell phone chirps. He views the caller ID.

Not now! Any other time, but not now! He presses the green button but says nothing. Maybe if he doesn't speak, the person will go away.

"Great Fortune Property Management?" A man's voice.

Horace holds his breath, then sighs. "Yes."

The boy interrupts. "Stop now!" he cries, kicking the back of Doby's seat for emphasis. Doby jerks his head around.

"Watch the road," snaps Horace, covering the phone's mouthpiece. He grabs the boy by the collar and replaces the phone to his ear.

"We've got a leak," says the caller. "Cheong Lok building, ninth-floor men's room. It's coming from under one of the sinks, and it's pretty much all over the floor now."

"I see."

The boy shouts again. "I want to go home!" Horace recoils from the noise.

"Can you send someone tonight?" the caller says. "Honestly, I don't like the looks of this."

Horace closes his eyes and tries to think, but opens them again to keep an eye on the boy and Doby. "I'll do what I can. Your name?"

"Eddie Leung, facilities manager. Use this number." The call ends.

"You can't do this!" screams the boy, standing up. "I don't know you! Let me out of this stupid truck now! It smells like cuttlefish!"

The boy thrashes till he frees himself. He kicks the front seat again. Doby brings his seat forward with a squeak and a lurch.

"What are you doing?" says Horace.

"Giving him more room."

"Never mind that." To the boy: "And you, stop kicking."

"Where are we going?" asks Doby, eyes on the road as instructed.

"Just drive!" Horace presses a speed dial number, dimly aware of the sound of his own grinding teeth in the earpiece.

"Ming Hang," answers a woman.

"Horace Yang, Great Fortune. Can you spare a plumber? We've got an emergency at the Cheong Lok building. Water leak."

"Now? No way. All my guys are working overtime."

The boy interrupts. "Where are you taking me?"

Horace shushes the boy again, then speaks to the woman on the line.

"I just need one guy to take a look," Horace says, "maybe do a temporary fix..."

"I'm not authorized to release anyone, sorry. We're flat out. You know about the big disco project in Tsim Sha Tsui?"

Horace cuts off the phone and dials a second number, noticing as he does so a red smear on his hand, another on his jacket cuff, a crimson sunburst on his shoe. The plan was to wipe off in the alley before getting into the van, but the boy made that impossible. He fumbles through his pocket for tissues, but they're missing. He manages to locate a pack just as his call goes through.

"*Wai?*"

"Stanley. It's Horace."

"Who?"

"Horace Yang. I'm managing Cheong Lok." He pulls out a tissue and wipes the worst of the blood off his hand.

"And?"

"I need a plumber—we have a bathroom leak. Ming Hang says they can't release anyone."

"No surprise," Stanley says. "They're all on the Great Wall Disco job."

"Can't one of them take off for a night?" He dangles the bloody tissue from two fingers. Where to dump it?

"They've got to get the interior walls in by Ching Ming. I don't think so."

Horace tries to concoct an argument that will persuade Stanley but his attention scatters as the van lurches to a halt.

"Why are we stopping?" Horace asks Doby.

"There's a policeman in the road."

"What?" Stanley's voice quacks in the earpiece. "Did you say something?"

"Uh, no. Hold on…" Squinting out the window, nose to the glass, he can just make out the figure of a police constable standing at the junction of Austin Road and Temple Street.

"What's that cop doing?" Horace says. Slowly he palms the bloody tissue and slips it into his jacket pocket.

"I don't know," says Doby.

"Hello?" says Stanley.

"Please, one minute," Horace says into the phone, barely aware that he's speaking. The van creeps to the intersection. No blockade, no torches, no radios. A traffic constable is directing cars past an open sewer.

I was this close to a policeman…

Horace shakes his head, clears his throat, and speaks into the phone. "Sorry, just a traffic problem. What should I do?"

"Well, you could call the contractor; maybe he could spare one. I doubt it, though."

Horace sighs again. "Give me the number." He wipes his finger on his jacket—it'll have to be thrown in the harbor anyway—and dials the hastily memorized number. Five minutes later it's taken care of. As Stanley predicted, the contractor can't spare anyone, but he's recommended another man who can handle a leak, albeit at overtime rates. Another memorized number, another abrupt exchange of words, and things are as they were.

"You'd better let me go," says the boy, straightening his glasses. "My *yeh yeh* will be looking for me."

"Who?" says Horace, his mind juggling plumbers and work orders, not grandfathers.

"Mo Tun. He's an important man. He's my *yeh yeh* and my father's boss."

Horace looks at the boy as if for the first time, takes in the short hair, the smooth, delicate face, the skinny frame, the navy blue acrylic pullover with a patch over the left breast designating the child as a student at Saint Peter's Secondary School, whatever that may be.

He senses a shift in the earth, an earth whose precarious tilt has until tonight kept Horace struggling for a foothold. Now at last, the horizon appears to be leveling.

A new plan forms in his brain. Riskier than the original, but with a much bigger jackpot. *Can I do this?*

He turns to Doby.

"Keep driving, but stay off Nathan Road," he says.

"Is Shanghai Street all right?"

"How do I know? Just stay off Nathan Road and Waterloo Road. Use the smaller streets."

"Where are we going?"

"I don't know yet."

"I'll have to cross Waterloo Road in a minute."

"Whatever. Just don't go along it. Understand?

"Understand" was perhaps the wrong word, but Doby would obey.

Chapter Two

Kowloon District, Hong Kong, Friday, 7:33 p.m.

"You might enjoy this, Herman."

Whether or not he might, Herman Lok lets Dora lead the dinner conversation. Usually, meals take the form of a briefing, with Dora holding forth on the children's accomplishments, the day's news, and proposed weekend plans.

"Daisy Cheu was complaining to me about her water bill," she says. "It's doubled these last few months."

"Doubled? Must be a mistake."

"They checked, no mistake."

Lok takes a mouthful of the simple weekday fare, a chicken and mushroom stir fry with *gai lan*. Only Lok, Dora, and Kitty are at the table. Kitty, now twelve, is uninterested in conversation. She stuffs her cheeks with the succulent food.

"A leak somewhere?"

"Nothing like that. They couldn't figure it out."

Lok is smiling already. She's preening, strutting, drawing out another of her deductive triumphs. "But you did?"

"I asked her how many boxes her *amah* took back to the Philippines at Christmas."

"So?"

"She said about fifteen or twenty."

8

"Pretty typical. Clothes and other Hong Kong stuff for relatives, I imagine." He's seen airline personnel cringe at the sight of a Filipino worker with a ticket home and a cavalcade of friends bearing boxes.

"And used clothing she's collected to resell there. It all needs to be washed, right? The *amah* was using Daisy and Rocky's washing machine, and of course, their water too."

Lok says nothing, but he's still smiling. *I had to learn to be a detective*, he mused once to a colleague. *She's a natural.*

Dinner done, Lok prepares once again to go out. These days, Dora doesn't ask where he's off to. She's memorized the "long hours" lecture and understands that his investigations take him many places, day and night. Public servants must be available when the public is, he's told her. She assumes he's working.

But Lok has never lied. If, some night, Dora decides to ask where he's going, he'll have to tell her.

He could postpone his shower till Dora leaves, but she'd notice the wet washcloth, the few extra points of humidity in the bathroom, the dried droplet on the mirror. That's how Dora is: without even looking for anything, she sees, deduces, concludes. Even when there's no suspicion in her heart, as in his case, she'll still notice that things are being hidden from her. Should suspicions arise, Lok could never erase them. Better not to risk it. Nothing remarkable about a shower anyway.

No question of cologne—Dora would smell it even tomorrow. But after he dries himself and dresses, Lok does manage a surreptitious check of his hair, thankful that mirrors don't keep notes on those who use them.

"Won't be too late," he says. He passes by Dora, who is checking over Kitty's homework at the dining table, and reaches for the door handle.

"Busy these days?" she asks.

"Yes." It's not a lie, except by intention. Anyway, it comes and goes too quickly to pull at his conscience. So slight, meaningless, and dull as to be indistinguishable from the truth.

* * *

Kowloon district, Hong Kong, Friday, 8:03 p.m.

Lok ascends a flight of stairs and walks through a colorless corridor to a gated apartment door. He grasps the tiny knocker and taps it three times against a steel gate, as if striking a gavel to adjourn the day and call the evening to order. Through the door float sounds having nothing to do with police work: maracas, congas, trumpets in tight formation, and over it all a singer pleading something in a language Lok knows not a word of.

The door opens, revealing through the bars a pair of dark eyes and a smile, which dispels the last of his misgivings. The woman utters his Chinese name softly, opens the gate, and lets him in.

Lok peels off his jacket. Somewhere he hears the soft keening of a kettle.

"I'm making tea," Lai-ping says, shutting the gate with a resonant clang. "Would you like some now, or after?"

"After," he says, tossing his jacket on the back of a chair.

Chapter Three

Yau Ma Tei District, Friday, 8:13 p.m.

Lento tops up Mo's beer glass in a gesture of deference. Mo Tun taps two fingers on the table in acknowledgment. Few words pass between them, not because they are poor conversationalists—though they are—but because Mo Tun stops into this particular restaurant to think in relative solitude, and Lento Chan knows it. Eventually Mo will have business to discuss, but until then, Lento keeps silent.

Mo Tun chose the restaurant—a dozen Formica-topped tables and a fish tank—precisely because it's not the kind of place one would look for a man like him. He can hide in plain sight, sip a beer, and catch up with his own thoughts.

Mo Tun is a businessman. He's sometimes called other things—high flier, criminal, whatever—but those names make less and less sense to Mo as the years go by. He's hammered away for the last six months on a business plan for the disco: working on contacts, forging alliances, gathering partners and choosing investors, and managing a workforce that expects to be paid. He's had to put together growth forecasts, consult architects and designers, listen to fire and health inspectors, sign contracts with building managers, and hash out advertising and media plans. All the while, he's been minding his reputation, keeping on top of the market, and staying ahead of the competition.

Call it crime or whatever you want. To Mo it's business. And he is a businessman.

Mo finally breaks the silence. "Where are we on the payment?"

"The escrow documents are ready. You'll have to go in for some signatures, and it's done. The work's proceeding, but they'll need cash in escrow by Monday to go to the next phase."

"That fire exit thing…"

"I can take care of it."

"No. Just cut a damn door in the rear."

"You lose some real estate that way. What did the guy say, two tables? That's…"

"Yeah, yeah, sixteen thousand a night. But even if you could fix the inspection…"

"Make it back in a month…"

"I'm thinking of worst-case. We have a fire, someone dies, they shut me down. Let's just cut the fucking door in the fucking wall and be done."

Lento nods. He writes down nothing and forgets nothing.

When Mo has drained his glass he stands, a prompt for Lento to throw cash on the table. It's a courtesy—no one would present a bill to Mo Tun for something as trifling as a Tsing Tao. They walk out the rear into the alley.

"Drop you somewhere?" says Mo. There's a lot of face in being dropped off by your boss in his limo, and Mo does it rarely. But Lento has been a great help at the disco.

"Just to the gym, if that's okay."

Lento opens the door of the Mercedes and stumbles backwards as if kicked in the stomach.

"Shit! What…?"

Goldfish Head Lau is sprawled on the seat, a kitchen knife lodged in his chest. Mo scans the alley, east to west. He bends down to check the man's carotid pulse.

"*Mut lun yeh?*" says Lento. What the fuck?

Mo stares inside the car, not at the body but at the vacant space by his driver's head. He inhales to calm himself, as his hand moves reflexively to his side to retrieve a weapon that's of no use.

"They've taken Bonitus," he says.

"What'll we do?"

"Call the police. But don't mention my grandson. I'll handle that."

Chapter Four

Wan Chai District, Hong Kong, 8:21 p.m.

"Get in there."

"No."

A shove from Horace sends the boy stumbling into the storage room. Ignoring the child's malevolent gaze, Horace takes a fast inventory: no tools, no ladders, no windows, nothing he could use to escape or make enough noise to be rescued. He removes a can of paint thinner and a coil of insulated electrical wire, just to be safe. He tests the lock and verifies that it can't be opened from the inside.

Doby looks on from the corridor. His instructions are to follow twenty paces behind and block the boy's escape if he should break free. But so far the boy has cooperated, apart from an occasional squirm.

The ride had been tense. While Doby drove, Horace sat deep in thought, sorting through his possible moves like a chess player, winnowing his choices down to one: kill the boy then and there. But where to dump him? Shorn of options, he sweated, fidgeted, and kneaded his fingers, waiting for inspiration to descend upon him. Descend it did, though, when his fingers nervously ran down his thigh and over the key chain in his pocket.

Shun Lok. Of course. As an account manager, Horace carried keys to some of the properties in his charge at Great Fortune. Not the great towers with 24-hour security, but a few smaller buildings that didn't employ a regular watchman. A couple of these buildings were closed and empty.

They'd taken the boy to the basement of the Shun Lok building, a stale gray pile in Wan Chai whose sixteen stories were once a source of pride and income for its owners. Trading companies and airlines installed their flagship offices at Shun Lok in the 1970s. By the nineties, those concerns had fled to the gleaming towers of Central and Tsim Sha Tsui. As Hong Kong office rents rose from exorbitant to astronomical to insane, the owners decided to obliterate Shun Lok and build a tower twice as high. Money is a religion with temples and ritual, but no relics.

Once the majority of tenants' leases expired, it was just a matter of bribing the laggards to empty the place. Now Shun Lok awaits the wrecking ball. Only Hong Kong's shortage of demolition crews has kept it from joining the city's rubble and dust. Annihilation is still a couple of weeks away. That will be time enough.

"We'll bring you food," Horace says. "Behave, and you can go home."

"I need the toilet," the boy says.

Horace points to a wastebasket. "There's your toilet." He's about to shut the door when a jingle wafts from the boy's pocket. Horace walks to him and extracts the cell phone. Then he shuts the door, locks it, and ushers Doby to the elevator.

"Take me home, and then bring him a rice box," says Horace. "Do you need money?"

Doby shakes his head. He's proud of the cash his driving job earns him.

"Good. Be careful. Don't talk to him, whatever you do. Just feed him and leave." Horace opens the back of the boy's cell phone and sets the battery free.

Chapter Five

Yau Ma Tei District, Hong Kong, Friday, 9:18 p.m.

Crime scenes have begun to look alike to Detective Inspector Herman Lok. Not that he would ever confuse one murder with another—his memory is too good for that—but arriving at the scene has begun to take on the feel of a day at the office. The sights and sounds repeat like symphonic themes: two or three constables standing within bantering distance of one another, scrutinizing the onlookers; the onlookers themselves, who gawk and murmur from behind the blue tape barriers; a herd of police vans streaking the pavement in red and blue light; friends of the victim, looking sometimes bereft but always bewildered; and at the center of the scene, the nucleus of stillness that is a death.

Lok and Lai-ping had only been at it a quarter-hour when Lok's cell phone chirped from inside his jacket. He'd caught it on the third ring and mumbled a couple of words, turning his back to Lai-ping, as if shielding her from the violence in his world.

When he said he had to go, she smiled in understanding, without a hint of protest or even disappointment. Homicide cases are curious that way. You just don't compete with death.

"Tomorrow night?" she had said, smiling faintly. A nod, and he was gone.

Clipboard in hand, Lok leads the team to the car. The victim is short, weedy, horseshoe bald with the beginnings of a wattle under his chin. On his neck is a pea-sized mole, no doubt pronounced lucky by a fortune teller.

The little man is sprawled on the beige rear seat, arms splayed in a grim parody of relaxation, legs a jumble on the floor. Just about perpendicular to his chest is the wooden handle of a knife.

Million Man is the first to speak. "Check out the leather in those seats. And the entertainment package—oh, this is some ride."

"That's what you're going to put in your report?" says Old Ko. "You're writing up the CD player?"

"Hey, it's a five-point-five litre V-12," says Million Man. His eyes run the length of the machine. "Five hundred horsepower in a city with a speed limit of 80kph."

"Good you know that," says Old Ko, "since you'll be assigned to traffic soon."

"Anyone got a name?" says Lok. By now the rhythm of his team is set, and although it works, Lok finds it on the noisy side: Million Man approaching each case like one of his sexual conquests, expecting to prevail by force of personality; Old Ko venting his ample supply of resentment on Million Man and Ears; Ears, who surprises him with some brilliant work when he's not just short of hopeless; and Big Pang, who seems to have figured life out better than any of them, including Lok himself.

A uniformed constable approaches, notebook in hand. "PC Ben Cheung, sir. The victim's name is Lau Fong-lok, known as Goldfish Head Lau."

"I remember the name," says Lok. "He got it from his bulging eyes, correct?" Goldfish Head is wearing a cheap mainland-made gray suit and a brown tie whose knot is too large. Not a big man in any sense.

"What's he doing in a car like this?" asks Big Pang. The right question, Lok thinks.

"He was a driver," says the PC, "working for Mo Tun. Mo's inside there." He points to the rear door of the restaurant.

Mo Tun. A picture forms in Lok's mind, a blurry montage of news clips, office towers, television gossip, the standard avatars of wealth and power that Lok can summon in his own admittedly meager imagination. The victim, it appears, worked for someone who mattered in Hong Kong.

"The place is called Wing Kee Restaurant," continues the PC. "Mo was in there with his assistant, a man named Lento Chan. Chan opened the door and found the body."

The PC doesn't need to check his notes for the names, Lok notes. Might be a bright kid, with that high forehead and a hint of a smile on his face, as if he's exactly where he wants to be right now.

"Have you called IB?" Lok says.

"Yes sir. I got to the scene…" he glances at his watch "…twenty five minutes ago. The restaurant owner, Fong Liu, called it in."

"All right, good work. We'll need an SOC officer, pathologist, government chemist." He waits for the constable to murmur into his shoulder microphone. The Identification Bureau will send a fingerprint man within the hour.

"Are you going to notify the DCS, sir?" asks Ears.

"Interrupt the District Crime Superintendent's dinner for one body in a car?" says Lok. "Not a good idea."

The constable releases his microphone and picks up what he presumes was a conversation with Lok. "The question is, what was he doing in the back seat…"

"Constable Cheung, thank you," says Lok. "If we get stuck on the investigation I'll send for you." The PC withdraws to the sound of the team's laughter.

"There's a guy who won't try to impress a CID officer again," says Million Man.

Mo Tun looks displeased but not particularly distraught, Lok concludes. Like someone who's just had his car towed for illegal parking, rather than a man whose employee lies stabbed to death outside a restaurant. Lok won't hold that against him; the emotions of the powerful will be as different from his as are their wardrobes and bank statements.

Mo is a tall man, his long, serious face topped by a thick head of gray-flecked hair which he combs back without a part. His suit is bespoke British wool, as impeccable as the charcoal gray coat that drapes over it. Lok finds him pacing the corridor, holding a cigarette and a cell phone and talking in low tones to another man. When Mo sees Lok he halts and drops the cigarette in a beer glass that sits on a metal shelf nearby.

Pity you couldn't order your skin, Lok thinks. Mo's hide is rough as an old riverbed, shot with flaws and tiny scars. The man beside him is Lento Chan.

"Not much to tell," Mo says, after introductions. "Goldfish Head drove me here and was waiting outside, like always. That was around seven-thirty. At around eight I came out with Lento, and we saw him." Mo speaks good Cantonese, but he isn't from the south, Lok judges. Beijing, probably.

"No one else with you?"

Mo shakes his head. Lento shakes his a second later. He's half Mo's age, dressed about as well, but smoother, a sanded down and varnished copy of the older man.

"Any idea why he was in the back seat?"

Mo nods. "I told him to clean out the ashtrays—they were filthy. Only place I can smoke now is in my own car, right?"

"Did you hear any sounds, any voices, anything?"

"No. Nothing. It's a long way to the back alley from where we were."

"Do you have any idea who killed him?" He looks Mo straight in the eye.

"No. No idea."

Lok watches for the signs: hesitation, uneasiness, fear. He wouldn't swear to it, but Mo appears to be telling the truth—about that, at least.

"Was he married?"

They shake their heads.

"Did he gamble?"

"Sure," Lento says. "Horses, Macau." Too quick an answer, as if he's eager to send Lok on the trail of a loan shark.

The cook and manager add little: Mo's limousine pulled into the alley, and Mo and Lento went in and had two beers each. A half-hour later, they walked out and saw the driver lying dead in the car. Unless the pair killed the driver themselves and staged the whole thing, which is absurd, they're in the clear.

Outside, Lok huddles his team into the van, away from the gawkers and the first of the reporters.

"All right, witnesses?"

They shake their heads.

"There might be passersby who saw something," says Ears. "People in taxis."

"Also, CCTV footage from around here," says Million Man. "Too early to say who'll turn up."

It's never early in a murder investigation, Lok could have said. It's always late. When we show up, the body is decomposing, the evidence is blowing away in the wind, the witnesses are on their way to forgetting what little they know, and the murderer is busy perfecting his story. It's always late, and it can only get later.

Two men burst from an ambulance that has just threaded its way past the EU vans. The men follow Lok's pointing hand to the body in the car, around which a swarm of technicians are gathering fingerprints and evidence.

"This is an easy one, gents," Lok says. "Just take him to the hospital mortuary when they're done."

The driver glances at the body. "But this guy's dead."

"Right," says Lok. "We want to close the scene down."

"But he's dead. You need the body box. Who called this in?"

"I did," says Lok. "It's late. I just need him taken to a hospital mortuary. We'll claim it later." Ambulances arrive in minutes, Lok knows. The body disposal van from Urban Services arrives when the stars and planets align just right, which could take a couple of hours, hours Lok would rather spend at the station writing up tomorrow's First Information Report.

"We're not running a dead body delivery service, Inspector. Bring him back to life and we'll take him to the hospital. Otherwise, he's not ours."

"Come on, guys."

"Call us if there's a resurrection." They hop into the ambulance and back out of the alley.

Pang approaches. "Good try, Sir," he says. "I'll stay and wait for the van."

"We've also got the car…" Lok says.

"No problem, sir. When the body's picked up, I'll escort the car to the pound and call it a night."

Lok sighs and slaps Big Pang on the shoulder.

Chapter Six

Kowloon District, Hong Kong, Friday, 11:01 p.m.

"I've had worse evenings," says Sylvie Mo.

The taxi hums through the Harbour Tunnel, ninety feet below the screws and bilges of the city's workhorse boats. Riding beside Sylvie is Eunice Kwan, tiny and wrapped in her customary Chanel. Sylvie herself has gone up a few rungs of formality from her work clothes, having donned a simple black cocktail dress that sets off her fair skin and blond hair.

"Better for some than others," says Eunice. "Phil Goh kept pressing me on that exam room he wants to poach from Endocrinology. He was so far up my arse he could have checked me for polyps."

"Really, Eunice!" Sylvie feigns amused disapproval but it isn't meant to fool the older woman. Hong Kong born, London trained, now head of Obstetrics at the hospital, Eunice Kwan has always been Sylvie's favorite, thanks to her miraculous ability to say what needs to be said at just the right time. It doesn't hurt that she says it in English as flawless and burnished as the BBC announcers of a generation ago.

Eunice. In America the last Eunices are lying in hospital beds, taking meals through tubes, having given up trying to remember their great-grandchildren's names. But in Hong Kong, teenagers answer to the name Eunice. Agatha, Florence, Doris, Mabel, Henrietta—the city is a Valhalla for old names that have died a Western death.

Sylvie recounts what made tonight's event worth the time: a good lecture on new robotic surgery techniques, the combining of the lecture with birthday cocktails for her department head, killing two birds, and leaving tomorrow evening free. And there was the party chatter, mostly medical shoptalk and lively at that.

"The open bar was a boon," says Eunice. "At least on Monday, I don't have to listen to everyone complain that there was nothing to drink."

They settle into silence. What changed Sylvie's mood, what placed the evening in need of redemption, was that silly British cow of a radiologist's wife, the one who worked for a PR agency. "My department is all Westerners," she had said in a private conversation over in a corner, just us girls, you understand. "Better, really—that way, we don't have to watch what we say."

Sylvie Mo, nee Maloney, nodded but said nothing, conscious of the color rising in her cheeks and hoping that the Grand Hyatt's subdued light would conceal her change in temper.

Brazen idiot, assuming that all Westerners trash the Chinese behind their backs. Sylvie has encountered bigotry in everyone—certainly in her fellow Americans—but she finds herself in awe of the British flair for dismissing entire races of people with a casual comment.

She was grateful when the text from her husband Ivan popped up on her phone. Eunice, too, was at her wit's end with Phil, who was angling for more elbow room for his department, so they made a quick escape together.

"How's Bonitus?" Eunice asks. "Haven't seen him in ages." The taxi emerges from the tunnel, and the hum ceases.

"Fine. Still naughty." Bonitus isn't naughty, not really, but the Chinese consider it boastful to refer to their own children as well-behaved. It took a while for Sylvie to understand why Chinese parents knocked their kids all the time, but eventually, "naughty" became her habitual answer, even with Eunice. On occasion she corrects Bonitus in front of guests, to give them face. But only when the boy deserves it, and never harshly.

"Keep up the New Scientist subscription. He's the one who's going to cure everything and put his mom out of business."

"Maybe he'll take after his father."

"Then he can get rich and donate a wing so Phil can have his bloody exam room."

The taxi drops off Sylvie first. She reaches for her purse, but Eunice waves her off and is gone.

* * *

Sylvie walks in to find Ivan sitting beside his father at the dining table. Mo has not removed his coat.

"*Tso ha*," says her husband. *Sit down.*

"*Dim ah?*" she says. *What's up?*

Ivan switches to English. "You know *Ba Ba's* driver, Goldfish Head?"

"Of course."

"He was killed tonight."

"What? What happened?" She lays her purse carelessly on the kitchen counter.

"Someone killed him. He was found dead in the car."

"You can't be serious. How horrible!"

Ivan nods. "Now listen, Sylvie. Bonitus was in the car with him, but we don't think he was hurt."

"What do you mean 'you don't think'…where is he?" These last three words quick and sharp.

"He's been taken."

"Taken…" Everyone is silent as her mind slowly grasps the euphemism.

"He's been kidnapped? Bonitus?" Her voice trembles. "No…you're wrong, he's not…"

"Sylvie, please don't worry, we're doing all we can."

All at once, she's out of breath. Her chest begins heaving, and her head starts to swim. She looks at Ivan's face for a clue of how to feel, how to respond. *Tell me this is wrong. That you're joking, mistaken. Tell me something.*

"Your husband's right," says Mo. "We'll take care of this. I have my people looking for him."

"Did you…. Have you called the police?"

Ivan says nothing.

"There's no need," says Mo, breaking in as if the exchange is beyond Ivan's abilities. "If we call the police, Bonitus might be in danger. It's safer this way."

She shifts her gaze from Mo to Ivan and back, but they stare at her as if she, and not her kidnapped son, is the problem to be handled right now.

Chapter Seven

Kowloon District, Hong Kong, Saturday, 5:58 a.m.

The siren rouses Lok: an ambulance is making short work of Waterloo Road. By the time his head clears, the siren is gone, replaced by the rumble of a pushcart. Probably a street vendor hauling his wares to the main road.

A dream awakened him. The usual nonsense—walks along streets that don't go where they should, long dead friends chatting with people they never knew in life. This dream took him to the station at one point, and something was out of whack—yes, he was dressed in beach clothes, of all things. What idiocy. Lok dislikes dreams—they're a waste of time, he once told Dora, who laughed for ten minutes afterward. He didn't see what was so funny.

"You dislike dreams because you can't solve them," Dora said. "They're not an investigation, you silly man; they're entertainment."

Not to Lok, they're not. Entertainment has a point, at least. Dreams are disordered, a procession of information that can't be understood or filed for future use. Worse, they seem to visit him when he's feeling nervous and vulnerable. As he is now.

Five a.m., and sleep is out of the question. Best to get to the station early—by eight, Doctor Lee will have peeled off his gloves, killed his memo recorder, and told his assistant to stitch up the body, having wrung from it every secret worth knowing.

He stands up and circles the bed with its motionless form. He won't disturb Dora; for years he's been able to navigate around a sleeping family like a jungle predator. He dresses and leaves.

On Waterloo Road the hiss of a propane stove confirms that he had indeed heard a pushcart earlier. The man bending over it is a bespectacled fossil of an earlier China, white-whiskered, with nut-brown skin and bow legs. Lok knows the type: an illiterate mainlander, too old for manual work, so his family scared up some cash to set him up as a hawker.

"Good morning," says the man in a two-pack-a-day voice. "You're my first customer. Buy some noodles and bring me luck, all right?" Steam billows from a stainless cauldron set in the cart's top.

"You're new here," says Lok.

"Construction going on at my old place." The old man jabs a chopstick in the pot and stirs it. "All blocked up, no use trying to work there. Ding is the name." His shapeless gray-blue smock hangs straight down from his frame, as if his shoulders were a wire hanger.

"Got a license, Ding?"

The query instantly deflates the man. He lowers his eyes.

"I'll go home, okay? I'll quit. Just don't confiscate the cart."

"If you're quitting, what do you need the cart for?

Ding shifts his gaze up and down the road, as if looking for rescue, then gives up and shrugs. At that point Lok, knowing all he needs to know, laughs a forgiving laugh.

Nothing people say of their own accord has any value. You can listen to someone talk all his life and not know him. To Lok, ready chatter is just like the static that lives between stations on the radio. To listen to it is to pick up the atmosphere of fraud and self-deception that surrounds us like air.

You get the truth the way you get diamonds, through pressure. Catch someone in a lie, light a fire under him, remove his defenses, and you'll find out more in ten minutes than you could from ten years of dinnertime chit-chat. Once a tool for work, this ploy is now a part of his manner, a way of ordering his life, of sifting and tabulating humanity by the type and magnitude of lies told.

"Don't worry, uncle," Lok says. "I won't take you in. I'm not Uniform Branch. What are you selling?"

Ding brightens immediately. "Noodles with dried shrimp and sesame oil. Good for breakfast. Here." Ding makes a cone from a sheet of wax paper and opens the tin pot, releasing fragrant steam skyward. He scoops a generous portion of noodles into the paper, dabs it with plum sauce, shakes a can of sesame seeds over it for a good two seconds. He pokes in some wooden chopsticks, and hands the cone to Lok.

"How much?" Lok asks.

"Free for you," he says.

"You want me to take you in? How much?"

"Six dollars. But I said no charge for you. What do you want to pay for?"

Lok hands him the coins, conscious of the spark of contempt that arcs from the old man's hand like St. Elmo's fire. To pay when you don't have to, that's for suckers.

Lok takes a mouthful of hot, fragrant mixture and watches the street wake up. The plum sauce is pungent, and the sesame seeds break with a satisfying crunch between his teeth in counterpoint to the soft noodles.

"What's with you police?" says Ding. "My brother used to run a snake restaurant in Wanchai. A cop would pay for his soup with a hundred dollar bill, and he'd get back a hundred and ten change. No one looking could tell what was going on."

"Long time ago, right?" Lok says between mouthfuls.

Ding nods. "I know some stories…"

"I've heard them, uncle." Lok finishes his noodles in silence, tosses the paper into a trash can, and walks toward the carpark, awake now.

* * *

Tsim Sha Tsui District, Hong Kong, 8:37 a.m.

"Our friend with the bulging eyes died in much pain, but very quickly."

Doctor Lee stands above the supine body of Goldfish Head Lau. The Doctor is a thin, fifty-ish man with a serious face and salt-and-pepper hair. He peers at Lok through gold-rimmed spectacles. An hour ago he removed the knife and placed it into the chain of evidence, leaving a pink buttonhole in the victim's chest. "The angle of the knife was perfect—it pierced the right ventricle, and death followed quickly." His fist, gripping an imaginary dagger, traces the arc of the knife's path in the air—a short, curving, upward motion.

"Why so little blood, then?"

"There are other ways to die besides bleeding to death, Inspector. This particular wound didn't need to bleed out to kill him. When the knife nicked the ventricle, blood filled the pericardium, putting pressure on the heart—what we call cardiac tamponade—and preventing it from beating. Essentially, the heart was squeezed to death by its own blood."

"Just the one wound?"

"That's all it took. One jab, one motion."

"But did the assailant know that?"

Doctor Lee nods, a rare acknowledgment of an intelligent question. "Doubtful. For one thing, the knife in question has only one cutting edge, not two, is fairly thin, and the blade is 13 centimeters long. One would not be sure of bringing about death with it, which, of course, does not stop one from trying. You remember the commotion in Shek Kip Mei last summer?"

The memory brings a smile to Lok's face. An advertising executive had come home late for dinner after a blissful hour in his secretary's bedroom. His furious wife heated the braised pork to boiling and flung it at her husband with a spatula, one portion at a time. Several volleys connected with his skin, burning him superficially on his chest and thigh. When her ammunition gave out, she threw the spatula and wok at him and then began to beat him with the wok lid. The cheap aluminum did no damage, but the husband slipped on the greasy pork and slammed his head on the kitchen counter. He died in the hospital a few hours later. Old Ko asked if he should put the murder weapon in an evidence bag or a take-out box.

"How did it happen?" says Lok.

"I am not omniscient, Inspector."

Caught once again by Doctor Lee. The man lives in a world without assumptions. Lok wonders if that is a world without hope as well.

"All right. What does the evidence suggest?"

A particle of satisfaction brightens the eyes behind Doctor Lee's spectacles, as if a trained dog has jumped to his command. "Let's assume for a moment—and this is just assumption, mind you—that the assailant knew what he was doing. In that case, the evidence suggests that he was aware of the best way to pierce the heart, stabbing upward from just below the sternum. He brought along just enough knife to do the job, for ease of concealment, perhaps. As he was attacking from above, standing while the victim was seated in the car, he gripped the knife so that it was pointing upward, opened the door, and thrust it in. He did not twist the knife."

"Suggesting that he was in a hurry?"

The Doctor glances to the floor for a second, implying that Lok's interruption was rude, irrelevant, or both. His own speech revives him.

"Perhaps. Now let us assume—and this is just assumption, mind you—that he did *not* know what he was doing." To Lok, he sounds like one of those bewigged lawyers from Scotland, where Doctor Lee once gorged on medical knowledge and character traits of that land: the stubbornness, the independence, the bluntness that rarely stopped short of effrontery.

"In that case," the Doctor says, "our assailant brings to the scene whatever knife he can get hold of. He opens the car door and has chosen to hold the knife pointing upward because it's easier to stab upward from below. He has no idea he's found the perfect angle, up behind the sternum and into the heart, but he stabs that way out of luck—his luck, of course, not our unfortunate driver's. He doesn't twist the knife because he doesn't know enough to, or he's too frightened to."

Lok would have made the same deductions. "I see. And that's all we know?"

"We don't even know that much, Inspector. We've just proposed two possibilities of differing degrees of likelihood. Other matters you can infer for yourself. For instance, the use of a standard piece of kitchenware means that the murderer is extremely unlikely to be one of our triad friends."

A small knife is a weapon of personal grudges: love, money, envy, that sort of thing. If Goldfish Head had insulted a 14K incense master, or fallen behind with a loan shark, he'd have been all but dismantled by a chopper. This murder comes with a "personal" label stuck to it.

And that's good: personal murders are the easiest to solve. A cheating lover, an argument, an unstable friend or relative who's gone round the bend—these leave traces that are easy to pick up. They're done on impulse, with little planning and worse concealment. A couple of days and this will be in the hands of the court.

* * *

Outside Doctor Lee's office Lok taps out a number on his cell phone. It's not on speed dial, but he knows the number by heart. A few rings, and Lai Ping answers.

"*Wai?*"

"It's me."

"I was worried."

"No need to be. How are things?"

"Good. Better. I'm glad you called."

"Seven tonight, then?"

"That's fine."

One part of him wants to shudder, another to dance. He claps the phone shut and stares at it for a long moment, as if the small silver device alone has twisted his life into the tortuous knot it's become.

Chapter Eight

Kowloon East District, Hong Kong, Saturday, 9:02 a.m.

At two after nine, Horace's phone bleeps. He's been staring at the gray cubicle wall, thinking about Mo Tun. Is Mo sweating? Having chest pains? Has he slept since last night?

Long ago Horace Yang came to Hong Kong for its fabled rewards. Mao's upheavals had stunted his education, so Horace joined the throngs of people who were improving themselves to grab a bigger piece of the Hong Kong pie. By day he completed a course in accountancy, while waiting tables each night at a Chiu Chow restaurant in North Point.

With his intelligence, the elite should have sought him out. They failed to.

The papers were crammed with ads for accountants back then, and he found a job. His plan was to work hard, follow the rules, think big, and move up. After all, he was brilliant, much smarter than these spoiled Hong Kongers who had everything given to him. Horace, remember, had made it to university in China, which was much harder. What happened afterwards was not his fault.

He found a girl, Winnie, and married her. Kenny was born a year later, Doby five years after that.

In the white-hot nineteen-eighties and nineties, jumping from one company to another was easy, and Horace did so, expecting that each change would advance him. He stayed an accountant, though; nothing above that opened up. For the big jobs they all wanted MBAs, which were handed out to rich kids who went to school abroad.

More education was the answer, so he worked nights to get a management degree, and took a job at Great Fortune Property Management as an accountant. His plan was to move up to senior management, if not CEO level.

But now everything was international. Great Fortune wanted someone with good English to bring in more business from American firms. Horace's new boss turned out to be Wayne Lai, an American-born Chinese fifteen years his junior. Carried a squash racquet under his arm to the office, stayed glued to his cell phone.

Horace kept his mind open. The man had attended Cornell in the USA. If he was sharp, he'd recognize Horace's intellect, value his experience, and promote him.

Wayne Lai turned out to be like the others, perhaps worse. He wasn't even Chinese, really, just some multi-national fabrication with a Chinese brand name and internal mechanism made in the USA. Oblivious to Horace, he was wrapped up in himself and his precious appearance.

Six weeks ago, Wayne Lai summoned Horace.

"Call me Wayne," said Wayne on that cold Monday. Everyone used his English name. "And have a seat. We haven't talked much, have we?"

Indeed we haven't. God, Wayne's Cantonese was bad, like most of the American-born Chinese. Horace would rather listen to a Hakka farmer talk than hear the language mangled by this banana. At least the Hakka is Chinese. This kid was just a *gweilo* brat painted yellow. Must have gone to Chinese school on Saturdays in San Francisco, probably made fun of his teacher, and whined about having to learn all those complicated Chinese characters.

"I promised some changes after the acquisition of Lung Fong, and they're happening."

Horace nodded. The same go-getters who hired Wayne acquired a competing property management company, and rumor had it that redundancies were coming. So this was it.

"We now have two different accounting systems, and we need to make a choice. It looks as if the one Lung Fong is using is more suited to our expansion plans."

Did the room suddenly heat up? Tendrils of sweat crept down the back of Horace's neck. He turned his head slightly to keep it out of Wayne's sightline. *Don't let him know what I'm feeling.*

"Now, rather than spending time training you in their system, it makes sense to migrate our accounts over. So I have a proposition for you."

Horace felt a wrench in his gut. *This cannot be good.*

"I'd like to bring you onto our account management team," he continued. "I realize it's a new set of responsibilities and not exactly what you're trained for, but I'm convinced you'd be valuable to us. Why not think it over and let me know tomorrow?"

"There's no way I could keep on in accounting?"

Wayne shook his head. "They're ready to make the transition—it should take a week, two tops. No need to add personnel on their side."

"I see."

"It could be really exciting—new people, you'd be getting out of the office a bit more. I'd have you shadow Petula for a while."

Wayne glanced at his gold Rolex. "Well, think it over and let me know. I think you'd do a great job."

And if I didn't take it, you'd fire me, so what choice do I have?

* * *

As painful as that change was, it was nothing compared to the change in Horace's life the day, three weeks later, that Mo Tun walked into Great Fortune. Up to that moment the Great Wall Disco was a spreadsheet, a collection of tasks: materials to be ordered, contractors to be briefed, certificates to be obtained, operations to be scheduled.

Mo walked in, tall, remote, oblivious to Horace, who was just another cubicled office drudge.

I mean nothing to him. None of us mean anything. He's just looking to see what good this all does him.

There was no doubt it was Mo, though, still the taut, wiry man he knew all those years ago, but with a slight fleshiness of face added to the unpleasantness of his expression. He wore pinstripes now, and his haircut was no longer the indifferent trim of the People's Republic.

Mo is alive. How could I not know this?

Horace never read gossip, never followed personalities in the news. Neither was he political—who in Hong Kong was, after all?—and his interest in financial news extended only to what new accounting regulations would be coming. He never followed the big *hongs*, the *tai-pans*, or glamour boys with their name-brand fashion franchises and sports car dealerships.

Mo has been in Hong Kong, thinking I'm dead, thinking he's been rid of me.

Well, Mo Tun, I am not dead. And you will never be rid of me. I, however, will soon be rid of you.

* * *

It's The Girl on the phone, of course, ringing to make sure that he's at his desk. She's looking for a weakness, a reason to dismiss him. But she won't have one.

"Could you come here for a minute?" she says. No hello, just an order, as if he's a servant.

Her name is Petula, but he calls her The Girl. She's half his age, dresses like a Wanchai whore, and thinks she knows everything. She knows nothing.

At first The Girl doesn't look up from her desk, just taps something into her phone. Texting, they call it. Horace called it ignoring a man to put him in his place. *If you knew what I did last night, you wouldn't be so cool. Think you're the only one who can handle power? I killed a man last night. I've got Mo Tun's kid. What have you got?*

Her texting over, The Girl looks up at Horace. "What's this I hear from Eddie Leung?"

"Eddie Leung?"

"At the Cheong Lok building. He called about a leak, and you sent a plumber."

"That's right. Last night, after hours."

"There's no such thing as after-hours in account management. Where did you dig up this plumber?"

How dare she instruct me. He regrets leaving the door open on the way in. Anyone could hear her.

"Ming Hang couldn't spare anyone," he says. "Stanley didn't have anyone else, but he gave me a number."

"Are you aware that we're in violation of contract?"

Horace says nothing. She finally looks up from her phone.

"Our contract states that all service personnel we use have to be licensed and approved. This guy was neither."

"No license?"

"No. Furthermore, how can I justify the charge?"

"There was a leak. I couldn't get anyone else."

"Approved alternates are in the handbook. Section 12." She points to a binder on her desk. Horace has an identical one on his own desk but hasn't committed it to memory. How can he be expected to?

"I'm sorry," he says.

She nods. "Well, it's done now." All she wanted, really, was to see him grovel, see him lose face to a twenty-something idiot in a miniskirt and absurd high heels. And with the office door open. She dismisses him without another word. No noises of understanding, not even a warning—as if he's beyond help.

I'm sorry, he had said, in a moment of weakness. *Not as sorry as Mo Tun is going to be. None of these people understand how power is going to shift in this place.* During lunch hour he'll make the ransom call. Till the money is paid, he just has to suffer these people.

As he walks out, he barely notices Wayne's assistant taking his photo.

Chapter Nine

Kowloon Tong District, Hong Kong, Saturday, 9:04 a.m.

I t was a small mercy that Bonitus was taken on the eve of her day off, so Sylvie didn't need to face her colleagues today. But Eunice, dear Eunice, saw the murder on the news, and now she's hopping in a taxi to comfort her best friend.

Sylvie's eaten nothing and slept little since yesterday. Ivan hasn't done much better, though he appears the more composed of the two. Sylvie passed most of the evening on the sofa, staring at the floor, occasionally glancing at Ivan, who busied himself with some contracts that had something to do with his father's new project. She watches him work, her admiration laced with the tiniest bit of resentment. How can he be calm enough to work? Is it strength? Or is his love somehow weaker than hers? The last thought makes no sense, and she banishes it from her mind as best she can. But it hurts.

As the buzzer announces Eunice's arrival, she wishes he could conjure up that same illusion of control. But Sylvie knows her peach skin will blanch and blush and spill her emotions out into the room no matter how she tries to conceal them. Resigned to the torture of conversation, she opens the door.

"You're all right, aren't you?" Eunice says. She walks into Sylvie's flat and closes the door herself to spare Sylvie the bother. Taking charge. She embraces Sylvie and pats her shoulder tenderly.

Sylvie nods. "Managing."

Eunice gives her the once over. "Managing to look like shit, you mean."

At least one person is honest with me, Sylvie thinks. Not that she can return the favor. They share a weak smile.

"Wasn't a good night last night."

"I can imagine. Got any sleepers?"

Sylvie shakes her head. "Don't like them. It'll be okay." One rough experience with pills, a few years ago, was enough.

"Do the police know anything yet?"

Sylvie doesn't want to answer, doesn't want to discuss the murder, doesn't want to skate around the thing that really terrifies her. If only Eunice would leave, but she can't think of a reason to turn her away.

"They're looking into it. Someone will be here later." The police don't even know that Bonitus is gone. What can they do?

"Look, Sylvie. I know it sounds selfish, but you need to be grateful that you're all right, that Ivan and Bonitus weren't there, that they're both safe. You need to concentrate on what's normal and stable in your life, on what's good. It's a terrible thing, but it's not the end of the world, right? You've got your family."

Sylvie reels, but catches her head so it resembles, she thinks, a nod. She cannot utter a word.

"So you'll be all right, then?" Eunice says.

Sylvie nods again.

"I'll go, then. I've got a C-section this afternoon. Glen Barstow's wife."

"Really?" Sylvie says, faking interest. "I didn't think she needed one. Looked like a pretty easy pregnancy."

"It was. But no natural childbirth for Dr. Barstow's wife. He wants her to stay nice and tight down there. A vaginal birth might hamper his sex life."

"Not him. You're kidding."

"Wish I were. Bastard. Oh, how's Bonitus? Does he know what's going on?"

Pause. "He's all right."

"Kids. They manage so well. We shouldn't worry so much about them. Listen, Sylvie. Keep busy. Come in to work if it would help. You'll get through this."

She pecks Sylvie on the cheek and is gone, leaving Sylvie scant seconds to lunge for the kitchen sink and expel the remains of last night's cocktail party.

Chapter Ten

Mongkok District, Hong Kong, Saturday, 6:40 a.m.

"Dinner tonight?" Million Man says, in a romantic gesture he instantly regrets. He's still in bed, covered to the waist. Icy Fong stands at his bathroom mirror applying lip gloss, head cocked forward, nose almost to the glass. She's dressed now in a white blouse and dark maroon slacks, a professional look that suits her. Where does she work? He racks his brain for a moment, but he sees her tracing red gloss on those lips and forgets what he was trying to remember.

He loves watching them dress, make themselves up, put themselves back together after he's taken them apart. He savors the restoration of all the little barriers that say "Look but don't touch" after he's had his fill of touching. The Hong Kong crowds must be content to view her composed, sober, professional front. But he's been around to the back.

It's not just sex, though. Million Man realizes he likes Icy Fong. She's older than him, by how much he's not sure. She also seems to want to have a good time without moving on to the dreaded Next Level. When they met three weeks ago at a bar, she had said, "They call you *man yan mai*, don't they?" The one millions fall in love with. He told her it was nowhere near a million. "You're still young," she said. He thought that clever, and the implied gulf between their knowledge of the world enticed him.

When told he was a Detective Constable, Icy didn't ask to see his gun, a ritual Million Man would have found tiresome if not for its obvious symbolism. No, she wanted to know if crime trends had changed after the 1997 handover, and what characteristics a good detective needed, and how the new force handled white-collar crime. Sharp questions, ones he hadn't ready answers for.

Electronics, that was it. She worked for some electronics firm. LF Industries.

He asked Icy out. An expensive place, of course, one with subtle illumination under the shelving at the bar, a wall-length aquarium stocked with blue tangs—always impress them on the first date. Later on, you can hit the food stalls if things work out. He waited for her jaw to drop when they stepped into the restaurant. It didn't, but they enjoyed themselves and ended up in bed a few days later.

It's been a good three weeks. And the lively conversation is a bonus, a welcome change in his after-work life. Hence his hasty dinner invitation.

"Dinner would be nice," says Icy. "Where?"

He thinks for a second. "Shanghainese? The one in Pacific Place?"

"I'd love that."

I'll bet you would, he thinks. *There goes my paycheck. How did I get into this?* But he knows exactly how.

The first date, for Million Man, is a show about him: who he is, what he is. Million Man the homicide detective (all right, detective constable, but he puts the tiniest stress on the word "detective" when he says it). Million Man, the sharp dresser, who knows how to treat a woman in public and who drives a Nissan Fairlady 350z coupe he can't afford—but his accounts are not part of the show.

He brings them home to an entirely respectable flat, a three-bedroom in Mongkok, which he shares with an often-traveling engineer. It's a good arrangement, rarely awkward.

But he's getting tired of what it costs to impress girls. He's tired of keeping up appearances, casually dropping money he doesn't have to put his stamp on each date. Sometimes he wonders if it's really worth it. Then Icy walks out and kneels on the bed, gives Million Man a slow kiss.

It's worth it.

All I need is a promotion, he thinks. *A little more money, and this will work out.*

* * *

Tsim Sha Tsui District, Hong Kong, Saturday, 9:01 a.m.

Million Man arrives to find Lok alone, leafing through the morning report that hits everyone's desk at 7:30. Million Man is relieved to be early. Old Ko needles him when he's late.

Not that Million Man cares about getting on Old Ko's good side; he wants to get on Lok's good side. The problem is, there appears to be no way to get on Lok's good side except by doing your job right.

Big Pang, Old Ko and Ears file in, all within the space of two minutes. Lok looks up from the report.

"We don't know much yet, and that's not good. Let's start with the victim. Tell me about Goldfish Head Lau."

"He did some time ten years ago for small stuff: illegal mahjong parlors, that kind of thing," says Old Ko. "Never into anything too dicey. But his boss, Mo Tun, is a big real estate guy, used to hang out with Greeny Ma, so he's probably neck-deep in triad stuff. Any tattoos on the body?"

Lok shakes his head.

"We can still check for triad associations," Old Ko says.

"That's yours, then," says Lok. "Find out everything about Goldfish Head. Did he have a girlfriend? Brother, mother, whoever, talk to them. Go to his flat, look it over. Find out where he ate, who he hung out with, where he bought his toilet paper. Check the computer logs, see if he's been the subject of a stop and search. He's a driver, so he'll have a cell phone; go over his contacts. Check his wallet for phone numbers, his voicemail—you know the drill. If he had an enemy, we need to know.

"Now, do we all get the feeling that this has more to do with Mo Tun than his driver?"

Nods all around.

"Ears, you need to look into Mo Tun's personal life, in case this is just a message sent to Mo to shake him up. You'll have to do some research on your own, because Mo won't give you much—he's playing this like an innocent man. Old Ko mentioned Greeny Ma. You know who he is?"

Ears doesn't.

"He's high up in the Sun Yee On, and maybe there's a connection with Mo. Not likely this is a triad dispute, given the weapon used. But just in case, you're going to find out if Mo's been seen with Greeny Ma or any other triad people, any disputes he might have had, any big rivalries that aren't on the radar now.

"Big Pang—you need to check Mo's finances. This could be some kind of territorial dispute, so we need to find out what his territory is. Any large loans through triad businesses, things like that."

He turns to Million Man.

"Million Man—the murder weapon has been released, so you need to follow that up. The knife looks pretty new—find out where it was bought and, if possible, who bought it. Then look for surveillance camera footage in the area."

Million Man doesn't conceal his disappointment. "The knife?"

"What's the problem?" says Old Ko. "Afraid you'll cut yourself?"

Chapter Eleven

Kowloon East District, Hong Kong, Saturday, 1:33 p.m.

Horace fumbles with the tiny card that refuses to slip into the new cell phone. Somewhere he's heard that these cheap phones cannot be traced, provided you pay cash for the SIM card, which he did just ten minutes ago at a nearby Watson's. But the new phone is stubborn, enigmatic, irritating—a smaller version of that kid he locked up in the Shun Lok building. Finally, after flipping the plastic sliver eight or nine ways and dropping it once, he shoves it home.

The murder of Goldfish Head Lau made the headlines this morning. Mo Tun, the car, the knife—it was all there. *Apple Daily* even managed to get a decent photo of the victim, bulging eyes and all.

But there was nothing about a missing kid. Nothing.

It made no sense. Kidnappings are big news. There should have been a manhunt, police updates, a tearful plea from a hysterical mother. An unknown man had a so-called great man by the balls: that should have been news.

Nothing. Police are making inquiries, it said.

That morning, after The Girl had confronted him about the plumber, things got quieter but not easier. In fact, the sheer normality of the day's routine irked him. It was Saturday, but everyone was working, so stiff was the workload. His colleagues, unaware of the boy imprisoned in the Shun Tak building, went on phoning clients and typing invoices. In this miserable office building only Horace was locked in a battle with nameless emotions. But in a way, that is how it's always been. Horace feels more, is aware of more. That is one of his burdens. That, and a deep, powerful intelligence no one seems to notice.

It's thirty minutes into lunch hour, and Horace is in Kowloon Bay Park because, after looking over restaurants and office lobbies, he had one of those flashes of ingenuity on which he prides himself: he could make the call outdoors. *The best cover is no cover at all.* He's getting good at this.

He presses the number.

A woman answers. "Diamond Rich Development."

"Mo Tun, please."

"He's in a meeting now." He's not—fictitious meetings are a secretary's verbal armor.

"Please tell him this regards yesterday's…matter."

"If you're a reporter…"

"I'm not. Tell him I have information that he's looking for. He'll know what it is. I'll call back in ten minutes."

"I can't…"

"You can. This is very important, and he will know it." Horace clicks off.

Contradicting that woman exhilarates him. Perhaps she's ridiculously young, self-important, and cheap, like the women at Great Fortune. Like The Girl.

He sits motionless on the bench. Very few people are motionless in Kowloon Bay Park at this time of day. One teenage couple is sharing a pair of earphones and eating. A group of women—probably secretaries—are sitting four to a bench with their rice boxes and chopsticks.

It occurs to Horace that he won't have time to eat.

When ten minutes has elapsed, he keys in the number again. The woman answers. This time, when he asks for Mo, she puts him on.

"This is Mo Tun."

Horace pauses. He hasn't actually prepared an opening sentence.

"We need to talk."

"We are talking. What do you want?"

"It's what you want. The boy."

Now Mo pauses. "Is he okay?"

"Yes."

"Prove it."

"What do you mean…?"

"What do you mean, 'What do you mean?' How do I know you haven't killed him already?"

"I haven't. I…"

"Well, prove it. Why the fuck should I take your word for it, you stupid dick?"

"Okay, I'll let you talk to him."

"I want him back now, dickhead."

"I…you'll get him back."

"You've got that right, dickface."

Horace has never been called so many filthy names, not since secondary school, at any rate. It's throwing him off.

"I want…ten million dollars."

"You have got to be fucking kidding. Eat shit and die."

Horace closes his eyes and takes a breath. "Ten million, or I keep the boy."

Mo switches to a business voice. "Five million."

What's going on? Is he really bargaining?

"Seven," Horace replies.

"All right. How do you want it?"

"I'll be in touch."

"Do you want my cell number?"

Horace winces. It doesn't look good for the victim to be making suggestions like that. He should have written down a script beforehand.

"Yes. One second." Horace fumbles through his pockets but can't find a pen. *Shit.*

"You're in a park, aren't you?

Shit.

"I'll call you back in a minute." Horace rings off and moves casually up to the secretaries to request the loan of a pen. A woman with gaudy highlights and red nails like kinfisher talons pulls a two-dollar ballpoint out of her purse and hands it over, her eyes lowered and distant.

He thanks her and once again keys in Mo's office number. This time Mo answers. He dictates his number as if each digit were a poison dart.

"I'll call you back so you can hear him. And I'll give you instructions for payment."

"You do that, and if you harm him, I'll pull your eyes right down to your ass, so you can watch me kick the shit out of you."

Mo closes the connection.

All in all, it went well. *Yes*, Horace thinks, *I'm getting good at this.*

* * *

Kowloon East District, Hong Kong, Saturday, 2:16 p.m.

He arrives back late from lunch—late for the first time in years—to find that Wayne has been looking for him. The boss could not have chosen a worse time for a meeting. He walks to Wayne's plush corner office, conscious of whispers and stares. Wayne greets him happily and asks Horace to sit.

"Horace, I'd like to know how things are going."

How things are going. What does he mean? His eyes circle the room, as if some clue might be planted there. But all he sees is a couple of framed documents in English—diplomas, probably, but he hasn't the patience to read them—a family photo, and that abominable squash racquet.

"Yes, how you're managing with your new assignment."

So this is what it's about. That bitch Petula has been reporting on him, telling him about his slip-up with the plumber.

"I…I'm learning. There's a lot to get used to, but I think it's…all right."

"Good…good. I've been hearing things—good things—and I wanted to verify that you're happy with work."

Hearing things? What has she told him?

He doesn't need this now. Everything depends on his staying calm, avoiding notice, and above all, avoiding upheavals. He's in the midst of the greatest undertaking of his life—the one he was born to complete—and this squash-playing fool is threatening to fire him. Maybe he's already fired him.

"You know," says Wayne, rising and circling to the front of his desk, "I realize this was quite a stretch for you. I'm very happy with the way it's working out." He leans back on his desk, looming over Horace. *He wants me to look up to him. I won't do it. I'll stare at his tie. I'll stare at the window. I will not give him the satisfaction of looking up to him.*

Wayne continues. "We want you to feel comfortable in your new role. I hope if any issues come up, you'll let us know."

Issues? Would you call that harpy Petula an issue? How about having to take calls about blocked toilets on my time off? Or snotty project managers who can't be bothered to help, so I end up sending in amateur plumbers? And throwing away years of accounting training for the privilege? Are those issues?

"Come on," says Wayne, standing up and gesturing to the door. "I'd like you to accompany me for a minute." As Horace rises Wayne drops a hand gently to his shoulder. They walk to a vestibule fronting one of the conference rooms. Most of the office personnel are in there, crammed shoulder-to-shoulder. The Girl is there, he notices.

"People," announces Wayne, "I didn't send a memo about this because I wanted it to be a surprise. We're instituting a new practice at Great Fortune. The most important asset we have is our employees—you're the ones who make this company a success."

A few of the employees smile and nod. Petula's face is frozen in a grimace that might pass for a smile to those unaware of her schemes. Wayne picks up an oblong panel sheathed in brown paper, obviously some sort of picture, which had been leaning against the wall behind him.

"So we're going to honor an employee each month— one of us who has shown that kind of drive and spirit that makes Great Fortune both a great firm to do business with, and a great place to work. I'm delighted to announce that our first employee of the month is…Horace Yang!"

As he says the name, Wayne rips off the paper, exposing a casual photo of the dumbfounded man who had exited Petula's office this morning.

The staff applauds. The ones who have in the past exchanged more than three words with Horace offer congratulations. Afterwards they all disperse to their desks except for Wayne's secretary Minna, who begins to hammer a nail into the corridor wall.

Chapter Twelve

Sha Tin District, Hong Kong, Saturday, 11:40 a.m.

"I'll need my street clothes, Oldfield," says Koon. The room boy, Oldfield Wong, nods and vanishes into the back room to retrieve Koon's suit. No boy, Oldfield must be sixty-five, though he is hale and vigorous, and his eyes gleam with cheer.

Chief Superintendent Koon pays Oldfield's salary, about four hundred per month, out of his own pocket. For that, Oldfield launders the District Commander's shirts, shines his shoes, and inspects Koon after he changes into his uniform each morning, adjusting his badges of rank and brushing off the odd fleck of dust.

"Taking the day off, sir?" says Oldfield, as he hangs the suit on a hook behind the back room door.

"No, I'll be back after lunch. Just have a function that calls for a suit."

It's unusual for Koon to change clothes at work, unless it's running shorts for a jog by the river. Police should be visible in their city, and if he's not proud of his uniform, how can others respect it?

Oldfield lays out a clean shirt for Koon's lunch date. When he found that a man twenty years his senior would be polishing his reading glasses, Koon considered abolishing the position of room boy. But he's come to see Oldfield's admiration as just another perk of his job.

Koon emerges from the back room and lets Oldfield dust him off with an immaculate paintbrush he keeps for that one task. Then Chief

Superintendent Koon, District Commander Shatin in New Territories South, walks out of the station and joins the herd on the MTR.

* * *

From the outset they've had a single rule: one never, ever, phones the other directly. Instead, a message traceable to Guangdong reaches Koon via the switchboard: Fatso says he'll be in Hong Kong soon. In fact, Fatso is not coming to Hong Kong. The message is Mo Tun's way of arranging a meeting, and Fatso called this morning.

At Shek Kip Mei, Koon walks from the MTR station to a *dim sum* restaurant, a cavernous red-carpeted hangar housing a quarter acre of round tables. Mid-week at noon, just a few diners scatter themselves amid the expanse of empty tables. Behind the front desk the owner sits reading the Sun's horse racing page, as the figures of *Fu Lou Shou*, the triune gods of luck, wealth, and longevity, gaze out from a shrine above.

Koon sits in the rear of the restaurant, with his back to the wall, orders *sui gow min* and a plate of *san choi*—dumplings in noodle soup and lettuce with oyster sauce—and waits. No *dim sum* because he wants no interruptions from the waiters.

Mo is on time. He knows that Koon dislikes disappearing on lunch hours; that's one reason these meetings are rare. Another is that the ponds they swim in are far apart these days, so far apart that when the waters mix, the fish can smell it. Koon is supposed to declare any association with "undesirable characters"—one of those charming terms beloved of the old Colonial force he joined decades ago. Should he learn of any suspicious conduct that Mo's involved in, it's his duty to report it. Such are the dangers of befriending the criminal fraternity—another one of those colorful terms, come to think of it.

Mo orders *won ton* and plain tea, and the two tally each other's gray hairs, gauge waistlines, perform the calculations of appearance and age that old friends do when they've been apart. Not that Koon and Mo are friends, exactly. But they go back a long way.

Their last meeting was six years ago.

Age has driven us apart, Koon thinks. *Or perhaps age has forced to the surface the differences we've always had.* Both of them wear expensive suits, but Koon's youthful, unlined face goes better with the chalk stripe British wool. His steel-gray hair sets off his glowing skin, while Mo's dyed black hair calls attention to every wrinkle. Mo has the look of the great indoors, as well: strong, but not what you'd call robust. His face shows his cunning rather than the native intelligence at the base of it. Probably still carries that knife. *No matter how well you dress, you can't hide the thug in you.* Was it a cop who said that to him, or a thug?

"Trouble," Mo says.

"Your driver, I take it. What don't we know?"

Mo raises his eyebrows, his version of a smile, at Koon's bluntness. "My grandson was taken," he says. "He was in the back seat with Goldfish Head. Got a ransom call."

"And you haven't reported this?"

Mo shakes his head. "It's a personal matter. An amateur with a grudge. Better I handle it."

"An amateur could be more dangerous than the 14K. You know, there's a lot we can do. Make a report, and they'll put CIB on it. Those men are good."

"Not safe. If it gets out, I could lose him."

They fall silent as the dumplings arrive in steaming bowls. Mo stirs his to dispel the heat.

"Criminal Intelligence Bureau runs a tight ship," says Koon. "You won't find them leaking anything to the press."

"You can control what the investigation gives out," says Mo, "but not what they dig up on me. And if word of this gets to the press, the reporters will be on my family, my businesses, everything I'm into. And it won't help that my son is married to a *gweipoh*. They'll love it. If my grandson's picture gets on TV, the bastard that took him will get scared. No telling what he'll do."

Mo has a point. Not that Koon would take Mo's route, gambling with a child's life. And the way he talks about getting his grandson back, as if the boy is some disputed piece of property.

"How are your son and his wife handling this?"

Mo replies with a small shrug that says, *as you'd expect—what can I do?*

They pause the conversation to eat and to be seen eating. Koon finally asks the question that's been on his mind.

"If you don't want the police on this, why did you want to meet?"

"I think I know who's got him."

"Who?"

"Man with a Beijing accent."

Koon halts with his *sui gow* in midair.

"You think it's Dollar-ten?"

"I'm sure of it."

"You spoke to him?"

"No—I spoke to some idiot, also Beijing. Must be his pal. He asked for 10 million. I got him down to seven."

Now that's a businessman, Koon thinks. *That's why Mo buys and sells buildings, and I have an office job with the government.*

"You can't be sure it's Dollar-ten," says Koon.

"Who else?"

"You've killed a lot of chickens in your time."

"True enough. But this feels like a money grab, not payback. More people need me than want to get rid of me these days. All right, so I made trouble for some bar owner fifteen years ago. Why would they be getting back at me now?"

"Could be someone you're making trouble for now."

"Then they've picked a stupid way to get themselves out of it."

"All right. Let's say Dollar-ten is behind it. What are you going to do?"

"Find him. Any idea where he is?"

Koon shakes his head. "Dead, I thought."

"When did you see him last?"

Koon raises his palms in a gesture of helplessness. "Twenty, twenty-two years. He was a construction worker then. He'd lost all his share."

"I need you to find him for me."

"I can't be involved. You know that."

"This is a kid, Koon. Twelve years old."

"Tun *chai*, the time when a cop could go in business for himself was over before I joined the force. You think I can just sit down at a computer and look up a name, print out an address? A search like that could take time, might need info from motor vehicles, immigration, Inland Revenue. I'm not an investigator."

"You know the detectives, though."

"Yes, and they have families and want to keep their jobs. It doesn't work like that. Here's what you can do: make a report, mention Dollar-ten, and if he's alive, we'll put his ass in the wringer and find out what he knows."

"I can't do that."

"Then I can't help."

Mo stares at him, the chopsticks motionless in his hand.

As if to answer the unspoken accusation, Koon explains. "We left everything behind because we wanted what was *here*." He thumps the wooden tabletop gently, as if it stands for all of Hong Kong. "Now you want me to throw it away? For what? You don't even know the boy's alive, or that finding Dollar-ten could save him."

Mo thinks as he pokes his chopsticks into the bowl and stirs.

"All right. Maybe it's best that I find him. But can you tell me something?"

"Perhaps."

"The man investigating Goldfish Head's murder is named Lok. Know him?"

"Detective Inspector Herman Lok. And you want to know …"

"… is Lok going to learn more than I want him to?"

Koon takes another bite of the lettuce, which is still warm in its coat of oil and oyster sauce.

"Take my word for it. He already has."

* * *

Kowloon Tong District, Saturday, 12:05 p.m.

It's been a good life. Is this how I must pay for it?

As soon as the thought appears, the guilt rolls in again, like a tide, this time because Sylvie chose to lament her own fate instead of her son's. Bonitus is the true victim, after all.

Still, Sylvie can't shake the notion that she's been asking for it all these years. Life up to now has been a procession of gifts unearned: two loving parents, old brick schools with small classes of bright and fortunate kids.

Gifts unearned: opportunities bequeathed by her mother's generation, who took the blows in the war for women's rights so that by the time Sylvie applied for medical school, smart women were in demand.

"In Grandma's time they'd call me a 'lady doctor,'" Sylvie told her mother the day she took the Hippocratic Oath.

"In grandma's time they'd call you a nurse," said her mother.

Gifts unearned: Ivan, who bathes her in unselfish love. His father's wealth makes no difference to her. But to God?

No one objected when Sylvie married a non-Catholic and a Chinese man to boot. Her family was too tell-the-Pope-to-mind-his-business progressive for that. If anything, it amused them. Her mother announced that Sylvie had "adopted a pagan baby," the term the nuns used in her day for sponsoring a child at a mission.

When Bonitus was born, she savored the feeling of completeness: she had everything. But maybe God figured a woman can claim just so much happiness. Maybe it had to balance out somewhere.

Catholic guilt, Ivan would call it. The Chinese had a different way of saying the same thing. When Bonitus was born Sylvie went on and on about his sweet face, his button nose, his handsome little mane of black hair. One of Ivan's aunts finally took her aside and told her not to praise an infant that way. She was just inviting bad luck—ghosts could overhear and snatch him away.

Perhaps that was why Sylvie insisted that Bonitus be raised a Catholic. Not that she was particularly religious; like many of her school friends, she shed her religion's outer carapace as soon as it began to restrict her movements. She stopped going to confession, then to church, and left her Saint Christopher medal in the top vanity drawer. But raising a child was a different matter.

Ivan wasn't crazy about the idea, but he was crazy about Sylvie, so he agreed. Besides, a good Catholic education had benefits; there were some fine Jesuit schools in Hong Kong. Their traditions of critical thinking and discipline would stay with Bonitus long after the doctrine fell away.

But shedding guilt was another matter. Sylvie's was buried too deep to reach.

* * *

Ivan walks up behind Sylvie and embraces her as she stares out at Lion Rock and the cinderblock canyons of Kowloon. His arms are warm and smooth. The day, like so many April days here, is gray.

"Do you remember what he looked like?" she says.

"Who? Bonitus? Of course. What are you saying?"

"When he was five? And three? And seven? I looked at the pictures in the bedroom and realized that, without the photos, I had a hard time recalling exactly how his face looked at each age. Why is that?"

"He's grown up so fast, Sylvie."

"Should I remember more than I do?"

"You remember plenty. You remember the names of his teachers, which is more than I do. You're a fine mother. Don't start trying to find reasons why you deserve this."

She says nothing.

"Sylvie, you're just like my superstitious friends, the one who claim they lost at roulette in Macau because they clipped their fingernails at night and were jinxed by ghosts. Stop looking for a reason."

She turns to face him, now in tears again. "But why is he gone? Why?"

In response, he tightens his embrace. "My father's on the way back with some news."

She buries her sobbing head in his chest and whispers, "I can't take this, Ivan."

*　*　*

Ten minutes later Mo enters the flat with his own key, the key Ivan gave him when they moved in. Mo bought them the place, after all.

"I got the ransom demand," Mo announces. "It'll all be over soon."

"Is Bonitus all right?" Sylvie asks, slipping from Ivan's arms and moving to her father-in-law. "Have you spoken to him?"

"I will, don't worry. I made that a condition of payment." Mo's manner is confident, but *lou je* is never as warm as Ivan. She's never certain of what he's thinking or feeling.

Mo looks at Ivan. "Have the police come here?"

"Not yet," Ivan says.

"I'm pretty sure who's behind it. We're tracking him down now."

"When will you know?" Sylvie says.

Mo glances again at Ivan, as if to say, *do something with her, will you?* He walks to the balcony, draws a Marlboro from a pack in his coat pocket, and lights it. Turning away from Ivan and Sylvie, he leans his elbows on the railing and inhales a lungful of smoke, watching a jet shrink to a dot in the distance.

"He's doing everything he can," Ivan says, walking to Sylvie and placing a hand on her shoulder.

"Everything but go to the police," she says.

"I thought you understood. My dad can handle this. In Hong Kong these things happen—they're private transactions. Better not to get the police involved. There's a kind of … a kind of understanding."

Understanding. Can anyone understand me? What I'm going through? And Bonitus?

"Bonitus must be alone; he must be terrified. It's … I don't know if I can do this!" She breaks from Ivan and starts toward the phone. Ivan jogs across the living room and clamps the receiver down with his hand.

"No, Sylvie. We agreed."

"You agreed. I need my son!"

"We all need him. And this is the best way to get him back. I promise."

She looks at her husband as if he's some stranger speaking a foreign language. As if, when Mo entered, he became a different person. She scans Ivan's face for a trace of sympathy, a vestige of shared pain. What she sees is fear.

Chapter Thirteen

Kowloon Tong District, Hong Kong, Saturday, 2:47 p.m.

"Mo *sin-sahng*, we're here to speak with Ivan," says Lok.

Lok would have preferred Mo to be elsewhere; he's simply too big to ignore in a room.

"What for?" Mo looks into Lok's eyes, ignoring Ears, who is standing next to him in the corridor.

"Standard practice for a murder investigation." Lok smiles an indulgent smile. *You know how it is—orders, rules.* It won't fool Mo, though.

"Ivan doesn't know anything about Goldfish Head," Mo says.

"Maybe not. But he works with you."

"He works *for* me." Mo steps back from the doorway, and they enter.

The apartment is spacious, bathed in light from vast windows that frame a picture-perfect harbor. It is the type of flat whose size and location advertise wealth even before a stick of furniture is placed in it. This one is a little sparer than what Lok is used to: few knickknacks or pictures, not one overpriced jade carving. Just a couple of Chinese scrolls whose quality Lok can't guess at, and a sideboard with a single vase on it, most likely a pricey thing from back a couple of dynasties. The type of thing Dora would like, if they could afford it.

Ivan, who is standing next to a blonde *gweipoh*, steps forward to greet Lok. A thirtyish man, tall, built like his father, except for his gym-pumped shoulders; Mo would never have had time for workouts, would have hardened on the job.

Ivan shakes Lok's hand. "How can I help, Inspector?" He sounds sincere. Ivan wears a tailored shirt and cuffed trousers. He appears alert and calm. The only slackness in evidence is the hue of fatigue in the young man's eyes, and his tie, which dangles loosely from his collar.

He introduces the *gweipoh* as his wife Sylvie. Lok has always been fascinated with golden hair, and it's clear why this woman would be thought of as a prize, with her translucent skin and features as sculpted and fragile-looking as a porcelain doll's. Only her smile is not radiant; it is dark and preoccupied. She excuses herself.

"Mo *sin-sahng*," Lok asks Ivan, "did you know Goldfish Head Lau?"

"Just to say hello to. I ride in my dad's car fairly often." Ivan's face is open, even kind, as unlike Mo's as one could imagine.

"Did you ever discuss anything personal with him? Friends, family?"

Ivan shakes his head. Ears says nothing, just takes something down on his notepad.

"Did you ever hear any arguments? Did he tell you about any trouble he was having?"

Ivan smiles sadly and shakes his head. "No, he didn't confide in me."

"Where were you yesterday between eight and ten p.m.?"

"Having dinner with some clients, Gerald Kwok and his wife Mary. I'll give you their number."

Lok nods. "Were you aware that Goldfish Head had a criminal past?"

"So does the police," says Mo from across the room.

Lok's eyebrow lifts at the unexpected reminder of the old days, the second one he's had recently. Mo would recall how it was back then; Lok had only heard stories in the canteen. Stories about brutal interrogations in the back of the wagon before the suspect reached the station. And of course, the bribes, part of the most breathtaking system of police corruption ever conceived.

"I didn't really know about Goldfish Head's past," says Ivan. "I understand my dad did, but he gave him a job anyway."

Nicely done—turn his father's sleazy association into a good deed. Maybe

Ivan is slicker than he looks.

Mo breaks in again. "If you're done, Inspector, we need to get going." He places his hands on Ivan's shoulder. Ivan looks at Mo but says nothing. Lok wonders if Ivan knew he had to get going.

"That's all right," says Lok. "You can go. We'll just speak with your wife for a few moments." Mo looks displeased but says nothing. After they leave, Lok and Ears walk over to Sylvie.

"I'm not sure what I can tell you," she says in excellent Cantonese. Her eyes are red, her complexion pale, even for a Westerner. This hasn't been easy on her. "Would you like some tea?"

"No need."

"Please. I'd like some anyway." She walks to the kitchen, which is married seamlessly to the living room, and fills an electric kettle.

"Do you work?" Ears asks. Lok has flipped his notebook closed, the signal for Ears to take over.

She switches on the kettle. "I'm at Hong Kong Sanatorium and Hospital. I'm a gynecologist."

Ears blushes. "Your Cantonese is very good," he says.

"Thank you."

"Most Westerners don't learn any Chinese," says Lok. "Even ones that live here a long time, ones that marry Chinese."

"I know. But I decided to jump in with both feet. Learn the language, the way of life." A faint smile. "My Chinese characters aren't very good, but you should try my shrimp dumplings."

Lok has a hard time imagining this slender blonde cooking up *won ton*, but he's seen stranger things. A priest from Poland who spoke Cantonese with not the slightest accent—on the phone, he could be your brother. An Irish detective, now retired, who whipped everyone at the station at mahjong. An American who got the better of a Shanghainese on a real estate deal—though that one might just be a story.

"That must make your husband proud," Ears says.

She thinks for a second, as if the idea has never occurred to her. "You'd have to ask him. We've both had to make adjustments. We live in Hong

Kong to be with Ivan's family, but visit the States at least once a year. We celebrate Chinese holidays, but our son …" her voice trails off, then picks up, like a radio signal that fades in and out. "…our son is being brought up Catholic."

"I see. What's your son's name?"

"Bonitus." As she says his name she turns to the kettle, which has boiled. She swishes some steamy water into a teapot, pours it into the sink, and then spoons some loose tea into the pot.

"I hope jasmine is all right."

"Thank you," says Lok. The Tun woman might speak Cantonese, but her taste in tea is Western. Jasmine isn't an everyday tea for most Chinese, but restaurants serve it to *gweilos*.

"Can you spell your son's name?" says Ears. Sylvie does, and Ears's writing slows as he carves out the English letters. Sylvie adds, "It wasn't my choice."

"Old style, I imagine," says Lok. By tradition, the paternal grandfather names the baby.

Sylvie nods. "Ivan's father hired a fortune teller to come up with a Chinese name, and he threw in an English one as a freebie. Bonitus was a medieval saint. Don't ask me how he found it. But it made Ivan and his father very happy when I agreed."

"Another one of those adjustments?"

"Exactly, Inspector. But it suits him now." She brings out two teacups; Ears had declined the tea.

"Did you know your father-in-law's driver?" Ears asks.

"A little. Not very well. He never came up here; he was always waiting in the car. I called him Mr. Lau."

"Does anyone else live here?" asks Ears.

"Just Ivan, our son, and our *amah* Myrna." In English, she'd probably use the word "helper," which is more respectful. But in Cantonese, Lok notes, she goes with the traditional word for nursemaid.

"Where are they now?"

"Where are…?"

"Your son and your *amah*?"

Sylvie nods in understanding, then pours the tea into the cups. Lok and Ears take sips.

"You were going to say where your son and *amah* were," says Ears.

Sylvie pauses, teacup poised at her lips. She looks to the floor, then away, apparently confused by the question. Finally she assembles an answer. "Not here. All this is so…it's too much, she took him…I had her take him to a friend's house to do some studying."

"Did you ever see Goldfish Head with anyone? A friend or acquaintance?"

"No, just on the job, and that was rare." She sips her tea but looks at the floor.

Ears looks to Lok, whose body language tells him that they're done. They thank Sylvie for the tea, and she escorts them to the door.

"One more thing, Mo *tai-tai*," Lok says. "You'll need to come to the Yau Ma Tei station to give us your fingerprints."

That news tends to unnerve some people, even innocent ones, but Sylvie just looks puzzled. "I don't understand."

"We want to rule out your fingerprints from the ones we collect in the car," Ears says.

"I see. Of course."

"Also your husband's and your son's," Lok adds.

She looks away, but nods.

* * *

"What do you think?" Lok says when they return to the Police van.

"I think she was lying, sir."

"Good, Ears. I thought so too. But about what?"

Ears pauses a minute. "Her son. She was fine talking about her husband. But when you asked her where her son was, she had something on her mind."

More than just something on her mind, Lok thinks. She looked as if she'd been shattered and hastily put back together for appearances' sake. Not the usual reaction to the death of one's husband's hired hand.

"Okay. Follow up on the fingerprints. It wouldn't be a bad idea to have

Airport talk to the son when he comes in."

* * *

Tsim Sha Tsui District, Hong Kong, 4:14 p.m.

Old Ko shucks his jacket and parks himself at the table across from Million Man. He digs out Goldfish Head's cell phone and starts keying names and numbers into a computer.

"Where's your gun?" asks Million Man.

"In my desk," Old Ko says, keeping his eyes on the screen. "Too big. Never liked the Sigs."

"What did they use when you started on the force? Swords? Axes?"

"No—brains. They stopped issuing them about the time you joined." He taps the keys slowly, scrolls to the next phone number, then taps more keys.

"Clubs? Spears? No, wait, crossbows. That's it. You joined during the Han Dynasty, wasn't it?"

Old Ko ignores him. Million Man ditches his mocking tone.

"So what's your problem with the Sigs? They're good guns."

"Give me something I can shoot with. These are too powerful. I already have a job as cop. Don't need to be judge, jury, and executioner as well."

Back when Old Ko started, guns were rare. *Lan jai* robbed jewelry stores with realistic toy pistols, or perhaps with a home-made bomb, most likely a fake. In those days, a long-barreled Smith & Wesson revolver loaded with short, useless rounds was all it took to walk tall on Temple Street.

Eventually the Black Star automatics showed up, military sidearms pilfered from some arsenal in a remote Guangdong outpost. A few triad characters in the old Walled City made a living renting out pistols for $800 a day. The police response was to issue Colt .38 Detective Specials: heavier, longer bullets, more punch.

In the decade before the handover, a wave of organized gangs began crossing the border from China to empty out banks and jewelry shops. On the sea, well-armed smugglers were ferrying DVD players into China. The police had to adapt. The marine police got MP5 machine guns, and CID got Sig Sauer automatics.

"Plus, I don't trust those things," says Ko. "They've gone off accidentally." He enters another number.

"No such thing as an accidental discharge," Million Man says. "Just negligence."

"Yeah, yeah. The voice of experience."

"You know, you can copy all the phone contacts right into the computer so they're easier to check."

"That so?"

"Yes. There's hardware that can read the SIM card. Fewer mistakes that way."

"Mm."

"Want me to find someone to do it for you?"

"You think I can't find someone if want? Worry about your own work. Believe me, it needs some worry."

Million Man tried to find out why Old Ko, now growing jowls and hiding gray hairs, was still a Detective Police Constable. After all, the man is older than Lok, who is a Detective Inspector and who could have gone even higher if he played along.

So far, no one seems to know.

Million Man thinks that the reason, when revealed, will confirm his judgment of Old Ko. Maybe Ko failed his promotion exam or misunderstood an order and fouled up an investigation. Somewhere in his record is a blot, a puddle of muck that slips up the old hack whenever he tries to step forward.

Ears doesn't buy Million Man's theory. The kid likes Old Ko, listens to his stories, fetches him the odd cup of coffee. "Look," Ears told him one time, "you've got a thousand cops going for maybe 50 places. Even if the guy's record's good, you can't promote everyone."

"Proves my point. There had to be some reason they didn't promote him."

* * *

They pound their terminals in silence for a while. Having run down the manufacturer of the knife—Double Shine Housewares of Shenzhen, PRC—Million Man has ordered a list of stores that sell it geographically, beginning with Kowloon shops close to the restaurant where Goldfish Head was stabbed.

That might be a mistake; the murderer could have bought the knife far from the scene of the killing to avert suspicion. But Million Man doesn't think so. This is a cheap kitchen knife, not a carefully selected weapon. And Wing Kee Restaurant was far from a routine stop for Mo, so he's working on the assumption that the murder saw his opportunity, bought the knife on the spot, and made a quick kill.

* * *

Causeway Bay District, Hong Kong, Saturday, 6:30 p.m.

Lai-ping, already seated and chatting with a young couple, is a fetching sight in a royal blue dress and black heels. He prefers meeting her like this at the hall; dropping by her flat feels risky.

When she notices him, she excuses herself and crosses the room to greet Lok.

Lai-ping is beautiful without a hint of artifice. She's twenty-three now, but to Lok she seems even younger, certainly the youngest one among the fifteen or so people in the room. *You're thinking too much about age,* he tells himself.

A woman's voice breaks in. "Wonderful to see you all. Let's get started, all right?" The speaker is an American woman named Beverly, around forty, with curly blonde hair. She's dressed in black stretch pants and a flowered top.

The people reluctantly cease the chatter. They separate into couples and arrange themselves about the room. Beverly poises a finger next to a button on a CD player.

"First, we'll just move a little in closed position, to get a feel for the rhythm. No need to try any steps out just yet, all right? Here we go."

The music starts, all popping congas and piercing trumpets, firing up the room with a sound that incites an almost guilty grin on Lok's face.

They move, tentatively at first, bodies positioned primly apart, Lok's hand drawing in the warmth of her body through the smooth fabric of her dress. Back and forth, as Lok recalls the basics drilled into him these past few weeks, his mind focused on the task at hand, the woman in his arms both a distraction and the point of it all. And then the swing, the rhythm, the trills and squeals of the brass, the voices of virile young men shouting their desire begin to heat their blood and take hold of their bodies. Three minutes and it's over, all too fast. Is that a slight blush on her neck, or just a trick of the halogen light?

"Great," says Beverly. "Now, I know you've all been listening to salsa twenty-four hours a day, the way I asked you to." Polite laughter. "So this should be easy. Let's count out eight beats and then do the basic for another eight, all right?"

Lok gives Lai-ping a sheepish grin. He can't listen to this music at home or at work, and he wouldn't dare keep CDs of dance music in his car—what would Dora make of that? Or his team? At first, he was resigned to his slow progress in the art of salsa dancing, but now he embraces his status as a laggard—it's all part of the deal. The horns and percussion have become for him a kind of sacred temple music, heard nowhere else, consecrating these ritual evenings with Lai-ping.

One, two, three, four, five, six, seven, eight. Feel the rhythm, stay relaxed...

* * *

Pok Fu Lam District, Hong Kong, Saturday, 8:18 p.m.

The Aberdeen Tunnel would have been faster, but Lok prefers taking the longer, winding Pok Fu Lam Road route, first west, then south to Lai-ping's home. A longer drive means a longer conversation.

They've already talked about the dance lesson and joked about the other couples.

Then: "Do you still think about him?"

"Sometimes," Lok says. "But that's not why I do this."

He regrets having told her, one night months ago, that he thinks of her brother. It only complicates things.

He owes Lai-ping nothing. He hadn't shot her brother—an Emergency Unit officer had done that, plugged the fool easily as he ran out the door of the jewelry store in Central, waving his Black Star automatic like an action hero. But Lok had been the one to unmask him, see the dread of death in his eyes, hear his final words.

"So what's your reason?"

"Why I keep visiting? You're good company."

"Then why don't we sleep together?"

The answer to that was another question, this one desperate and final, uttered by a dying man. *Elder sister. Who will take care of her?* Lai-ping's brother Lai-man had spoken those words to him as he bled out on the pavement.

The dead boy had been right to worry about his sister. Both parents were gone, and now the old aunt who had tried to raise them was wasting away in an institution, with little mind or body left.

The boy had given up on school and taken up with the 14K, despite his sister's pleas. *We need money*, he said. *What kind of job could I get with my brains? Pumping gas with those old mainland geezers? Parking cars? You stay in school, elder sister—I'll take care of the money.*

A gang from the mainland organized the robbery, brought the weapons, even drove the van. Lai-ping's brother was just a lookout, the kid who knew the streets in Hong Kong, the one posted stiff and sweating at the door while three others smashed cases and crammed duffel bags with watches and gold. Awash in a sea of alarms and broken glass, they barely heard the sirens. A Police van swerved into Pottinger Street and cornered them between the store and their getaway car. Nothing to do but shoot it out. They all died, two on the concrete, two on the gurney. Lok reached the scene in time to hear the boy's last question. Only later did he discover that he was the answer.

Lok found Lai-ping in one of the anonymous towers of Wah Fu estate, a dingy set of public housing blocks in southern Hong Kong, and informed her of her brother's death. She was nineteen.

At first, it was a visit every month or so, ensuring she had food to eat and clothes to wear, with an occasional word to the patrolman at Wah Fu to keep an eye on her. Then came the odd meal. Lai-ping never asked for more or less than Lok gave her, which in his eyes was very little. Just a compassionate ear, some advice on whether to take a full-time job now or go for more schooling, that sort of thing.

Lai-ping grew older and more attractive. The contrast with Dora was only too obvious. His wife, who'd enjoyed the attention of men from an early age, handled them with grace and ease. Lai-ping hadn't the slightest idea of how to flirt, or contend with men who did. That she was unaware of her allure served to increase it.

Conscious that he was leading himself into temptation, Lok did the sensible thing and told Lai-ping to go out and meet some young people. She was smart and good-looking, after all, and maturity would come.

At first she'd agreed politely and ignored his advice, but eventually she began to seek more company. Lok got reports of a Lantau cookout here, a concert there, a slow accumulation of a circle of friends. She didn't mention men specifically. Never had, in fact.

Still, Lok visited almost weekly, and during one of those visits, Lok almost succumbed to what would have been the only indiscretion in all the years of his marriage. He wouldn't admit it, but he'd been overcome by jealousy at the thought of her achieving independence from him. She had a job and no longer needed the folded hundred he pressed in her hand when he said goodbye. Soon she would need no guide or benefactor, and he felt too old to be a friend. What else was there?

He found out one night when they returned from a dinner at a Sri Lankan restaurant. It was a balmy October evening, and they were relaxed and laughing. With no warning, Lai Ping unbuttoned her blouse to expose a band of pink lace. Lok pulled at his tie and was about to remove it when his eyes swept the room, looking for a place to lay his clothes so that they wouldn't pick up any unfamiliar wrinkles, fragrances, or other clues that might arouse Dora's suspicion.

He could never risk it, he realized. He didn't fear discovery, but he did fear losing Dora. He slid the knot back up to his collar and told her to stop.

She said she understood. *What does she understand?*

Perhaps she understands that he wants to be in her life, but can't throw away his marriage. The compromise, so crazy that it seems to make sense, is for him to take dance lessons with her.

Up to tonight, he thought it was settled. Had he been sending the wrong signals? Looking at her too fondly, too intently? Or was the dancing itself a danger?

He says nothing, just drives on, leaving her query unanswered. After a minute, she takes a small paper bag from her handbag.

"Have a walnut?" she asks.

"No thanks."

"You should eat them. They're good brain food."

"Why is that?"

"Because they look like brains."

The Chinese are a symbolic people, he thinks. Everything means something. He takes the walnut and pops it in his mouth.

Chapter Fourteen

Wan Chai District, Hong Kong, Saturday, 4:16 p.m.

What did *Ba Ba* say to do first? *Unlock the door. Crack it open slowly. Plant your foot near the threshold to block the door, in case the boy tries to burst out.*

The boy makes no move, however. He's crouched in a far corner, hours of contained bile overflowing into the glare he casts at Doby through his eyeglasses. He has a few little dark spots around his nose. Doby doesn't remember seeing a Chinese kid with them before.

The room stinks: the boy has had a bowel movement already. The wastebasket sits by the door.

"I brought you some lunch," Doby says. Silence. Doby lays the rice box on the floor, removes the wastebasket, and locks the door again. He carries the foul basket to the sink in the janitor's closet down the hall, holding it as far from his face as he can. He fills it halfway with water and empties it into the toilet across the hall.

When he returns, the boy is wolfing down his food.

"I'll be back tonight," says Doby.

"I need my homework," says the boy, his mouth full of rice.

"What?"

"My homework. If I don't do it, I'll get behind in school. Can you bring me my bookbag?"

"Uh... I don't think so."

"I'll get in trouble. It's not fair."

Doby thinks for a minute. This requires some kind of decision. He's not good at decisions—that's *Ba Ba's* job. *Ba Ba* makes Doby's decisions, and *Ma Ma's*. *Ba Ba* makes decisions for other people at work, too, he says. They all ask *Ba Ba* to decide things because he always knows what to do.

Doby never knows what to do.

"I'd better ask," he says.

"It's just a book bag. What's the harm?"

"Why do you want to do schoolwork?" Doby hates schoolwork. He sighed with relief the day he was allowed to quit school. People always wanted to know stupid stuff, like what was this word and how much did this add up to. He doesn't care about those things. *Ba Ba* understands that. *Ba Ba* is clever.

"It's boring here," says the boy. "I need something to do. And my *Ba Ba* won't like it if I get behind."

My Ba Ba *won't like it.* That Doby understands. He clicks the door closed and retrieves the bag, which his father had shoved in a broom closet.

"Thanks," said the boy. "What's your name?"

"Doby." Is it okay to tell him my name? *Ba Ba* hadn't said not to tell him his name. Or had he? *Don't go in the room, don't talk to him, just give him the food and clean the wastebasket,* he had said.

Don't talk means don't tell him my name. He's disobeyed *Ba Ba!* In panic, he shuts the door and runs to the elevator, as if to distance himself from his own folly.

* * *

Tsuen Wan District, Hong Kong, Saturday, 7:32 p.m.

The mile from the Tsuen Wan MTR station to Horace's flat is an irrelevant one, crammed with businesses that don't interest Horace: vision shops, fashion stores, a cell phone accessory depot, an herbalist, and a jeweler. The signs are colorful, the conversations at the bins spirited. Not for years has

Horace paid much attention to surroundings, not since he first arrived in Hong Kong, a young man still sore from his wound and his humiliation. Back then Hong Kong was a narcotic, a non-stop rush of stimulation that drowned him in novelty, more new ideas in a day than China had offered him in five years. Only gradually did he come to understand that Hong Kong taunts you with everything but gives you nothing. It's like that diamond in the jeweler's window, gorgeous to look at, but not to be possessed, ever.

He arrives at his building and shares the elevator with two other silent commuters. Like gamblers at a roulette wheel, they stare at the numbers above the door, waiting for theirs to come up.

By the time he opens his apartment door his wife has appeared. Winnie knows to be there when he comes in, so he doesn't have to address an empty room. Winnie is small and thin, with a narrow face and a head of long, coarse hair tied in a ponytail. She has spindly arms and a slightly dark complexion. In their early days together, her skin drew mild derision from Horace. *I'm marrying a Haklo fisherwoman*, he would say from time to time. *What would my parents think?*

"Is dinner ready?"

"Almost," she says, putting the best face on things. Much better to say *almost* than *not yet*. "The market was crowded today, so I had to wait to get the pig's ears."

He nods. Pig's ears are good, though Winnie doesn't do them quite as well as his grandmother did. Horace's grandmother died when he twelve, in what he learned, many years later, was a great famine brought on by stupidity. How ironic that he should escape one country crippled by stupidity and end up in a city that thrives on it.

"How was work today?"

"How do you think it was?" Horace says, though he expects no reply. Her last few inquiries about work resulted in a full account of The Girl and her disgusting personality. That put him in a filthy mood all evening.

Winnie asks where Doby is. Often, Horace and Doby come home together.

"He'll be home soon. I needed him to do something for me."

"What was that?"

"Why do you care? Mind your own business."

"I'm sorry." She smiles a broad smile. "I was just wondering when he'll be home…"

"Then ask when he'll be home. Don't poke into things that don't concern you." Winnie nods and returns to the kitchen. Horace switches on the TV.

As Winnie brings the steaming braised pig's ears and *bok choy* to the table, Kenny arrives.

Kenny is taller than Horace, taller even than Doby, with bright, clear eyes. His oxford shirt clings to a body that is hard but not over-muscled. The spoon looks like a toy in his large hand as he ladles himself some rice. He's twenty-seven and perfectly groomed, with a dash of gel restraining a shock of hair above his forehead.

Kenny greets Winnie, but passes by Horace in silence. After washing his hands in the bathroom, he sits down. "Pig's ears again?" he says with a laugh. "Any other parts of the pig for sale lately?"

"Your father likes them," says Winnie as she takes a chair opposite him.

"How about you? I know Doby doesn't care for them."

"I don't mind them," she says.

"Just eat," says Horace.

"What's new in school?" says Winnie. Kenny teaches mathematics at a secondary school.

"Not too much. Next year Old Lau is leaving, so there might be an opening for department head."

She beams. "That would be wonderful."

"Can't pay that much more," says Horace.

"Not too much more," says Kenny.

"Could you support a wife on it?"

"I'm not married," he says. "And I'd rather help out here." Kenny has given Winnie part of his salary since his first job as a teaching assistant. Money has always been tight; Winnie had to leave her bookkeeping position at a department store when Horace learned that her salary had crept above his. She's a secretary now.

"Isn't it about time you got married?" Horace says.

"Haven't met anyone," says Kenny.

"At your age? You must meet plenty of women. I never see you going out with anyone. You just hang out with your friend, that Reggie Ko."

"Sure."

"Remember that Bonnie Fong you used to spend time with?" says Winnie.

"Mmm."

"She was a nice girl. I know her father. He tells me she's still not married either."

"So I hear."

"I wonder why not. She's a pretty girl."

Kenny concentrates on his food. Pig's ears are pure cartilage, but the surrounding flavors of garlic, soy, and cinnamon have a way of soaking in.

"If I were you, I wouldn't associate with Reggie Ko," says Horace. "What is he, a bartender?"

"A maitre d'. At a very good restaurant in Lan Kwai Fong."

"Maitre d', whatever. And I hear things about him."

Again, Kenny says nothing, just paddles a bit more rice onto his plate from the cooker.

"What things?" says Winnie.

He lowers his voice. "They think he's a *gay lo.*"

Winnie's eyes widen. "Really? Reggie is gay?" She turns to Kenny. "Kenny, did you know that?"

Kenny shrugs. "Not illegal."

"It was in China," says Horace. "I know of a couple who were put down like old cats. That was in the sixties."

Kenny's eyes narrow for a moment as he looks at Horace for the first time tonight. "It's not that way now. Not in Hong Kong. That's why you came here, wasn't it? To get away from that kind of thing."

"To see those people roaming around free? No."

"No, you came to get rich."

Horace stops chewing for a second, stares at his own half-full plate of pig's ears. On TV, an announcer is reciting the day's stock prices.

Winnie breaks in. "I read somewhere that there's a thing in the brain that they're missing," she says. "There are doctors in China who can cure it. They use herbs, or electricity, or something."

Kenny shakes his head. "They're just in it for the money."

"What's wrong with that?" says Horace. "Making a living doing something worthwhile…"

Kenny stands, his legs sending his chair back with a judder and a screech. Winnie looks up, her face a mask of anxiety, as it almost always is by the time Horace has been home an hour.

"I have papers to grade," Kenny says. He vanishes into his bedroom.

"Is it wrong to want a grandson?" says Horace.

Winnie smiles. It's a habit now, smiling when speaking with her husband. "It will come. Kenny is such a handsome boy. He picked me up from work the other day, and the other ladies almost swooned. They told me he was a real catch."

"It isn't as if he has all that much to do."

"He's a teacher. He works hard."

"We all work hard. Don't talk to me about working hard. I worked hard, and I gave you two boys."

They finish the meal in silence, apart from the chatter of television announcers and the consistent cheery cacophony of ads for watches, cars, fashion, food.

* * *

Doby arrives as Winnie is washing the dishes in the kitchen sink. He nods to his parents and then sits down to the meal his mother has left him on the table.

"I'm late," he says. "I couldn't help it. I had to…"

"It's all right, Doby," says Horace. "You had things to do."

Winnie pauses at this sudden display of understanding, then goes back to the dishes. Horace leans over Doby until their heads almost touch.

"Everything go all right?"

Doby nods.

"Lock up after?"

Another nod.

Doby shovels the rice in his eager mouth and stares at the TV screen. A commercial flashes by, causing Doby to halt for a moment.

"We carry those," he says.

"What?" Winnie has been distracted and doesn't understand.

Doby points to the TV. "Ming Wah Dried Cuttlefish Snacks. Also Ming Wah Chili Peanut Snacks. We carry them both."

"I see. Did you deliver any of them today?"

"The cuttlefish. To a store in Kowloon Tong."

"Good," says Winnie.

After his meal Doby retreats to his room with its waiting stack of comic books. Winnie looks over the paper, and Horace watches TV. Nothing new on the murder of Goldfish Head Lau. Lau's ID card photo appears on the screen, an indifferent black-and-white snapshot that arouses no emotion in Horace. That switches to a picture of Mo Tun. Horace stares into the eyes as if Mo had burst into the room.

Winnie looks up from the paper. "By the way, when I was hanging up your jacket, I found a second cell phone in your pocket. Is that yours too?"

"Mind your own business," he says. He can't tear his eyes from the screen, though Mo's face has vanished.

Chapter Fifteen

Kowloon District, Hong Kong, Sunday, 9:51 a.m.

Lento finds one of them on every building site: an old guy living out his years in a pantomime of his former job. Aged sixty, older sometimes, in need of a shave, lean as a stray cat, and just as wary. Too old to haul lumber or hoist girders, but able to dig a hole here and there and fetch tea or a magazine at the break. This particular site, the fifth one on Lento Chan's list, is an office-tower-to-be in Causeway Bay. A new steel skeleton looms above a pit three or four stories deep and a quarter of a block in length. Down below, in the dust and clatter, men are pouring concrete and setting rebar. Young, tough men: mainland Chinese, Filipino, a Nepali or two. But Lento won't find his man down there among the sweating and aching muscles. The guy he wants will stay in the shade, on the rim of the abyss. Lento rarely has to walk far to find him.

* * *

There are places Lento would rather be. He had to cancel Mo's bank appointment to do this; the escrow matter would have to wait. Mo was not pleased about putting anything regarding the Great Wall Disco on hold, as it stands to be his largest and most profitable business, the one that will change the character of his operation and add zeroes to his bottom line. But they both know this matter must be taken care of, and Mo insists that Lento handle the footwork.

Having given the yard man face by asking his permission to question his employees, Lento heads toward the most grizzled man on the site, whose name turns out to be Old Chong. He's a willowy man of at least seventy who is dragging a sack of something somewhere. Lento asks Old Chong if he remembers a worker named Dollar-10 from many years ago.

Old Chong lets go of the bag and uses his fingers to form two circles around his eyes, mimicking coins of different sizes.

"Dollar-ten. One big eye, one small eye, right?"

"That's right. You know him?"

"Worked with him on a couple of jobs. Not too much use, if you know what I mean. Talked a lot, didn't do much besides follow his horoscope in the paper and collect his pay."

"Any idea where he is now?"

Old Chong shakes his head. "Haven't seen him in maybe ten years. Don't think he's doing this anymore. Maybe his luck changed. He sure worried about it enough."

Lento thanks him, keeping the discouragement out of his voice. His boss got where he is through persistence, after all, and Lento intends to show him that he's made of the same stuff. And he had better be, because he will never run out of construction sites in Hong Kong. With the handover settled and China pouring money in, the territory is feeding its insatiable addiction to growth and renewal. As he steps off the dirt onto the pavement of Jaffe Road, he can see his next site already, the cranes shifting slowly to and fro in the smog above the rooftops.

Chapter Sixteen

Kowloon District, Hong Kong, Sunday, 8:18 a.m.

Breakfast is congee, a fragrant rice porridge into which Esmeralda has thrown chopped scallions, peanuts, and small slices of chicken. Apart from weekend *dim sum*, it's Lok's favorite breakfast, and he's content to let Dora talk while he devours it.

"You'll be happy to note that Edna has gone back to her original hair color. Or an approximation of it."

Lok smiles. Their daughter has the habit of proclaiming her independence in ways that have nothing to do with real independence, and everything to do with annoying Lok. A blonde dye job was the most recent of these.

"So you were right, she came around. What's Kelvin up to?"

"I told him to start thinking about university. Have you seen his grades?"

Lok shakes his head.

"He got a B in English."

"Well, I'd get a C in English if I took the test now."

"Herman, the kids he's competing against have all A's."

Dora is right, but the thought of placing his kids under constant pressure makes him uneasy.

Lok doesn't know much about universities, never having attended one. But a degree is an escape to a job and a Canadian passport. Even the cops want graduates. When he joined the force a university education had been out of the question. Now it was more or less a requirement. Occasionally you got a kid like Ears who was so bright and motivated that you could overlook the lack of a degree, but not often.

"Your friend Rocky Cheu is cheating again," Dora says, though she doesn't appear too distressed by the news. Her tone is more like a mother reporting on a child's mischief.

"How do you know?" says Lok.

"He bought Daisy earrings. Gorgeous pair, diamond."

"That doesn't mean he's cheating. You think it's guilt?"

"No."

She says nothing. On this point they differ, Lok preferring to deliver information without fanfare or teasing.

"All right, let's have it."

"They're from Wing Lo Jewelers in Central."

"And that tells me…"

"Wing Lo is having a sale. Buy one pair, get the second for half off. Big signs in the window."

"So?"

"So, do you think with a sale like that, Rocky just bought one pair? I'm sure the other pair went to the night shift."

There is something chilling about Dora's mind, that ability to take any line of thought to the obvious conclusion, no matter what it says about humanity. Still, it's just a report, not a veiled reference to his own escapade with Lai-ping. Dora doesn't veil anything.

* * *

Sham Shui Po District, Hong Kong, Sunday, 11:12 a.m.

Rarely has Old Ko seen a room this barren. A full inventory of the flat takes him less than a minute: a small worn sofa set to face the television, a coffee table bearing a few copies of the Racing News and a pile of cigarette butts under which, somewhere, lies an ashtray; and, in the southwest corner, placed correctly for this year according to astrologers, a shrine to Pi Yao, protector of gamblers, its dragon head open-mouthed, fierce, and unaware of its recent dismissal for cause as a good-luck token.

The closet-like kitchen displays emblems of Lau's solitude: a tiny refrigerator stocked with beer and nothing else; a charred and dented kettle on the hot plate; some instant noodles and tea bags in the cupboard; a bottle opener on the counter; a few bottle caps in the trash.

For a moment Old Ko wonders if it's all a deception, if Goldfish Head Lau really lived somewhere else than this little flat with its dusty cream-colored walls and floors of mottled baby blue ceramic tile.

But the deception would have been a poor one—nothing here adds up to a real life, anyway. No pictures on the walls, no calendar, no rug, no ornaments apart from cobwebs. No deck of cards, no extra coffee cup or bowl or pillow or chair—not one provision for a second human being in Lau's life. For the only other human being in this man's crabbed existence was his boss. Lau's sole purpose was to ferry the big man from office to property to restaurant to club to alley to wherever else he made his just-this-side-of-the-law deals.

Ko searches the drawers, and finds some clothing, but no documents to speak of apart from salary notifications, a checkbook, and a tax bill. No family photos, no computer, no money, no magazines apart from a pile of porn on the far side of the bed, next to the cell phone charger and a boom box. The porn is standard stuff, nothing exotic. Nowadays only old men buy the magazines. The Internet serves the younger generation.

"Find out who did it?"

Ko follows the voice to the door, where a young woman leans idly against the door frame. She's in her twenties, petite, pretty, expensively dressed, carrying a bag that would cost Old Ko a month's salary if it isn't a back-alley fake.

"Who are you?"

"Cinderella Chu. I own the flat next door. It was on the news, what happened. Did you catch whoever did it?"

"Not yet," Ko says, walking over to the door and opening it a bit wider. The woman draws back slightly, conscious that she's being inspected by the older man. Her face is open but her haircut looks masculine, a short and fashionable razor job that seems severe to Ko, not a fitting counterpoint to her delicate face.

"Did you know Lau?" says Old Ko.

"Not really. To say hello to. He kept to himself. I know they always say, 'he kept to himself,' but it's true. He was never around, went out early, came back late. Like my grandfather. No life at all."

"Your grandfather?"

"Sold fish in North Point. Lived on Cheung Chau, took the first ferry in at six with his prawns and mackerel, came back on 11:30 every night. Died on the ferry, in fact."

"I think I remember that. Maybe eight, ten years ago?" People die everywhere in a city, Ko thinks. On ferries and trains, in parks, restaurants, and streets. And limousines. The best kind of death, an unexpected one—less time for everyone to suffer.

She nods. "I work damn hard, but I want a life too."

"Some jobs are demanding of time. Where do you work?"

"Bennett Kwok Creative Partners. Advertising. I'm an account exec."

To Old Ko it sounds at once complex and uninteresting. "Did you ever see any visitors here?"

"Never. Not a one. The guy was a monk."

"A monk who played the horses."

"Right. I could hear the races on the TV sometimes."

"Did his employer ever come by?"

"That big man? Come here? No way. I had no idea who Lau worked for till the news report."

"Did you ever see him with a woman?"

She shakes her head. "He struck me as the prostitute type."

Old Ko silently agrees with her: Mongkok hookers on payday or when the horse came in, perhaps a trip to the New Territories for something cheaper when money was tight. And for the lonely, penniless nights, the magazines.

Scanning the room one more time, Ko concludes that Goldfish Head Lau was no monk, despite the privation. Monks have an ideal, a direction in life.

Austerity can be a sign of character—Ko had seen sparse rooms occupied by wealthy men who wanted no distractions, no clutter, no impediments between them and their ambitions.

But this was different. This was the room of a man without ambition. And a man without ambition is a man without enemies.

"Please write your name and number here," Ko says, holding out his notepad for her to scribble on. "If you think of anything else, give a call." He hands her a business card.

"I don't think I could take a life like his," she says. "No friends, work all day and night, and then you gamble a little on your time off. Is a cop's life like that?"

Isn't everyone's life like that, Ko wonders. The job comes first for everyone here. "We work long hours, I'll say that."

"Hope you got something good for it." She slips away and into her own flat.

Thanks for putting my career in the past tense, lady.

* * *

Tsim Sha Tsui District, Hong Kong, Sunday, 2:04 p.m.

Million Man is tracking down the knife; Old Ko is checking out Goldfish Head Lau's flat; Big Pang is sifting through Mo's banking records; Ears is attempting to collect fingerprints from Mo's family. Mo Tun himself has no fingerprints on file, Lok is surprised to find. On occasion Mo has been fingerprinted in connection with choppings involving triads linked to his operations, but always for elimination purposes. By law the prints are tossed afterward.

Lok is comparing Mo's statement with his son's, looking for inconsistencies, when Airport pokes her head inside the door.

"Sir?"

"Come on in, Airport." Since joining the team a year ago, WPC Carrion

Kwok has undergone the transformation that policewomen must make, the one that occurs solely in the minds of her male peers. Airport began as the team's little sister, the girl they all advised and protected. They teased her, all right—the Sig on her belt practically dragged on the ground—and the nickname came to CID with her. The joke was that when they flattened out Chek Lap Kok to build the airport, they used her chest for a model.

She took it in stride. After all, to get where she was, Airport had to be twice as good as any man. She could throw an armlock on a drunk Filipina who outweighed her by forty pounds, and her repertoire of curses was as large as it was varied. No one teases her now.

"I've been trying to track down Mo's grandson, Bonitus," she says. "No luck yet."

"What's going on?"

"I asked the mother if I could drop by, but she said it wasn't convenient. Some kind of appointment—she was pretty vague."

"Well, keep trying."

"I have, sir. The first time the *amah* took him to a doctor, the second time he was at the movies with a friend. Doesn't sound right.

"Did you confront them?"

"No sir, I thought it best to talk to the *amah* first." The domestic helper is the weak link in a Chinese family—some discreet prodding can release a gusher of information. Hong Kong's minor aristocrats might be smug, stubborn, devious. But their maids will be petrified of the police.

"And?" Lok says.

"Guess what? The *amah's* on holiday."

"Since when?"

"Mo *tai-tai* says Friday, but let's see what the maid says. I got her name from immigration. That way, the family doesn't know I'm going to talk to her. If she's really on holiday, it'll be tough to track her down. But if she's just been told to lie low for a while, I'll find her."

Chapter Seventeen

Tsuen Wan District, Hong Kong, Sunday, 5:38 p.m.

Kenny is still in his room preparing classes and grading papers. Horace watches the television news, Winnie in a chair beside him. The murder story leads the broadcast, and Horace sees again the limousine, now immersed in garish TV lighting. *Easy to see with all those lights. Maybe if I'd have had those spotlights I could have seen that the man in the limousine wasn't Mo.*

But the lights and cameras are only there because of him. The thought that the reporters, cops, and witnesses are really talking about him makes him clench his knees together in…what? Fear? Excitement? Horace isn't sure what he's feeling, but it's more than he's felt in years. Since the old days with Mo.

At nine p.m. Horace grabs a light sweater and leaves his flat. Winnie doesn't ask where he's off to, Horace having made her regret doing so in the past. For a few blocks he wanders, stopping once to stare through the window of a cafe in which people have gathered to eat, drink, shout, and laugh. Just past the restaurant, he brings out his second cell phone, but the 39M bus, a red-and-yellow Dennis Dragon, trundles by and breaks his concentration.

On a quiet side street lined with steel-gated garages he fires up the phone and presses the one number in the Recent Calls list.

"*Wai?* Mo answers on the first ring. In the background a television reporter is nattering; Mo has been watching the same news report.

"Here's what I want you to do," Horace says. "Get the money. Put it in a bag in one hundred dollar bills…"

"Stop there, dickface. Seven million in hundreds? That's seventy thousand bills. Do you have a truck with you? A crane? Have you any idea how much that weighs?"

"Thousands, then! Put it in thousands, and be ready at 10 p.m. the day after tomorrow. I'll call you with instructions."

"I told you I wasn't doing anything until I heard that Bonitus is all right."

"He's fine, I told you. I'll let him speak to you when I give you your instructions."

"If you do anything to him, I'll pull you apart like a doll. You think I don't know who you are?"

He can't know, thinks Horace. He's bluffing.

* * *

Wan Chai District, Hong Kong, Sunday, 6:20 p.m.

The last few days have been full of new things, and Doby is never sure what to think of new things. At school, his teachers had brought out new things all the time, things that always seemed to defeat him: stories about places around the world that only made him tired, math rules he forgot as soon as he heard them, characters full of confusing strokes that he had to practice for weeks to remember, while his schoolmates giggled at the awkwardness of his Chinese script.

But these new things are from *Ba Ba*, and that was different, because *Ba Ba* understands that Doby is different. The math rules and Chinese characters didn't stay in his mind for very long. But *Ba Ba* knows how to tell him things so that he remembers them. That's how *Ba Ba* taught Doby to drive, a step at a time, spending days on the left turn, days on parking. *Ba Ba* doesn't get tired of him the way other teachers did.

The aroma of pork curry fills the van. He wonders if the kid will like it.

Drive past the building and look for people.

If someone is there, drive away.

If no one is around, drive two blocks and then park.

Walk in the shade. Wear your cap. Pull the brim down in front.

When you get to the building, look once again to the left, the right, and across the street. If no one is there, unlock the service door and go in. Be extra quiet. All right, now what do you do first?

Drive past the building and look for people.

No one is in front of the building. Did *Ba Ba* say to look across the street? He does it anyway. Empty.

If no one is around, drive two blocks and then park.

First block….second block… it's almost three blocks before he finds a gap in the cars wide enough for the van. He'll have to explain to his father later, but he doesn't think he's really disobeying.

Walk in the shade. Wear your cap. Pull the brim down in front.

The brim of his cap makes it hard to see.

When you get to the building, look once again to the left, the right, and across the street. If no one is there, unlock the service door and go in. Be extra quiet.

When Doby cracks the door open, the boy, who is lying on the floor, raises his head and stares in Doby's direction, but he doesn't meet Doby's eyes. Doby places the bag of takeout by the door. The boy studies it.

"I need something to drink," he says. "You brought me food, but no drinks. I'm thirsty."

Had his father told him to buy a drink? He doesn't think so. Can he do it now and still be obeying *Ba Ba?*

Put down the food. Empty the wastebasket in the toilet and rinse it out. That's all.

He didn't say anything about drinks.

In the bathroom he drains the wastebasket, keeping his head as far as he can from the foulness of it. Halfway down the corridor is the janitor's closet, with a large sink for rinsing the container clean. He returns to the room and is grateful that the boy has not tried to escape. His father keeps warning him that the boy might barrel out of the room as Doby returns with the basket. Just in case, he braces his body against the door as he opens it.

But the boy doesn't try anything. He's sitting down by the far wall, reading a comic book. Doby moves his lips as he reads the characters of the title: Legends of the Green Warriors.

"What are you looking at?" says the boy. Defiant, testy.

"The book." In the drab shadows, the colors of the comic transfix him.

The boy is silent for a moment. Then: "Do you want to read it? Get me a drink and I'll give it to you."

Doby closes his eyes. How is he to navigate this new maze? He's been told not to talk to the boy, just feed him. But he's been offered a comic book.

"I…I don't think I can."

"Why not?" The boy jiggles the magazine in his hand, presenting his case. "It's yours. It's good, too."

"Wait here," Doby says. He closes the door, leans against it, and thinks.

Chapter Eighteen

Kowloon Tong District, Hong Kong, Sunday, 10:00 p.m.

The call is on time to the minute. Sylvie's and Ivan's eyes meet at the sound of the ringtone. Mo presses the green button. They're huddled on the couple's living room sofa.

"*Wai?*" he says.

"Okay, this is what you wanted. You'd better listen." It's the same voice, that cretin who made the ransom demand. Mo presses the speaker button and lays the phone on the coffee table.

"*Ma Ma?*"

"Bonitus!" says Sylvie.

"*Ma Ma*, they won't let me go home. I'm sorry."

"It's okay, Bonitus. Are you all right?" The sound of her breathing competes with her words.

"Yes."

"Anyone hurt you?"

"No."

"We'll get you out of there," says Ivan.

"I want to leave this place. They don't have a bathroom. There's nothing to do." Mo hears a slight echo in the boy's words, as if they're being uttered in a bare room.

"Don't worry, Bonitus. We're getting you home right away."

"I'm sorry, M*a Ma*."

"Don't be. It's not your fault. Your grandfather will get you home." She's weeping now. Ivan, usually calm, is clutching his mouth as if he might vomit.

"That's enough," says the man's voice. "Is the money ready?"

"What do you think, dickface?"

Silence on the line. The insult has thrown him off, established Mo as the one running the conversation.

"Take it to the corner of Shantung Street and Reclamation Street. Now. Bring this phone, and the money. Do not tell the police, and don't have anyone following you."

"I'm sending an assistant."

"I want you to deliver it."

"Can't do that. The moment it's delivered, I'm picking up my grandson. I presume you and the money will be somewhere else. I just want the boy. Who gives a shit who hands you the money?"

Silence again.

"All right. No police, no guns, no extra people. Wait for further instructions."

The phone clicks off.

"It's almost over," says Mo. He fumbles in his pocket for a cigarette, finds none, then leaves.

* * *

Tsim Sha Tsui District, Hong Kong, Sunday, 10:51 p.m.

Lento will know he has truly legitimized the operation when he no longer has to supervise people like Jelly Pong. To hire a secretary or computer engineer, you just put an ad in the paper and choose the best. But when a fish seller is behind in his protection payments, and you need a man to kick over crab tanks, you can't advertise. You find your men where you can.

The paradox taunts Mo and Lento daily: you try to outsmart the police with an army made up of losers, people who were outsmarted by life at the outset. Most of your prospects leave school early, so they won't be good at much. They'll be crooks and thugs: needlessly violent, uneducated, sloppy, disinclined to learn, and worst of all, they'll have absolutely no desire to do hard work. That is, Mo reminds him, why they become crooks and thugs in the first place.

Lento hands Jelly Pong a gym bag full of cash. Jelly is twenty-three, slim and short with a head of hair that appears to be the sole purpose of his existence. It stands a good two inches above his scalp, arching back like a wheat field in a breeze, thanks to professional waving and daily brushing. Apart from keeping his hair neat, Jelly excels at one job: waiting in line when a new block of flats goes on sale, hogging the front places, and dislocating the fingers of anyone who tries to knock them back. The flats usually jump some twenty percent in value in the first few weeks after Mo buys them. Jelly and each of his pals earn $1500 for a morning's work. Mo nets a fortune.

Lento has yet to find Jelly suited to a more challenging task. Perhaps bag man for a kidnap payoff is it. Lento offered to go himself, but Mo forbade him. You can never tell what a crazy person will do. That's what people like Jelly are for.

Lento bought the gym bag on the way to his banker. He chose one that would be large enough, knowing as he does that seven thousand bills makes five stacks, each six inches in height. He's made similar cash payments before, but never to a stranger. He knows who the stranger is working for, however, and in time the money will be back where it belongs.

Worse than the size of the payment is the timing: Diamond Rich Development is cash-poor. The disco has been a massive money drain, and the ransom just about cleans them out of cash. Most of this money should have gone into escrow for the construction people.

The waiting is what bothers Lento. Nothing should hold up the disco, as far as he is concerned.

They go over the instructions one more time. Go to the appointed corner. Wait for the call. Do not bring a gun. Make the handoff. Be polite. Leave.

* * *

Yau Ma Tei District, Hong Kong, Sunday, 11:48 p.m.

Jelly Pong arrives at a small, dingy, godforsaken industrial building in a remote corner of Yau Ma Tei. The lobby is dark, and that's unusual; does nobody work here at night? No uncle or grandpa dozing in a chair, uniform hat tossed on top of a dog-eared magazine. Only a stray beam from a streetlight keeps him from walking into a wall.

An hour ago he called the one number on the phone, the way Lento told him to, and took instructions from the man on the line. Got the money? Yes. Go to the corner of wherever and whatever and wait for another call. The dreary routine went on and on, corner to alley to corner, until he ended up at this building.

The elevator is lighted, but there's nothing to see except the framed inspection card. Some fellow named Wong Tai-wo showed up every six months, looked at the elevator, and signed the card. How much does Mr. Wong make as a lift inspector? Not much, Jelly supposes, and he pays taxes to boot, the sucker.

Jelly checks his hair in the glass of the frame.

The door opens upon a darkened corridor. He feels for the reassuring weight of the Black Star 9mm pressing against his back. It's fine for Lento to tell him not to be armed. But what if the other guy starts something?

He steps into the corridor. As the elevator door slides shut, Jelly hears a voice.

"Over here."

"Turn on a light. I can't see."

Jelly hears a low, rumbling hiss. Before he can make sense of it he's knocked to the floor by something hard and cold as a sledgehammer. It slams the breath out of him, chokes him, presses down on his face, his chest, with an urgent pounding that he can't fight.

Only when the rumble ceases does he recognize what knocked him down. His eyes begin to adjust to the darkness. He reaches for his weapon, and dies.

Chapter Nineteen

Kowloon District, Hong Kong, Monday, 10:09 a.m.

"Bless me Father, for I have sinned. It has been..."

Hearing the familiar prologue to confession in English startles Father Kan just a bit. Filipinas occasionally come to confess their sins, but the congregation at St. James's is mostly Chinese, and Cantonese is the language in which the priest does his work. And in any case, this is not the English of a Filipina.

"...four years since my last confession."

The woman sounds American. This will be a change. Funny how everything can become routine, even the sins and plaints of the confessional. Love affairs, lies, and questions—so many questions whispered through the grille that both joins and separates the sinner and confessor.

The woman falls silent for a moment, and the only sound he can hear is a coin dropping into the offering box. Across the apse, a supplicant is lighting a candle to Saint Francis.

It has its challenges, being a Catholic among Taoists—"pagans," they used to say, but the word is fortunately out of favor. Father Kan is sometimes asked if it's all right to attend an uncle's Taoist funeral, and if so, can they light incense? Have their fortune told? Should they accept the gift of a household shrine from a parent? One girl was terrified of ghosts until she discovered she could pray to Jesus, and the ghosts would flee. It took Father Kan a while to sort that one out.

"Father, I need to speak to someone. My son is in danger."

"What kind of danger?"

"I can't say. I promised I wouldn't."

"Promised whom?"

"My husband." These words spoken softly, as if the thought shames them both.

"Is your husband the source of the danger?"

"No. But he's asked me not to tell anyone, and I'm scared."

He has heard confessions long enough to recognize real fear in a voice. Wives who are abused to the point of insanity, children who will jump off the roof of their building if they hear their parents fight one more time. Men terrified of losing their family after—but only after—their overnight with the maid was found out.

"Tell me about it. You're safe here."

"I promised them…"

"The seal of the confessional means that I can never disclose anything you say to anyone. Whatever you've done, it's between you, me, and God."

It all pours out, a fantastic tale of kidnapping and murder. The priest hears the hopelessness in her voice, the conflict tearing at her soul. When she finishes, he asks a few clarifying questions. Has this happened before? Does your father-in-law seem worried? The answers give him little confidence that he can help. The woman is going to suffer no matter what.

"You must tell the police," Father Kan says.

"But my husband and his father both forbid it."

They forbid it? He didn't realize one could forbid a Western wife to do anything.

"You have a duty to your husband, of course," he says. "But you also have a responsibility to your son, and to God. Your son has been entrusted to you by God. He's been placed in your care. That's the reason no bond is stronger than that between parent and child."

He feels safe saying that, as long as he banishes from his mind the story of Abraham and Isaac. Of all the tales in the Bible, that is the one he's had the hardest time coming to terms with. To kill your son, even under orders from God—what would he have done, had he been Abraham? Thirty years as a Catholic priest, and he still doesn't know. It's the one paragraph in the contract he couldn't sign off on.

"If I went to the police, it would be a betrayal," she says. "I'd feel like Judas."

This is not a confession, not really, so there is no absolution, no forgiveness from God. In fact, God can do very little for this woman.

"Judas," says Father Kan, "had his part to play as well."

* * *

Kowloon District, Hong Kong, Monday, 1:34 p.m.

"Just good police work, really. It began when we nicked a couple of kids for illegal street racing in Kowloon."

ADC Admin Roger Chu is speaking between sips of beer. He and Million Man are having lunch at an English bar where off-duty policemen can hold conversations a bit more private than the YauTsim Canteen allows.

"It was two in the morning. They were burning rubber along the West Kowloon Corridor when they ran up against our roadblock. We impounded the cars and did a full forensic search at Ho Man Tin. The team didn't find anything, so they were about to release the vehicle. I was a DPC like you back then. I took a look inside the car and noticed a second ashtray, just a small bowl shoved in the cup holder. The crime lab had checked it for drugs, found nothing."

Despite himself, Million Man is enjoying this. He invited Roger Chu for a beer under the pretext of hearing about some of his old cases. Like many senior officers, especially ones sidelined in their later years, Chu enjoys reliving his old triumphs. Million Man's purpose is not to hear anecdotes but to get Chu on his side, persuade him to put in a word when promotion time comes.

"The problem is, they hadn't examined the bowl itself, a brown clay thing with a design on it. It looked kind of familiar, so on the off-chance, I took a photo of it to a cousin of mine, an antiques dealer. It turned out to be a neolithic bowl, perhaps five thousand years old. Why would a bunch of road racing kids have a beautiful object like that in their car?"

ADC Admin Roger Chu was no longer solving crimes, or supervising the men who did. Rumor had it he'd lost the plot. His enthusiasm for police work had vanished, or perhaps other enthusiasms had overtaken it. Whatever happened, his superiors noticed, and now ADC Admin Roger Chu processes leave applications and issues carpark labels.

"We came down hard on the driver, and he was surprised, I can tell you that. We had him for road racing, all kinds of infractions, and here I was asking him where he got that fucking bowl he stubbed his cigarettes into! He told us he lifted it from his girlfriend's brother's flat. The brother, it turned out, had a first class antiquities smuggling operation. He'd brought in thousands of pots and vases from China."

"I suppose that got you noticed," says Million Man.

"It didn't hurt, but I had a good team. Who's on yours?"

Million Man goes over the list, most of whom are known to Roger Chu. "Good man," he says of Lok. "Not a political bone in his body. Ability's what got him there, and that's what's going to keep him there, I think. Not really the type to do supervisory work."

Big Pang he knows too. "Too handsome for his own good, but he's on his way to DI, no doubt about that. It helps that he keeps away from his mates' wives, eh?" Million Man can't imagine Big Pang preying on anyone's wife, despite his looks.

Ears is new to Roger Chu, but he's interested in the young man's story—perhaps too interested for Million Man's comfort. "Is he the earnest type?" Chu asks.

"Yes," Million Man replies. "Always studying, always asking for more work, but he doesn't have much life experience. On one case Inspector Lok sent him to some topless bars…"

"He'll get the life experience," says Chu. "But the earnest character is what makes the difference. I've seen young men like that go very far. Why don't you bring him around next time?"

"I will, sir." This was not going the way he'd planned. He mentions Old Ko.

"Oh, yes, he's from my era. Too bad, he was a good man."

Million Man nods, a gesture that instantly makes him feel cheap. "He's the oldest on the team, I think."

Roger sits back and inhales, as if about to recount an old, old story. "Happens, sometimes. Good officer, and then something goes wrong, and you just can't recover."

"What was that, sir?"

"Mmm?" Chu seems lost in thought.

"What happened to Old Ko?"

"Not sure, exactly. Something about associating with undesirable characters. That's a sure way to dig yourself into a hole, you know."

They chat a while longer, and Million Man offers elaborate thanks for the chance to hear about Chu's police work. Million Man sees the ADC Admin into his taxi.

Undesirable characters. Million Man had bet that Old Ko had screwed up a case or something, but this is even better. His teammate, twenty years his senior, is hiding something unsavory, perhaps illegal. A whiff of a criminal association can stop a police career dead, and someone smelled it on Old Ko. He wonders what his teammate is really made of.

* * *

Yau Ma Tei, Hong Kong, Monday, 2:42 p.m.

Not bad, this one: a snow leopard from Xinjiang, killed not a week ago. More flesh on him than on the one he skinned last month, though it's still on the rangy side, like most of them these days. From a wall rack, Soddy Leung draws a steel scimitar knife.

He slices through the belly skin, then removes the innards, carefully snipping the membranes that hold them. He makes a dozen more cuts to the meat and bone, in an order that hasn't varied for years. Once the flesh is trimmed, he will pack it in ice and truck it to a chef who is waiting in Sha Tin. The bones—not as potent as tiger bones, but good enough to treat the odd burn or ulcer—will go to an herbalist just two blocks away. The penis, of course, will sell for thousands. Once again, nothing compares to what a genuine tiger penis will bring, but the snow leopard's organ, swimming in a jug of rice wine, will juice up some lucky man's sex life. It didn't seem to work when Soddy tried it himself, but he's no expert on Chinese medicine.

The thighs yield some good meat—you need real muscle to chase hares and goats over frozen Central Asian slopes. But the cat was killed a year short of adulthood, so it's nowhere near the full length—three feet long, perhaps, not counting the tail, which might make a good soup on its own.

He snips the whiskers as close to the snout as he can—they pay him by length, after all. An herbalist will make them into charms for curing toothache. Alas, there are no takers for the skin in Hong Kong—in some countries, the wealthy Chinese display it as a trophy—but the rest of the cat makes enough profit, so the waste isn't a concern.

Soddy Leung was not always a supplier of exotic animals. He threw away the first third of his life selling cameras, stereos, and other electronics from a shop off Nathan Road. He could handle the low margins, but the rents killed him: more than $420,000 per month for a small storefront. It was like buying fifteen goddam Jettas a year. No one could possibly survive with overhead like that, so Soddy did what every merchant on his block did: he cheated people. It was built into the system, and everyone seemed to know it except the customers. Certainly the police did. Yes, they took care of those alert few who whined that their new Nikon had been switched for a used one at the last moment. But for every tourist who discovered the cheat, there were a dozen who didn't. And the police never came around when no one complained.

Soddy became adept at pushing customers toward whatever he had in stock, telling them that the old model they wanted was obsolete. He had a local print shop fake some international warranties for products that didn't have them and weren't supposed to. Anything to make the customer happy.

After a few years, Soddy tired of the tourists, the complaints, the consumer watchdogs, and the Hong Kong Tourist Association, who seemed not to understand the economics of running a shop on Nathan Road. Nor was cheating people in his nature; essentially, he was an honest businessman.

Ashamed of making a crooked living and tired of making a meager one, he quit to join his brother in the restaurant supply business, selling stoves and griddles. The margin was slightly better, but nothing great.

One day a customer asked Soddy's brother to find a sea turtle for a banquet. As it was illegal, the man had set a budget of $20,000. Soddy's brother, it turned out, knew an exotic wildlife broker in Macau, a man named Fat Gary.

Soddy became Fat Gary's Hong Kong agent. Golden coin turtles, $8000 each. Egrets, fishing cormorants, civets from the mountains of Fujian province, Siberian white foxes, ibex, all kinds of birds. Tibetan antelope, arriving in chilled boxes with processed chickens and seafood, ready to ship to wealthy gourmets intent on impressing their VIP guests in private dining rooms.

Soddy took over the restaurant supply business when his brother died. Now he operates three successful outfits. He supplies restaurants with everything they need from napkin holders to steam tables. He also sells specialty cutlery from his Nanking Street storefront. Finally, in the back room he dresses wildlife, separating the meat from the parts that have medicinal value, and sells them both to a select but ravenous clientele.

The money is good, but Soddy is most proud that he now makes an honest living. Customers are getting what they paid for.

* * *

The man who flashes the police warrant card is young, almost too young to take seriously. He's dressed in a blue blazer and gray trousers, clothes a bit too somber for his age. Some of the younger F&B people at hotels are like that—they dress well to let you know how important they are, but you can't buy authority or respect off the rack.

The young man pulls out a photo.

"Did you sell any of these recently?" he asks.

"Why do you want to know? Is someone in trouble? Am I liable or something?"

"No, uncle. We're just trying to find a person who bought this knife."

Soddy studies the image. Yes, it's the same cheap kitchen knife—the one that hyperventilating weirdo bought the other night.

"Sell a lot of knives," Soddy says.

The detective looks around. "Yeah, but you've got a pretty high-end shop here. Lots of German and Swiss stuff. Maybe you noticed someone buying a cheap Chinese-made knife."

"Thirty-four fifty. Sold one a day or two ago. This exact one—you can see it over there." He points to a rack on which the knife hangs, encased in bubble wrap.

It occurs to Soddy to deny it, of course. Usually one denies everything when talking to authorities. But he knew something was wrong that night as soon as he laid eyes on the stuttering, sweating, trembling guy. Probably stabbed his wife, and now they're chasing him. When he's caught, he'll tell them he bought the knife here. Better not be caught in a lie.

"Can you describe the man?" the cop asks.

"Don't remember. Just a man." Soddy recalls a head bald and yellow as an onion, just a few wisps of hair combed over it, the thin lips, the reedy voice, the waxy complexion.

"You don't have a security camera here, do you?"

Soddy shakes his head.

"Was he tall? Short?"

"Short. A little shorter than me, maybe. I didn't look."

"Could you remember the face well enough for us to make a sketch?"

Soddy shakes his head again. "Sorry, he was just a customer."

"Do you remember how he was dressed?"

A herringbone tweed jacket, Soddy remembers. A tan sweater underneath it, even though it wasn't particularly cold that day. The type of man who worries and complains about his health. Navy trousers. He wore a tie, too. Soddy forgets the color, but he remembers that the man's chicken neck poked out over a fastened collar. You don't fasten a collar unless you wear a tie as well.

"No, sorry. I don't remember anything."

"How about the time? When exactly was he here?"

That evening he'd been in the back, plucking an owl. The bird had been picked up just before closing, so it had to have been between five and six.

"Evening sometime. Not sure, sorry."

The cop thanks him and leaves.

That was a first, he thinks. Cooperating with the police. *Soddy Leung, you are not only an honest businessman, you're a citizen as well.*

* * *

On the street, Millon Man reports his success to the Station Sergeant. As an afterthought he rings Icy Fong.

"How's the big murder case going?" she asks.

"I can't talk about it—you know that," he says. "How about dinner tonight?"

"Oh, so it's going well."

"Let's say I'm doing my job. Eight, okay?"

"Sure. What kind of food?"

"I'll surprise you."

She laughs. "Just what I need—a good surprise. Pick me up at work at eight. Nothing too fancy—no time to change."

Nothing too fancy. He has about one hundred fifty dollars left in his current account as of yesterday. Dinner will cost over six. He'll need to carry a balance on his credit card for a while. But Icy, he hopes, is worth it.

* * *

Pok Fu Lam District, Hong Kong, Monday, 6:17 p.m.

Lai-ping walks in with a teapot and cups on a tray. She's looking especially lovely, even in her cheap lavender cotton top and black shorts. Her feet are bare, as they always are inside her flat. She senses she's being observed, returns his gaze, then pours the tea.

No time for dancing. Lok doesn't really have time for any of this, but she asked him to stop in to hear some news.

"Thanks for coming," she says. "I know this is difficult for you."

"It's fine, Lai-ping."

"Keeping this secret, I mean. You have all the problems of a love affair, but none of the pleasures. I've thought of that too. I have the same problem, in a way. You're like a married lover who has to return to his wife every night."

All of the penalties, none of the compensations. And a risk that, when dwelt upon, makes him dizzy. What would he say if Dora ever caught a whiff of perfume, found a ticket stub in his pocket for a movie that she hadn't seen? Would she divorce him?

And then Lai-ping says: "I'm seeing someone."

For a quarter minute, his body takes over. Blood rushes to his ears. He consciously commands his breath to stay even.

Good, he wants to say. You need someone your own age who can take care of you. A young, handsome man who's not confused about his intentions. Someone who can dance with you for the joy of it, rather than for some crazy symbolic reason. Someone who can share your bed.

But he says nothing.

Chapter Twenty

Tsuen Wan District, Hong Kong, Monday, 7:49 p.m.

Police are making progress with the case. What kind of progress? Do they know the child is missing? How is Mo handling this? Why is there no footage of a distraught Mo, begging for the return of his grandchild?

From the television Horace has endured what seemed like hours of nonsense—weather, horse racing, politics—before gleaning a few details about the chauffeur, and something about Mo and his operations. But nothing about the kid. Nothing about Mo's pain. They call this news reporting?

He sits at the table and takes small, distracted bites of Winnie's egg and fried cabbage while staring at the television. Already his Sunday breakfast has been interrupted by an idiot client: the site manager of the Seaview Medical Building called to tell him their billing system was down. Horace told them to call their IT support and don't bother him.

He returned to his egg and fried cabbage.

That's the way to deal with things. A firm hand. That's how he showed that punk who was boss last night. Disabled him first, then finished him off with the fire ax.

His plate empty now, Horace sips tea until a fierce little man from an IT firm calls, shattering his daydream.

"I just heard from the Seaview Medical Building," he says.

"Yes? They've got some IT issue. I told them to call you." He speaks absently, thinking not of doctors, but of the payoff man's bloody corpse. He tried to pry open the elevator door to dump the body down the shaft, but the door fought him. So he left him in a bathroom stall. The building is closed anyway.

"It's not an IT issue," the man says with some grit in his voice. "The network is down because the server room is overheating because the A/C is out. That's not our department. Please don't call us again about this."

Horace has no air conditioning people on his cell phone. Rather than call The Girl, he leaves for the office, grumbling under his breath.

* * *

East Kowloon District, Hong Kong, 8:51 p.m.

Most of the cubicles are empty at this time of night; only the workaholics, the drudges, and Horace are present. He leaves a message for the HVAC people—of course, *they* wouldn't be at their office tonight—and then waits for a callback. There's no TV in the office, not even a radio that he can find, so he sits back and casts his mind to the previous night.

Horace stashed the payoff man's body and the gun that dropped out of his belt in a toilet stall. He then washed the blood into the drain in the janitor's closet and hid the money in the basement of the building, not daring to bring it home. On the way to the office this morning he picked up the double-wide valise. The money is stashed in the locked bottom drawer of Horace's desk. No one will look there.

Once he finishes this ridiculous business, he'll call Mo again and twist the knife. Mo had sent an armed man, probably to shoot him. The money was just for show. But the man is dead, and the money is his. It's taken thirty years, but Horace finally has the upper hand.

The phone burbles on its cradle. It's the building manager.

"The aircon man said that his equipment is fine," he explains. "There's no electricity going to the A/C. You need an electrician for that. Why can't you people get this right?"

Horace dials the first electrician on the list, who tells him that all their men are on the disco job.

As he hangs up, his cell phone rings.

"I just got a call from Seaview Medical," says The Girl. "What in hell is going on?"

* * *

Tsuen Wan District, Hong Kong, 10:03 p.m.

That kid was right. The Legend of the Green Warriors is good, very good. Doby labors through the pages of the comic, stopping at each unfamiliar word, studying the pictures to piece together the meaning. Finishing the story is a good two hours' work. When he's done, he stares at the cover picture—three men, swords poised for combat on the rampart of a Middle Kingdom fortress—and begins to read again.

It's his favorite kind of comic book, a tale of ancient fighters. The story is about an old king in China who is not satisfied with his own land; he wants to conquer the neighboring western kingdom, so he can collect more taxes and be richer.

In one panel, the king wonders how he can win a battle. He has an army, but so does the western kingdom. He has weapons, but so does the Western kingdom. Finally, he gets the idea of hiring some special fighters: three great swordsmen, known only as the Horse, the Rabbit, and the Snake, after the signs of their birth.

"Help me conquer the western kingdom," says the king to the swordsmen. "I'll give you all the gold you want."

"We are men who protect kings—we don't attack them," says their leader, Horse, in another panel covering half a page. The Old King offers them land, but they refuse. He will even let them marry his beautiful daughters, but they won't attack an innocent king.

This infuriates the Old King. He orders the guards to arrest them. But the swordsmen are too good. Hands and heads fly all over the place—Doby has a hard time tearing his gaze away from the pictures of the fight in the palace, with the blood and the faces twisted in agony.

Within minutes a hundred palace guards are dead, and the three warriors have escaped.

Now the Old King is sorry he ever thought of conquering the western kingdom. His best soldiers, the ones he had picked to keep him safe, are lying in pieces on the throne room floor.

But that's not the end of it, because the Old King's son has his own ideas. He wants to inherit a great kingdom from his father some day. "You can't let those warriors go free," he tells his father. "They'll go to the western kingdom and offer themselves for hire. They'll come back with armies and conquer us."

That makes sense to the Old King. He sends his whole army—thousands of soldiers—to capture the three men. The army catches up with the three warriors, and after a great battle, drives them back to the palace to face the King.

The prince wants his father to kill the three fighters. But the Old King's daughters speak out. "Don't kill them," they beg. "It would be a shame to waste such good fighters. They might fight for you some day." And they might marry us too, they think.

The Old King loves his daughters. So instead of executing the men, he throws them in a dungeon, declaring that he'll release them when they change their minds and agree to serve him.

The prince knows that the three warriors will never give in. Worse, they could escape and warn the Western kingdom. Then he gets an idea: he orders the three warriors to be dyed green all over and put in green clothes, so that if they escape, everyone will know them and they can easily be recaptured.

End of Part 1.

Doby flips the book back to front and begins to read again.

Chapter Twenty-One

Tsim Sha Tsui District, Hong Kong, Monday, 8:23 p.m.

Mo dials, hears the phone go to voicemail, and hangs up. He has already left messages containing, apart from his full vocabulary of profanity, two questions: where is the boy, and where is Jelly Pong?

Could Jelly have run off with the money? He doubts Jelly has the courage, or even the imagination. The man is a blight. A 49, the lowest rank in the Sun Yee On Triad, Jelly Pong has none of the qualities needed to move up either in the triad ranks or in Mo's organization. Up until last night, he was of vague use as an errand boy. Now he is trouble.

Mo is alone at Diamond Rich enterprises, which does business from an office in Tsim Sha Tsui, above a Granville Road dress shop. A visitor might think he had ended up at a third-rate trading company, one of the thousands of outfits that shuffle pens, toys, and dish towels from China's sweat-soaked factories to the world. The two-room office has no pictures on the walls, no photos of the boss shaking hands with the Chief Executive or a Tai-Pan. The rooms could use some paint. There's a desk for Mo, a plain wood-and-metal affair from the department store, and an identical one across the room for his secretary. The back room, with nothing but a few tables and chairs, is where Mo and Lento convene out of the secretary's earshot.

Mo has been sitting at his desk since early morning. Mostly he thinks of what he will do to the kidnapper when he finds him. The kidnapper, and

Dollar-ten, who is behind it.

Halfway through an imaginary evisceration, his phone beeps. The kidnapper.

"*Wai?*"

"He was armed! I told you no guns. Now I'm going to kill the kid." The man is talking too fast.

"Wait…" He needs to think about this. Jelly, armed? Mo wouldn't put it past him. To keep his thinking straight, Mo lights a cigarette and inhales a lungful of smoke. Smoking is permitted at Diamond Rich. His office, his rules.

"Where is the boy?" Mo says. "Let's not get excited…"

"What are you trying to do to me?"

"I'm trying to pay you and get the boy back." Mo thinks of adding "dickhead" but refrains. "Did you get the money?"

The kidnapper says nothing.

"You got the money, right? So we're good. Is the boy safe?"

"For the moment."

"What about Jelly Pong?"

"The one you sent to pay? What do you think?"

Mo takes another drag on the Marlboro. "You've got the money. Why not let the child go now?"

"Your man had a gun. I said no guns. Was he going to kill me?"

"I told him not to come armed. He disobeyed me. You know what it's like." The next words came hard to Mo. "I apologize."

"You lose, Mo. You like to be a big winner, but now you lose."

"Don't kill him. Listen to me. Think about it. No one's looking for you now. If you release my grandson, we're done. You can go on your way, spend your money, do what you want. But if you kill him, the police get involved. You'll have them breathing down your neck. They'll find you. They take kidnapping seriously. And child murder?"

Silence on the line. Mo takes a last drag of his *Ma Bo Lo* and stubs it out.

"Okay. Another seven million."

"What?"

"You heard me. I'm doubling the ransom as punishment. And you will bring it yourself this time! No flunkies. And no guns. I am serious, believe me."

"Look, you got all my cash."

"I know what your holdings are worth. You have plenty."

This isn't good. "Four," he says, an automatic reaction.

"No bargaining. Seven, just like before."

"How do I know you won't keep him and ask for more?"

"I'll give him back to you. The extra money is to teach you a lesson. You've gone too long without a lesson."

"All right. But I need time to raise the cash. You've got everything I had on hand. I'll have to borrow on my assets, then put it into currency. That takes some time."

"Don't bullshit me, Mo."

"I'm not. I'll get you the money, and then we're done, right? You'll treat the boy well and release him. Correct?"

"Get the money. And do it right this time."

"One more thing," says Mo. "A favor?"

"What?"

"Have you dumped Jelly Pong's body yet?"

No sound on the line.

"If you haven't, can you keep him out of sight as long as possible? I don't need any more attention."

The kidnapper mumbles something, and the phone goes dead.

Mo dials Lento.

"*Wai?*"

"Find Dollar-ten. Get help if you need it. But find him now." He kills the phone.

You've gone too long without a lesson. What did he mean by that?

Chapter Twenty-Two

Kowloon Tong District, Tuesday, 9:17 a.m.

"Oh, Inspector…Lok, is it? My husband isn't home." Lok's unexpected arrival seems to puzzle her, which suits him fine. Ivan isn't in, and alone, she might be less secure, more prone to manipulation. Puzzled is a good start.

"No work today?" Lok says.

"I'm taking a bit of time off. This has all been…very trying. Would you like some tea?"

He would like some tea, and she makes it well, but this time he declines, so as not to let her occupy her hands. He needs to remove every comfort. Lok himself, however, senses the need for a prop. He draws his notebook from a breast pocket, flips it open, and runs his eyes over the top page.

"I see you provided your fingerprints for reference," Lok says.

"Yes, at the Yau Ma Tei station, this morning." Once again he marvels at her Cantonese. Funny accent, but she's speaking it, and that's something.

"We still need your son's fingerprints. You didn't bring him with you?"

"No, I…I didn't…it wasn't convenient, to tell you the truth. I'll make arrangements to do that. Are you sure you wouldn't like some tea? Or coffee?"

An espresso machine gleams on the kitchen counter. Westerners make such a fetish out of coffee. The Chinese have been brewing tea in clay pots for thousands of years.

"No, thank you. Just a few questions." Again he pretends to scan his notebook—just taking care of details. "You were at a party when the murder occurred."

"Yes, a lecture and cocktail party at the Grand Hyatt."

"And you went there from work?"

"Yes, directly from the hospital."

"And your husband was at work?"

"A dinner with clients, he said."

"And who picked up your son from school?"

Sylvie pauses and glances off to one side, as if trying to recall. "That would be Myrna, our helper."

"What time would that have been?"

A tiny pause; she's uncomfortable lying. "Three-thirty. She would have returned here by four."

"So when you got home, your son was here?"

"I'm not sure why you're asking…"

"We do need an answer."

A longer hesitation. "He was home."

"And did he sleep here that night?"

"I don't see…"

Lok waits.

"Where else would he sleep?" she says finally.

He flips the book closed. "Mo *tai-tai*, your helper Myrna De La Cruz says that his grandfather picked him up that day." Airport came through with that information yesterday, having found Myrna at Statue Square, where many of Hong Kong's Filipinas gather on Sunday.

Sylvie inhales, causing her chest to rise. Her shoulders stiffen as well. "Yes…"

"Is that true?"

A whisper. "Yes"

"And that night your husband told her to take a holiday?"

Her head rocks a degree or two. It could be a nod.

"Where is your son now, Mo *tai-tai*? We need to speak to him."

A key rattles in the door. Ivan walks in, briefcase in hand. "Meeting canceled," he says in Cantonese, before noticing that Lok is in the room.

"The Inspector was asking where Bonitus is, Ivan."

Ivan does not hesitate with his answer. "He's visiting relatives in Yuen Long. Why?"

* * *

Tsim Sha Tsui District, Hong Kong, Tuesday, 10:51 a.m.

"Ah Lok!"

The scratchy baritone sounds from behind the Assistant District Commander's door just as Lok passes by.

How does Kwan know it's me? He pokes his head in.

As if reading Lok's mind, K.K. Kwan says, "I know your footsteps, Herman."

Kwan gestures for Lok to enter. He looks distracted, which is unusual, and tired, which is more unusual. Kwan is short and wiry, one of those compact dynamos that power everything at the station. His head is completely smooth, shiny as a stainless steel wok, and despite his age—over sixty, Lok figures—he is strong and fast. He sits behind a desk even more loaded with manila folders than usual. Must be a filthy week.

"I hate to say this," says Kwan, "but you're behind on paperwork."

"Sorry, sir. Which paperwork?"

"I thought you could tell me."

A sigh erupts before Lok can suppress it. "Sir, I'm up to my neck with the Goldfish Head murder…"

"And I'm up to my neck with the Commissioner. It seems SQW did a customer satisfaction survey. Our satisfaction rate went down from eighty-two percent to seventy-four. The press has been hounding the Commissioner about it."

"About what, sir?"

"About why the public is less satisfied with us, what do you think?"

Eighty-two to seventy-four? Kwan might as well be talking about sunspot activity.

"Anyway," Kwan says, "SQW is compiling some new reports to show that we're performing better than ever. They must have asked you for statistics for your team."

Lok vaguely remembers a memo from the Service Quality Wing, a ghetto of pen-pushers who hire consultants and print out reports while Lok and his men are facing triad killers.

"Sir, I don't have time to do that right now."

"You need to make time. The Commissioner is frantic for some good news for a change."

"So you're having SQW manufacture it out of statistics?"

Kwan raises a hand in a gesture of helplessness. "Herman, I know it's bullshit. But I need the Commissioner on my side, which means wasting the occasional odd hour on this stuff. I want to see you wasting your hour, too. Now, where are we with Goldfish Head?"

Lok takes a seat. "Nothing much from forensics. We're reviewing CCTV footage. There's a camera down the street from the shop where the killer bought the knife. But this is what's interesting: Mo Tun picked up his grandson Bonitus that day at 3:45."

"Was he in the car at the time of the murder?"

"We don't know. But the boy hasn't been seen with the family since then."

"Do you think the kid saw the murder? And Mo's hiding him till he deals with the killer himself?"

"Sounds like Mo Tun. But it's also possible the child was kidnapped."

"No report from the parents?"

Lok shakes his head.

"Nothing you can do, then. Talk to the Chief Super of CIB if you want, but without a formal report, there's no kidnapping, no going to a high court judge for wiretaps. What do the parents say?"

"That the boy is with relatives in the New Territories. But if Mo is hiding a witness, he's obstructing the investigation."

"Don't even think of it," Kwan says. "Try to charge him, and Mo will have some crooked lawyer filling out a complaint in ten seconds. Better to bring Mo in and pry what you can out of him, find a discrepancy between his story and his son's. Maybe even convince him that we can do a better job than he can."

"Mo's the type who likes to be in control," says Lok.

Kwan kicks the leg of his desk. "So am I, dammit! Follow him till you get something. Follow his toadies, too. He probably has them looking for the killer."

"Yes, sir."

"And please, Herman, get those fucking statistics to SQW."

Lok wonders what this case will do to those statistics. The first rule of Hong Kong kidnapping is kill the victim.

Chapter Twenty-Three

Tsuen Wan District, Hong Kong, Tuesday, 11:05 a.m.

Doby clutches the edges of the comic book tightly enough to whiten his fingers. If he could squeeze out the next chapter of the tale from the paper, learn what happens to the Green Warriors, he would.

When he finally stirs from his daydream, it's eleven in the morning. Father said to feed the boy around noon. He'll start now, stopping off first to pick up the next chapter in the series.

The shop doesn't carry it, however. It's not a new item, says Mr. Cho, the man with a toupee and a thick Chiu Chow accent at the corner news shop. So Doby drives the streets of Kowloon, visiting store after store, asking for volume 2 of the Legend of the Green Warriors. *Never heard of it. Out of stock. Maybe six months ago, maybe a year. Sorry.* By the time he gives up the quest, it's after two o'clock.

Late! What if Ba Ba finds out? He stops at a fast food restaurant, buys a pork chop-fried rice takeaway and a bottle of water, and makes his way to the Shun Lok building. Once in the building, he stops, seized by the thought that he's messed up his instructions. His belly tightens as he recites to himself what he can remember of *Ba Ba's* rules.

Drive past the building and look for people.

If someone is there, drive away.

Walk in the shade. Wear your cap.

When you get to the building, look once again to the left, the right, and across the street...

Doby has done none of that. What if he's been seen or heard? He shuffles from foot to foot as the elevator descends to the basement, where the boy and his stinking bucket are waiting for him. This time he finds the boy sitting back against the far wall, fingering a paper airplane made from a page of his notebook.

Doby drops the food by the door, grabs the fouled trash bin, and once again performs the cleaning ritual. When he returns, the boy is still sitting against the wall, glaring at him. Doby has seen an expression like that before. On *Ba Ba*'s face. On Kenny's face too, when he fights with *Ba Ba*.

"I read the comic book."

The boy says nothing.

"Do you have the next book in the series?"

The boy's expression eases a bit. "Maybe," he says.

Maybe.

"Can I read it?"

"Maybe. I know where it is. But first, you need to do something for me."

"What do you want?"

"I want to go home."

"I can't do that. *Ba Ba* won't let me."

The boy slumps, shoulders collapsing like an accordion for a moment. Then he speaks.

"Then I need some things."

"What things."

"Toilet paper. Some ice cream. Something to draw with."

Doby juggles the elements of the list in his mind. "Toilet paper?"

"Yes. Also something to clean my hands with. And ice cream. And a drawing pad and crayons."

Four things. No five. Doby recites them to himself.

"And you'll tell me where to find the second book?"

"Yes."

Doby turns to leave.

"Why are you keeping me here?" asks the boy.

Doby says, "My father."

"Why does your father want me?"

Doby has no answer.

* * *

Once in the van, Doby scribbles the boy's items on the clipboard that holds his route list. Toilet paper. Ice cream. Pad and crayons. What else was there? One other thing. Oh yes, something to clean his hands with. What would that be? He'd have to ask *Ma Ma*.

Then, his mind free again, he begins to ponder the boy's question.

"Why does your father want me?"

Ba Ba already has two sons. True, Kenny talks back and doesn't respect his father, but Doby is a good son.

Why does Ba Ba need another son? Is he going to take him in and send me away? What am I doing wrong?

Chapter Twenty-Four

Shek Kip Mei District, Hong Kong, Tuesday, 12:48 p.m.

This time, when Mo Tun arrives, Koon is waiting in front of the restaurant. The Chief Superintendent is wearing his usual pinstripes and gleaming black wingtips, but no coat: a spring shower has left the air moist and warm. Mo is taking a few last restorative puffs from a cigarette.

"Never mind the noodles," Koon says. "Let's take a ride." At his bidding they hop into a taxi. Far from being vexed by the change in program, Mo is eager to dispense with the backdrop of the ritual meal. Appearances are not on his mind right now. Lento has just told him that construction has stopped on the disco. Until he can put another six million in escrow, the site has been shut down, workers gone home, everything on hold. He hates that idea. A nightclub is the best money laundering device ever invented.

But first, the disco must be built. And to do that, it seems, he must get his money back from Dollar-ten, and then kill him.

For a moment the face of Bonitus emerges in his thoughts. He hopes the boy is okay. Dollar-ten would never kill a kid. He wouldn't dare. This whole thing is some addle-brained prank, a drunken fantasy that a fool decided to make real, without a thought of the consequences.

"Wong Tai Sin Temple," Koon tells the driver.

A rare smile tightens Mo's lips. "Are we going to get our fortune told?"

"Maybe."

Mo was surprised yesterday when he heard the voicemail, with its innocuous coded summons to meet at the noodle shop. He hadn't expected Koon to be working much on his behalf. Koon would not be concerned with their friendship, which is, in any case, tepid, and like most things in their lives, rooted only in self-interest.

But Koon is here. Perhaps something put the scare into him, and if so, Mo knows what it is: the dark mire they both escaped from forty years ago. The two men grew up in a country where independent thinking was a contagion, its victims subject to cure, quarantine, or euthanasia. A country where any aim, any desire larger than a bowl of rice was lopped off like a gangrenous limb. Where ambitions were not just defeated; they were meaningless.

Mo and Koon made it out of the swamp. Now they maintain their lives, their friendships, their working habits with the single goal of ensuring that they do not end as they began. It's a flight masquerading as a pursuit.

Not that the two men were ever the same. Koon has no instinct for the kill, no need to seize power; society's methods of advancement work well enough for him. In his young days, Koon carried an English dictionary in his pocket. Mo carried a knife, tucked in his belt and covered by a jacket. These days Koon has no need of the dictionary. But a pocket is sewn in each of Mo's jackets, a slim thing just long enough to hold his old army knife in case of trouble. His tailor thinks it's for a cell phone.

"What do you remember about Dollar-ten?" Koon says. He's speaking Mandarin now, the better to keep their conversation from the driver.

"Not too much, to tell you the truth. Those stupid eyes, of course. His gambling—he lost his whole share of money on horses. The Jockey club probably built three hospitals with the cash he pushed through the betting window. But then I lost track of him."

"Right. So did I. But you remember the gambling. Horses, lotteries, cards, mahjong—always doing whatever he could to boost his luck. And that reminded me of how superstitious he was."

"Of course," Mo says. He stares out the window at the shell of an apartment building, decked in bamboo scaffolding on which builders hang like flies in a web. Maybe Dollar-ten is working there. Lento has enlisted an associate, name of Yank Lee, to canvass construction workers and find the kidnapper.

"He did it all," Mo says. "Feng shui, lucky charms, talismans…"

"…fortune tellers. So if he's alive, he'll show up at the temple sooner or later."

Wong Tai Sin is Hong Kong's main exchange for the supernatural. An immense concrete clearing amid the towers of Kowloon, it offers the religious a scattering of temples decked in Chinese grandeur: red pillars, lanterns, arches, ornate pavilions trimmed in gold, gardens, and coils of incense smoldering away above the heads of worshipers.

The taxi discharges them onto a paved walkway. They pass long troughs of sand in which supplicants have placed their burning joss sticks, filling the air with a haze of agarwood, bamboo, and camphor.

"We might even fall over him," says Koon, gesturing to the men and women kneeling in prayer in the courtyard.

Ignoring the main temple, they enter a long side building that resembles a market lined with stalls. Instead of food, though, the stalls house fortune tellers. The walls in each cubicle are covered in astrological charts, palm diagrams, and descriptions of the methods of divination on offer.

"I forgot how many there were," says Mo. "Where do we start?"

"I used to know a couple of them."

"You get your fortune told?"

"Not much these days. But before. No sense in taking chances, right? My whole team would end up here after a *bai gwan dai*, drunk out of our minds, and we'd find out how our case was going to work out." He waves a hand toward the row of stalls that snakes along the north side of the building. "You work that side. Just mention his eyes. These guys always take in a person's face when they do a reading."

"Hate to think of what they'd make of mine." Mo stops at the first stall in which a fortune teller sits idle: a woman, mid-forties, wearing a simple print suit. Her smile is pleasant, her manner cheerful.

"Would you like to know the future?"

"No thanks. I need to know a little about the past."

"The past?"

"A customer. Do you ever tell a fortune for a man who has one big eye and one small eye?"

She glances away to think, shakes her head. "No, I'd remember that. What do they call him?"

"Dollar-ten." He loops fingers in each hand to mimic large and small coins. She chuckles, shakes her head again.

"I wish I had advised him. Your face points to your destiny, you know."

"I hope not." He walks along to the next man, a palm specialist, who gives him the same answer as the next three: no one knows Dollar-ten. Mo finds Koon and tells him that it's a lost cause; he'll station Lento at the temple to keep an eye out for him. Yank can keep doing the construction sites.

"How many of these guys did you talk to?"

"Maybe half—the ones who were free."

"If I know Dollar-ten, he'll take this seriously. He'll find the fortune teller he thinks is the best, and stick with him. Like drinking XO."

"So we find the fortune tellers with the best reputations."

"In other words, the longest lines." Koon glances at his watch. "I have to go."

Mo nods his thanks. After Koon departs he lines up for the busiest fortune teller in the building. It's a time-consuming operation. An hour later, he's spoken with three—two men and a woman—with no results, apart from one offer of help: one spiritualist said he could find Dollar-ten with his fortune-telling birds, two pigeons trained to peck at cards, which are then read and interpreted.

The oldest fortune teller—and the busiest—is Ong, a man of at least seventy-five with a long white beard that makes him resemble Tu Di Gong, the god of wealth. *That can't hurt business.* Mo describes Dollar-ten to him.

"I know him," old Ong says in a gentle soft tenor.

"What can you tell me about him? When was he here last?"

"Fortune first," says Ong.

Mo sighs in resignation and lowers himself onto the stool opposite the old man. "I'm pressed for time," he says.

You have all the time there is, until you die. The same as all of us. When were you born?"

Mo tells him. The man offers an almost inaudible grunt, as if he knew it all along.

"We'll use *chien tung,*" he says. He hands Mo a wooden container filled with bamboo sticks. Mo shakes the container until a stick falls to the table.

"One more," says Ong. Mo obeys, and the fortune teller lays out the sticks and studies them. He says nothing for a while.

"Your number is 53," he says finally.

"Can't be good," says Mo. "5354." The numbers *ng sam ng se* sound like *not living, not dead.*

"Depends. You could say that if you're not born, you can't die." The man gestures to Mo's right hand. Mo extends it, and the man lifts it slightly, places his thumbs on the opened palm, and draws them apart as if trying to smooth a crumpled piece of paper. Mo watches for a few seconds, then lets his eyes settle across the room, bored with the display of mysticism. But everything here is mysticism. Reading coins, palms, cards, the actions of birds, the dictates of stars. People want to know their fate because they can't control it. Mo learned early on to control his, however. He has no need of mystics.

"You're wealthy—your hands tell me that."

"The lines in my palm?"

"Don't be silly. Your hands are soft. You haven't labored with them. And your clothes are expensive."

Despite himself, Mo admires the man's honesty. "So, am I going to get richer?"

"How should I know? I don't read the future. I read you. I tell you what your life is."

"I know what my life is."

"Do you? Then why are you here?"

"I already told you—to find a man."

"He has something you want."

"Good guess."

"Money is involved."

"Another good guess." A sliver of impatience works its way into Mo's voice. He scans the room again.

"This is something you were not prepared for," Ong says. "You're not on familiar ground."

Mo regards the man closely for the first time. Up to now, he'd just seen the beard. But there is a face behind the beard, eyes that show some kind of intelligence. He's not just a huckster playing up to fools in the temple.

Mo tries to look through the beard, the incense smoke, the robe, and mystical trappings. Ong returns his gaze, and seems to revel in the scrutiny. *You're reading me, just as I read you.*

"The wheel of a cart turns on its axle," Ong says, making a circular motion with a delicate hand. "The rim moves fast, the center slowly. That is how it should be. Until the wheel comes off the cart and spins and rolls out of control. Then the center moves fast." He mimes a wheel rolling away.

"What are you saying?"

"You are the center of the wheel. You should be turning slowly, while those around you turn more swiftly. But now you are moving too fast. That tells me that you have come off the cart."

"You can tell this from the sticks?"

"I don't even need *chien tung*—I can read your life. You carry your life with you. You drag it through your home, into the streets, onto the bus, and it's with you right now. It's in your face, your clothes, your voice, your breath. Everything you've ever done, every betrayal you've suffered, everyone you've..."

"Everyone I've what?"

The man lays his eyes on the sticks once more and goes silent.

"Never mind," says Mo. He drops a banknote on the table. "Thanks for the reading. Now what do you know about the man?"

"They call him Dollar-ten."

"I know that. Has he been here recently?"

"All the time." The man smiles. "Always two days before race day."

"The Wednesday or Saturday race?"

"Both. He likes to bet on both races. He asks me which horse to bet on, and I never tell him. But I tell him other things, and from that, he decides if it's a good idea to bet that day.

"Two days before, you say?"

"Yes, he's a regular Monday and Thursday afternoons."

"Then that's what I want to know."

"Is it?"

"Now what are you saying?"

"Dollar-ten is a weak man," says Ong. "He won't be strong enough to put the wheel back on the cart."

Mo slips his wallet into his pocket and leaves the temple.

* * *

Kowloon Tong District, Hong Kong, Tuesday, 5:12 p.m.

Ivan pours a second cognac and collapses on the sofa. Usually he changes out of his business suit when he comes home, but for the last hour he's been lounging in his tailored shirt and trousers.

Frightening as Bonitus's disappearance is, it's Sylvie's state that worries Ivan most. Mo has assured Ivan their son is safe; otherwise, he'd be a wreck like Sylvie. His father knows about these things, these symbolic kidnappings that happen quietly to teach others to keep silent, or pay up, or otherwise give in.

Why isn't it over, then? They must really want to put the scare into him. Well, they're doing it.

Get the disco going, that was the plan. Build up real cash flow, do some property deals, major ones, and we're done. *Ba Ba* can fire the Jelly Pongs in his organization and preside over a small, professional real estate empire. Eventually the operation will come to Ivan, scrubbed clean of the brutal but necessary tactics that created it. Then life will be good for Sylvie and him.

Sylvie. Where is she?

Ivan rises to his feet, ignoring the heaviness behind his eyes, and walks to her study. She's sitting at her desk, on which she's laid some papers: Bonitus's drawings, photos, schoolwork. Her face is raw and bereft of makeup.

"Look at this," she says, staring at a crayon drawing of two figures: a woman with bright yellow hair and a man next to her holding a briefcase.

The caption reads *My* Ma Ma *is a doctor. My* Ba Ba *is a lawyer.*

"He had to show his class the picture, talk about his parents. He said I was a doctor, and I cured diseases. You were a lawyer, and you helped people in trouble."

A few of his classmates at law school became criminal lawyers. They do help people in trouble; Ivan only helps his father, by giving him the gift of distance. He files motions and delivers envelopes so that Mo Tun can stay removed from street thugs and bribes paid to mainland officials. He helps *Ba Ba* read contracts whose clauses could come back to bite him, and when *Ba Ba* hands others contracts to sign, Ivan is the one who files the teeth good and sharp.

Sylvie's desk is covered with crayon pictures. Beside it, on a chair, is a kindergarten photo, with its row of tiny faces lined up against a banner.

Ivan realizes that he's looking at a shrine to Bonitus. A chill works into his skin.

"Sylvie, I promise it'll be all right. It's one of *Ba Ba*'s associates, and he'll return Bonitus any moment now."

"Associates?" She doesn't look at him, stares at the drawing of the couple. *My* Ma Ma *is a doctor. My* Ba Ba *is a lawyer.*

"Well, it's not someone we want to deal with. But he's got *Ba Ba's* attention, which is what he wants."

"That's what he wants, is it?"

"Sylvie, you know where Bonitus is? He's in a flat somewhere with some woman who's feeding him ice cream and shoving him in front of a TV with a video game."

"He said there was no toilet, Ivan."

The chill works deeper into him.

"Please, Sylvie."

"Please, what?"

Chapter Twenty-Five

Mongkok District, Hong Kong, Tuesday, 1:11 p.m.

With neither Mo nor his sidekick Lento to be found, Old Ko and Big Pang are tailing one Yank Wong, a one-time petty thief who reports to Lento. Yank, who wears a shiny black blazer and shades, has been visiting construction sites and talking to foremen all morning. He's on his fourth site, an urban renewal project on Yim Po Fong Street. Big Pang and Old Ko are parked down the street in their unmarked Mazda.

They sit back and watch Yank approach a young, wiry man in a hard hat. From this distance the worker's face looks thin, his body language indolent. Ko takes an instant dislike to the worker, for reasons that become apparent when the curl of a dragon's tail peeks from under his open collar. The man is a triad. There are plenty of gang people on construction sites—this part of Kowloon is ruled by the 14K. The builders might have been forced to hire him—just another way of taking protection money. Or he might work for a subcontractor set up by the triad. If so, the developer will have to pay to have the work re-done by someone competent.

"Same deal," says Old Ko. "He finds a guy in a hard hat, talks to him, leaves a card."

"That's more or less what we do," says Big Pang.

"Except he's paid a lot more. I don't even own a silk jacket. Wonder what he's asking them. Hmm, did the other ones he talked to have yellow hats?"

"Think so, why?"

"Yellow Phoenix is running in the second at Sha Tin. Five year old, did well at the 1600 meter and one trial. I've been seeing yellow a lot lately. Might place a bet."

"It's your money."

"And you don't throw any cash away?"

"Sure. But at least I have control. With mahjong I know who I'm playing with."

"Then why did you have to borrow five hundred from me two months in a row? At least with horses, my chances don't go down with every beer I—there he goes." Old Ko nods toward the site, where Yank is handing the man a business card.

Big Pang says, "What do you say we play our hand?"

They exit the Mazda. Pang approaches Yank and identifies himself, while Old Ko disappears.

"What's your interest in construction workers?" says Big Pang.

Yank looks confused. Up close, he's mid-twentyish, with a scar on his upper lip and an expression just short of intelligent.

"Nothing."

"Nothing? This is a pretty strange place to be doing nothing."

Again Yank stares at him, whether in defiance or bewilderment, Pang has no idea.

"Look," says Pang. "Something serious is going on, and you'd better not be involved in it. I promise you, we mean it—we're not doing this because we're bored." He hands Yank a card. "Think about it. Then either call me, or call Lento. But once you call Lento, you're part of it. Understand?"

Yank takes the card in silence. Pang walks away, not bothering to look back as he says, "And if you do call Lento, mention my name."

* * *

At the car Pang meets Old Ko, who had been keeping watch on Yank from afar. "He made a call," Old Ko says. "Let's go."

127

This time the two men confront Yank Wong together.

"What did I tell you?" Pang says in a tone of exasperation. Pang shoves his hand in Yank's blazer, digs his cell phone out and tosses it to Old Ko.

"Hey!"

"Never mind, you'll get it back." Pang closes in on Yank, nose to nose. "Do you know what the punishment is for obstructing an investigation?..."

While he talks, Old Ko takes Yank's cell phone around the corner and stations himself near a bulldozer whose motor is churning away. He presses redial and hears exactly what he wants to hear: Lento's voice.

"*Wai?*"

"Too much noise here," Old Ko says in a voice an octave higher than his own. "What did you say before?"

"Dickhead! I said ignore the police. Keep at it till you find someone who knows Dollar-ten from Beijing. Then do nothing, just call me. Is that too complicated for you?"

Old Ko shuts off the phone and walks back to where Big Pang is still intimidating Yank. He chucks him the phone.

"Let's go," says Old Ko.

* * *

Kowloon District, Hong Kong, Tuesday, 4:48 p.m.

The sky is a charcoal sketch of gravid clouds that will soon burst upon Kowloon. As he makes his way down Waterloo Road Lok watches the coming rainstorm tune up the city, tighten up its wires and springs. People walk faster, push themselves in and out of buses a little more urgently, get to the point sooner in conversation, all in an effort to stay ahead of the rain.

Lok pulls into his parking space and checks his messages. Big Pang has some news; he calls and gets the update from their surveillance of Yank Wong. That gives him something to do tonight.

Guilt suddenly stings him. Why did he feel relief when faced with an excuse for working tonight?

He loves Dora. He loves his children. Does he love his job more? Perhaps his concern for Lai Ping is more than fatherly, and the need to escape his flat is prelude to a deeper need that will some sad day reveal itself.

* * *

The street hawker Ding stands on the corner by his building, heedless of the coming rain.

"It's the police officer," Ding says, lifting a square steel lid and prodding the noodles under it with a pair of chopsticks.

"Detective Inspector," Lok says.

"Sure. Want some noodles?"

"Ding," Lok says, "would you like to earn some money?"

Ding looks up from his food cart. He's still unshaven, still wearing the same blue shirt that covers him like an empty rice sack, sleeves spilling over his knuckles.

"I need you to ask around your Beijing clan. I'm looking for a man from there, nickname Dollar-ten."

"Why Dollar-ten?"

"I don't know. But I've never heard it before. Don't think there's more than one."

"What's the reward?"

"Let's say a big cow." The five-hundred dollar bill is brown like a cow.

Ding thinks for a second. "I find this guy, you bring me the money?"

"You can sign for it at YauTsim station."

"I want you to bring it to me. I heard about someone who gave information for a reward. They made him go to the station to get it. A few days later he was fished out of the harbor."

A true story, probably a few times over. A triad within police ranks would inform on informers.

"This isn't a big organized crime case, Ding. We just need a little help finding someone we want to talk to. Your name won't come up."

"I'll think about it. Want some noodles?"

* * *

Tsim Sha Tsui District, Hong Kong, Tuesday, 9:14 p.m.

What would I tell Big Pang, or anyone else, if they pulled this stunt? *You're an idiot and a glutton for punishment, Lok.* But he tells himself that his course is rational, that right now pretending to flip through an oversized and overpriced architectural magazine, while fixing his eyes on the building across the street, is in everyone's best interest.

He had no intention of being here. An hour ago, he was at Diamond Rich listening to Mo Tun deny knowing anyone named Dollar-ten.

With the lie on record, he set out for home. But on an impulse, Lok phoned Lai Ping, then took a drive, parked in the shadows, and double-timed it to the sundry store across the street from Harbor Palace Seafood Restaurant. That is the workplace of a certain man Lai-ping has been seeing from time to time, she says.

All he wants is a look at this new man in her life. He needs to make sure she'll be all right.

Lok toys with the idea that knowing her schedule helps him keep her safe in a hostile city, but he rarely knows where his eldest daughter is these days. No, there's no logical explanation for his behavior, and that's what infuriates him. That, and the fact that he doesn't really have time to be skulking in mini-marts.

The city having been taunted with an hour of frenetic winds, the rain comes, and within moments it is pooling in gutters and tapping against the storefront window. When it stops the water will evaporate, bathing everyone in steam.

It's not his childhood rain, though. On his island of Cheung Chau the rain pelted with abandon. He'd walk home in ankle-deep water, enjoying the squish of the rain filling up his sneakers. Here in Hong Kong, the wind and rain have been civilized, for the most part.

A figure approaches the doorway. Lok leans into the window and sees that it's a man in his early thirties, short hair, slim build, wide shoulders. In defiance of the rain, he's wearing just a T-shirt under a sport jacket.

The man matches the description Lok extracted from Lai-ping by laboriously feigning enthusiasm about him.

I know him, Lok thinks.

He hurls the magazine onto a shelf and stamps out of the store.

Chapter Twenty-Six

Tsuen Wan District, Hong Kong, Wednesday, 9:02 a.m.

Winnie and Kenny have left for work. Doby is still asleep. From his usual chair at the kitchen table, Horace stares at the television. Fifteen seconds into the morning news his hand goes limp and his spoon falls as he confronts, on the old cathode screen, the face of the man he stabbed.

The seller of the knife that killed Goldfish Head Lau, chauffeur to property baron Mo Tun, has been located. Police have declined to comment, but our sources say that the knife was bought the same day as the murder, perhaps even just hours or minutes before the killing.

Abandoning a half-eaten cup of instant noodles, he leaves for the office. On the way he buys his usual newspapers, but doesn't read them, preferring today to stare at other commuters, who are lost in their chatter, their earphone music, their sleep-starved dozing.

Are things breaking apart? He's not sure. It began disastrously, to be sure; he was supposed to kill Mo. Instead, he killed some man he'd never heard of and had nothing against.

He was supposed to slip away and get on with his life, content that he'd outlived Mo Tun. Instead, Mo lives. Worse, Horace is playing babysitter to Mo's grandson, a witness to the whole thing. Moreover, his job is a form of slow extinction, and at home, Winnie and Kenny deliver one vexation after another.

And now the police are finding things out.

Only Doby does what is asked of him. *That's who I have to depend on,* Horace thinks. Poor Doby. He doesn't know anything. And it's better that way, really. The less Doby is told, the better he'll manage.

The arrival at Horace's station jostles his mind back to the problem at hand. On the street he passes a shop in which a radio is blaring. *The knife store has been located...* The police are talking to the seller, who can no doubt identify Horace. He should have been more careful. But how? Wear a mask? The whole thing was so unplanned, so rushed. *It wasn't supposed to be like this.* It's amazing Horace has the upper hand. But he does. Mo is suffering, and he'll suffer more.

A vibration tickles his breast: his cell phone. Not the secret one that he talks to Mo on, but the other one, the one that brings him nothing but trouble.

"*Wai?*"

"Galen Bing, I manage Yuen Po Building? They're smelling smoke on the 14th floor."

"Has anyone checked what's going on?"

"Their boss called, said his people won't go into the office. You've got to take care of this right away."

Horace sighs his first sigh of the day. "I'll take care of it."

He calls one of the numbers he placed on his phone after his last talk with The Girl, and tells the electrician to check out the smoke.

Ten minutes later Horace enters the office and walks past his Employee of the Month picture, mentally calculating the days till that thing is taken down. He wanders to a bathroom stall, opens the newspaper, and flips through the pages while sitting fully clothed on the toilet. Nothing new. No news of the knife. It must have happened too late for the morning papers.

Horace remembers the knife seller, an oily man with full lips and a slouch. What is he telling the police? Probably describing his face, his clothes. Will Horace wake up tomorrow morning to find his own picture on the news?

Back at his seat, he switches on his computer and begins to run through the work order system.

AB3-1410 - Install new hand dryers in bathrooms, Lung Fok bldg. Pending.

AB3-1411 - Network cabling, Eversun building. In progress. That should have been done by now. Horace makes a note to call.

He checks his calendar for maintenance that is due for scheduling. God, what boring work.

And worse, his time is no longer his own. As an accountant, he could leave work at six and not have to think about the job until morning. Now he gets calls before breakfast, after dinner, anytime. Oh, clients are asked not to phone after hours with simple questions, but they do. How do I order an extra key for the lobby door? Who organizes the fire drills? People think nothing of rousing him with idiocy like that.

Now The Girl plans to make him visit all his sites once a week. A waste of time, and she knows it.

His eyes shift from the monitor to his bottom desk drawer. Strangely, he hasn't thought much about the money—what it buys, what it means to have it. He could just quit this job. But what would he tell Winnie? How would he get this money into an account so he can pay his mortgage? And what would Inland Revenue do if he suddenly tried to deposit seven million dollars?

The desk phone rings; it can only be The Girl. No one else calls him on this line.

"Just heard from Yuen Po Building," she says.

"Yes. They smelled smoke. I called an electrician..."

"Right. First of all, why did you call him?"

"Because all the others are on the disco job..."

"The disco job has been put on hold, didn't you know that? The site is dark."

"I didn't know..."

"Furthermore, he wasn't even needed. It was just a laser printer that went bad. Didn't you even check first?"

"I... he said the staff weren't going in the office. I figured they were losing money. So I..."

"You know who's losing money around here? We are!" The phone goes dead.

Horace lowers his head into his hands and slowly rubs his eyes.

Time to end things and move on. Time to kill the boy.

* * *

Wan Chai District, Hong Kong, Wednesday, 3:03 p.m.

Drive past the building and look for people.

If someone is there, drive away.

If no one is around, drive two blocks and then park.

Walk in the shade. Wear your cap. Pull the brim down in front.

Be extra quiet.

Was there something else, Doby wonders, as he slips in the service entrance.

A film of dust is beginning to settle inside the building. Doby moves through the deserted corridors and unlocks the room. He lays down a shopping bag containing a box of *char siu fan*, a grape soda, and an ice cream bar. Also a twenty-pack of toilet paper, a large drawing pad, crayons, a pack of wipes.

The boy looks weak. He sits against the wall, but his arms fall lazily against his sides, and head is bowed down, as if in shame.

"I brought everything."

The boy looks at him, but doesn't say thank you. "When can I go home? I want to see *Ma Ma* and *Ba Ba*."

Doby doesn't know. His father hasn't told him what's going on.

"You said you'd give me the rest of the story," Doby reminds him.

"Why can't you let me go? I didn't do anything to you. I hate this place."

"Can I have the story?"

"How would *you* like to be here? I have to shit in a wastebasket. It's hot in here too. There's no window, and no air conditioning."

"You said you'd…"

"I have no one to talk to."

The boy keeps changing the subject. He's hard to follow sometimes.

"I brought what you asked for," he says.

The boy looks at the bag, thinks for a moment. Then he points to the bottom of the wire shelf that stands against the wall by the door.

"What?"

"Underneath."

Doby slips his hand under the bottom shelf, which sits an inch above the floor. He removes a comic book. *Part 2.*

He resists the urge to open the book then and there. He grabs the doorknob and starts to leave.

"Wait," the child says. "There's another part to the book."

"Yeah?"

"Part 3, yeah."

"Do you have that?"

"I might know where to get it."

"Where?"

"I want something first."

"What?"

"I want to use your phone."

Doby remembers seeing *Ba Ba* take away the kid's phone. This doesn't feel right.

"I don't think I can."

"I just want to let *Ma Ma* and *Ba Ba* know I'm all right. They'll be worried about me."

"I can't."

"Please. I love them."

Doby studies the floor. He hates, *hates* when something new comes at him and he doesn't know what to do.

Finally, he says, "I'll ask my father."

"No! He'll say no. But you know I'm your friend. I gave you those comics, right? I just want to let *Ma Ma* and *Ba Ba* know I'm okay. We don't need to tell anyone else. That's okay, isn't it?"

CHAPTER TWENTY-SIX

Doby closes his eyes, thinks, thinks again, but it's so confusing.

"My phone…I left it in the van."

"Just bring it to me. It'll just take a second, I promise. Then, next time, I'll get you the third part of Green Warriors."

"Okay, wait here."

He walks two blocks to his van, opens the door, spots his cell phone on the center console, where it's recharging. All the boy wants to do is let his parents know he's all right. But *Ba Ba* took away his phone. He must not want the kid to talk to anyone.

Why not? What's the harm of him talking to his parents? He wishes he knew more about what's going on.

He grabs the phone and detaches it from the cord. As he moves to close the van door, a group of men—three in all—walk by the van toward the building where the boy is hidden.

Look for people.

If someone is there, drive away.

A shiver wrenches Doby from head to knees. He jumps in the van and drives away, wondering what he could have been thinking.

Do I want Ba Ba *to replace me with the boy? I must be crazy.*

***

The three warriors are trapped in the dungeon now, painted and dressed in green. Nevertheless, they plan to do exactly what the Prince feared—warn the western kingdom of the coming attack. Snake has a plan.

Good stuff, Doby thinks as he flips to the next page. Every once in a while he comes upon a passage or two with easy characters, ones he learned early on in school. He wishes they'd stick to those.

The jailer, a stupid-looking guy with missing teeth, brings the three warriors bowls of slop and places them in the cell. Horse takes a sip and says, "Hey, they gave us pork! No one told me that they fed the prisoners pork here."

"What are you talking about?" says the jailer.

Horse mumbles, "This is really good," as he stuffs the food in his mouth. "There's roast pork in here. From a really fat, healthy pig. Nicely prepared, too. Please congratulate your cook."

The guard laughs. "Have you gone crazy? It's boiled grass and seeds, maybe some tree bark for seasoning."

"No," says Snake. "This is delicious." They dig in. Rabbit says he can't remember tasting anything this good.

The jailer is puzzled. His own food isn't that good, just taro root and radishes. But look at them dig in to their rations!

"Oh, my stomach is going to hurt from eating so fast," says Horse. He asks for more.

There is no more, the jailer says—no one ever asks for more. So the three men leave some food in their dishes, saying that they'll eat it later—no sense making such good pork disappear all at once.

Then they lie down and close eyes, leaving the half-full food bowls on the floor.

On the next page, Doby sees the guard scratching his head, trying to figure out why the prisoners had been given better food than he has. "When was the last time I had pork?" the guard thinks.

The temptation is too great. Once the three men are snoring loudly, he unlocks the cell door and tiptoes in to steal the tasty pork for himself.

The three warriors leap up. They were just pretending to be asleep! The fighters set upon the jailer, tie him up with strips of his own clothes, lock him in the cell, and vanish from the jail.

At a nearby stream, the warriors try to wash the green color from their skin, but the dye won't come out. So they decide to travel only at night, when they can't be seen.

Their problem is food. They can't beg, because people would see that they were green, and soon word would get back to the King. So they walk through the night toward the western kingdom, far away, getting hungrier and hungrier.

Right at sunrise, when they're about to go to sleep, Rabbit goes off to hunt for food. He steps on to a trail and sees…

Doby turns the page. Whoever made this comic book likes to save the surprises for when you turn the page.

...a demon, a red-faced devil with black burning eyes! Rabbit screams, but the demon screams too. He's afraid of Rabbit.

"Leave us alone, demon!" says the demon. "You have no reason to punish us."

Rabbit sees that it's no demon at all. It's an actor in costume, working with a local troupe. Rabbit explains to him why he's painted green and hiding in the woods. The actor, relieved, takes the three warriors back to the troupe's camp and feeds them.

The actor has a good idea: the three men can travel with the troupe. They can play green demons in a play. No one will suspect who they are.

So the three men journey with the actors to the western kingdom, to find the ruler and warn him of the Old King's plans to attack.

The warning comes too late, however. The Western ruler has no time to prepare, and though they all fight bravely, the Old King's armies have the advantage of numbers and surprise. Once again, the three swordsmen are captured and thrown in the dungeon.

"You see what happens when you show mercy, Father," says the Prince. "These men will always be your enemy. You must execute them." This time the Old King agrees. However, it's the eve of the Autumn festival. They're planning a big victory celebration. It would be bad luck to execute them before the festival is over.

End of part 2.

Chapter Twenty-Seven

Kowloon District, Hong Kong, Wednesday, 3:39 p.m.

It's Dollar-ten, all right. He's skinnier now, a shade lighter, with chin and cheeks covered in gray stubble below his trademark mismatched eyes.

And a limp. No, worse than a limp, the guy is a cripple, leaning heavily on a metal cane and swinging a useless leg behind him. Old Ong didn't mention that.

He's about to hobble to the fortune teller's booth when Mo places a hand on his shoulder. Dollar-ten looks up at Mo—he's almost a head shorter, thanks to his bent frame—and his eyes widen to the best of their differing abilities.

"*Ya!*" he says. "What are you doing here?"

"Looking for you. Let's talk."

They move into the courtyard, away from worshipers and tourists, into a clear patch under a gray sky. Mo doesn't care for the outdoors, but he wants no one to overhear.

Mo offers Dollar-ten a cigarette and lights it, giving the shorter man a tiny morsel of face. He lights his own, takes a drag, and says, "What are you trying to pull?"

Dollar-ten looks truly startled. "What? What are you talking about?"

"You know exactly what we're talking about, Little Eye."

In response he shakes his head. "They call me Dollar-ten now, remember?"

Mo does. He was Little Eye in China, but the Cantonese dubbed him Dollar-ten the moment he crossed the border. Funny people, these Cantonese.

"My grandson," Mo says. "You took him. I paid you. Now I want him."

Mo looks in the man's asymmetrical eyes, sees no hint of recognition, much less guilt.

"Answer, dickhead. Where is he?"

Dollar-ten shakes his head. "What the fuck are you talking about?"

Lento breaks in. "Someone from Beijing has been fucking with us. Mo *sin-sahng* says it's you."

"Well, then Mo *sin-sahng* is a stupid dickhead." He starts to shuffle back to the fortune tellers, but Mo brings his hand down on his shoulder again, this time pressing hard.

"Listen, you old whorefucker. I don't want to know you or see you. But I've got a problem, so you'd better talk to me."

"Or what?" shouts Dollar-ten. "Break my other leg? Take all my money away? What can you do to me that hasn't been done?"

Lento assumes the duty of looking nervously from side to side, making sure they're not attracting attention, while Mo stares at the broken little man.

"You're saying you have nothing to do with this?"

"With what? Have you gone crazy? I haven't seen you or thought about you in … twenty-five years? More? What the fuck am I supposed to be doing? And how the fuck am I supposed to be doing it when I can't even cross the street in the time it takes for the fucking light to change? You didn't know I fell off a scaffold twenty years ago?"

"So who is it?"

"What?"

"Who is it? It's one of us."

Dollar-ten seems to know who *us* is, despite the passage of what feels like eons since they were in an enterprise together.

"Someone kidnapped your kid? For ransom?"

"My grandson. Killed my driver. And it has to be one of us."

A faint smile brightens Dollar-ten's leathery face. Inappropriate, Mo realizes, but information in itself.

"Has to be the other one."

"Can't be."

"Has to be. No one else."

Mo releases his hand, backs up a few paces, and stares out into West Kowloon. Dollar-ten, his only lead, is useless. It has to be the kid, indeed.

The kid, the one Dollar-ten calls the other one, is dead. But Mo can't tell anyone how he knows that.

Red Terror

" If a man wants to succeed in his work, that is, to achieve the anticipated results, he must bring his ideas into correspondence with the laws of the objective external world; if they do not correspond, he will fail in his practice."
— Chairman Mao Zedong

Chapter Twenty-Eight

Beijing, China 1967

A good set of teeth was a matter of luck. Even one decayed molar and Mo Tun would have failed the physical for the People's Liberation Army. But he didn't fail. The tall, wiry youth with the serious manner was army material all the way. Once he got in, luck had done its work. The rest he could do on his own.

The army wanted Mo, but the feeling was never mutual. Like everything in Mo's life, the military was just there to hoist him to wherever he was going. There was much to do, much to have. Most of all, Mo wanted power and the things that came with it. And you don't get that in the Army.

Drilling, chores, assembly, inspection; the stupidity of it all turned his stomach. Worse was the drudgery of faking a devotion to the Party. Endless dreary meetings, the need to quote from memory the Chairman's thoughts, the constant chiding of comrades who were lax in matters revolutionary. It was tedious—he hated reading and writing and wasn't good at it. One thing he could do well was lie, well enough, he hoped, to get into the Party. The army was a path to the Party, and the Party a path to everything else in China.

Unlike the dolts who saw no shame in serving the government in a low capacity, Mo kept his eyes open. He'd watched sleek and pampered Party officials motoring along Chang Lu in chauffeured cars. He'd seen high-ranking cadres wearing tailored wool uniforms so unlike the ill-fitting cotton one that draped his own gaunt frame. He imagined their spacious houses stuffed full of Western luxuries. And most important, he knew that those men were no smarter than he was.

Mo had the qualifications: intelligence, a clean record, and a good family background. And he could make an impression if called upon. During his first party indoctrination meeting, the leader, a homely woman in a baggy Mao suit and too-large eyeglasses, asked him what inspired him to further his political education.

"It was Lei Fung," he answered, citing the soldier whose diary was being held up as a model for the country's youth. "I realized how much I could learn from him. He didn't care about himself—he was concerned about his comrades, about the Revolution. Even though he never rose to a high rank, I want to be like him."

It was all bullshit, of course. Bao, his army doctor, mused about the book once in an unguarded moment. "I myself could never write poems so stirring, nor prose so elegant as the uneducated Lei Fung," the doctor had said. "Not that I doubt them for a second, you understand. But if one didn't know what an extraordinary young man he was, one would suspect a fabrication."

Dr. Bao had sensed that Mo was a kindred soul—one who could recognize bullshit when he saw it. But Mo said nothing. He had no need of a confidant. Hanging out with fellow malcontents might even slow him down. Friendship could wait; it would all pay off when he was invited to apply for Party membership. The commissars couldn't fail to notice his performance. Once Mo got his Party card, nothing would stop him.

But it never happened. The invitation never came, despite the fine show he made in training, despite his performance in instruction classes. Months and finally a year passed, and he was still marching back and forth, wasting bullets on targets, parroting slogans at meetings, pissing away his life.

A year and a half, two years. He took his discharge.

Mo was handed a job at Fengtai District Electronics Factory No. 2, which made power transformers, definitely not what he had in mind when he joined the army at eighteen. He showed up at the factory each morning at seven, watched the conveyor belt looping around and back, on and on in endless circles. The symbolism was obvious to the point of insult. His plan was shot to hell.

It got worse that summer. Up to then, Mo had understood the chain of power. The Great Chairman and the party on top; his factory boss directly above him; a political instructor haunting the floor to watch him for signs of eroding revolutionary will; and his dear friends, of course—the believers who would inform on him if he bared a true thought.

That order he understood. But a new power had emerged, one that confounded Mo: the Red Guards.

Old Chairman Mao, realizing that China was slipping from his shriveled talons, began preaching to kids: *you are the Revolution.* China needs you to defend against the capitalist roaders who are undermining socialism. Denounce your teachers, your parents, anyone hostile to the Revolution.

Fucking students were determined to take authority away from the army, Mao's own army. And they even had Mao's go-ahead to do it. The kids, moreover, came cheap: a bowl of rice a day to the Red Guards, no matter where they were, kept the party under Mao's thumb. Mo knew how the Red Guards would end. After the job was done, the Chairman would tell them what the Army told him: *well done, my children, now kiss my ass and go back to the farm.*

The smart ones would conclude. as he did, that it was time get out of China. That would take a plan, and planning meant observation. He studied the Red Guards, skulked about at meetings, listened to gossip, and learned.

One thing you had to admire about the Red Guards: the fear they inspired. Loyal party members, men who had been knee-deep in the shit and blood of the revolution in the 1940s, were suddenly terrified of what some Beijing University botany major might accuse them of.

This was, he concluded, the new order: the Party had China; the Red Guards had the Party; Mao and his wife Jiang Qing had the Red Guards. Not even Deng Xiaoping could oppose them. No way could the army shield that old, clever conservative much longer. Deng was finished.

The plan came to Mo one day as he read an item about the Guards in the newspaper. He realized that these idealistic, stupid kids were his ticket out of China.

Get weapons from the arsenals. In a stroke of irresponsibility testifying either to genius or dementia, the Great Leader had ordered the Red Guards to arm themselves. It was insanity, of course; kids have no training. What use is an army that can't disassemble, reassemble, maintain, clean, and load its guns, much less aim and fire them? Mo had the answer: the young army was an engine of fear.

A detachment of Red Guards had formed near Mo: mostly students, but some workers from his factory as well. They called themselves the 18s for the date they were formed. A poster said they would be gathering at his factory lunchroom.

Mo showed up to listen. The speeches reminded him of the cant of his army days when party slogans bubbled up spontaneously. But soon all the chatter made the kids restless, a feeling Mo knew well.

"Slogans! You're chanting slogans as if they'll do your fighting for you," said the group leader, a youth named Yang Wai-kit. Not the way Mo would have put it, but this student seemed to have a brain, at least. The boy was no poster model: medium height, slight build, weak chin, a high forehead topped by limp hair. But his eyes had fire in them, and the others were silent when he spoke. The Cultural Revolution had liberated something in Yang's gut, something that had yet to take form. "We need weapons," he said.

"What for?" asked one of the Guards.

"That's the Chairman's directive, you should know that," Yang replied, his voice crackling with impatience. But there was more to it, Mo knew. There were rumors about another Red Guard detachment, the Brothers of the Flag, who had gotten hold of some rifles already. The 18s would not be outdone.

There came questions. What kind of weapons should we get? Handguns or heavier artillery? How much ammunition? Enough for one onslaught against corrupt former landlords and rightists, or enough for a prolonged campaign against all the lackeys of the old feudal regime we might meet?

"Who cares?" said a Guard. "Let's go!" There were shouts, raised fists, some laughs, too many smiles for a matter so serious.

"Hold on," piped up a bespectacled youth. "Is this a policy decision, or an operational decision?"

Mo groaned inwardly, and he saw in Yang's face the same hopelessness. These kids were utterly unfit for any kind of job, much less an armed revolt.

The meeting broke down into arguments and chatter. Mo knew the problem: they were scared shitless of picking up a gun. When the meeting ended and the students had dispersed, Mo approached Yang, who sat staring at the wall, deep in the contemplation of his own inadequacy as a revolutionary leader.

"Look, weapons are dangerous," Mo said. "You need to know how to handle them. I was in the military. I can show you."

Yang showed no reaction, apart from a flicker in his eyes. "Why should we trust you?"

"You think you can do it on your own?"

"That doesn't answer my question."

"I think the Chairman knows what's best for China. He got us this far." It was a new variation on a lie Mo had plenty of practice telling.

"What do you get out of it?"

The kid was sharp, Mo gave him that. "I'm a little older than you. I know what it was like, what those counter-revolutionary bastards are trying to preserve. My own family was ruined by a landlord. He stole our farm. We had to beg for food until Mao's land reform put things right." Pure invention—his father had been a watchmaker. Now, of course, his father's shop was shuttered—watches had been declared a luxury, like large houses and romantic love. But Yang bought the story.

It was in the army, during a unique form of torture called the political instruction session, that Mo met Koon. Mo was infantry, and Koon was attached to the quartermaster's staff at the 8th Regiment, Beijing Garrison. Koon was a good boy, a politically active class struggler from a solid worker background. A handsome boy with wise, penetrating eyes, he was a true believer. Koon had eloquently denounced the Four Olds and capitalist roaders at the meetings, praised the Chairman and the heroes of the Long March, and, like Mo, had set his sights on a Party membership.

And like Mo, Koon had been rejected. His family history hadn't been as pure as he had thought: an uncle, one he'd never met, had fled to Hong Kong. Somehow, Koon kept his army position, but his sisters and brother had been sent to a rural district for reeducation. That tiny bug-ridden sewer of a village lacked running water and rudimentary sanitation, but there were plenty of overseers to make sure the ungrateful students shoveled pig shit from dawn to dark. Half-starved and withered with fatigue, Koon's sisters were easy prey when typhoid ripped through the village. But even after the loss of his beloved sisters, Koon still believed, going on at meetings about how China was being reborn and how proud he was to take part in this great event.

Then, one night, Koon's brother was caught listening to foreign radio. Only fifteen, he was arrested and beaten until he went blind in one eye. This time Koon, and not China, had been reborn.

Koon did nothing to advertise the depth of his resentment, but neither did he hide it very well. At meetings he answered questions and nodded his head at appropriate times. But losing both sisters and the best half of his only brother stole the revolutionary fire from his heart.

Mo said nothing, just filed it away until he needed something from Koon. That day came after Mo attended the meeting of the 18s and saw how they lusted for guns. Immediately he tracked Koon down and met him at the Defend the Worker's Revolution Noodle Restaurant, formerly Huang's Fine Dumplings.

It was a summer evening. They watched the workers, men and women, clatter back and forth on their bicycles. A truck clattered by, laden with rubble from a nearby demolition. Mo was reminded that where they were once looked out on the old city wall, which had stood for half a millennium. Now there was a ring road. Where a wall once protected the city, cars now ran in circles.

A group of teenagers passed by, the little red bible of Mao sayings peeking out of their pockets.

"You see what's happening, don't you?" Mo said. "Soon those kids will own China."

Koon looked up from his noodles. "Those kids?"

"I hear they're plotting to raid the arsenal."

The words had the intended effect on Koon. "Do they know at the base?" he said. "Could be trouble."

"Depends," Mo said. He had thought about what to say next. Koon no longer had a stake in the Revolution; it was obvious. But just how far would he go?

"Let me ask you something," Mo said. "What happened to your cousins from the South?"

"Gone." Mo knew damn well what had happened to them. They'd made it over the border to Hong Kong six months ago.

"Ever hear from them them?"

It was the riskiest thing you could say in modern China. If he'd misjudged Koon, he could be reported and sent to prison. The labor camps were full of people who thought they knew whom to trust.

Koon just nodded.

"Let's go somewhere we can talk," said Mo.

* * *

"I don't like it," Koon said. The whole thing stank of something foreign, something reckless and outside of his control.

"We'll be following the Chairman's orders," said Mo.

"You joke, but this isn't a joke. We can't give the Red Guards guns. Kids against soldiers is risky. All it would take would be one soldier who didn't feel like taking shit, and a student would be dead. Then things would be out of control. We might be responsible."

"I don't intend for them to use the guns in the city. But they need to see them, try them out, so they feel important, so they'll do what we want. Trust me."

Trust him? A tall order. Oh, Mo would never turn him in. They both detested the true believers too much for that. But Mo was hard to like, truth be known. The ex-soldier with a gaze like flint and a voice like sandstone revealed so little of himself and yet seemed to know so much about Koon.

150

Mo was a little scary, to tell the truth.

Koon spent a day mulling over Mo's proposal, thinking also of the whispered rumors of what Hong Kong was like. People who dressed in bright colors and ate lots of tasty meat. No loudspeakers blaring revolutionary hymns. And best of all, no political instruction anywhere.

Four days later, Koon delivered a crate of Type 56 rifles and another crate full of ammunition. It had been easy. He didn't even have to worry about his superior: the quartermaster was in business for himself as well, selling what he could on the black market for extra cash. If the quartermaster ever did a check and found a crate missing, he'd be the last person to start an investigation. At worst, if discovered, Koon might have to pay him off.

And there would be money soon. Money to pay off the quartermaster, if he had to, and money to take Koon all the way to Hong Kong.

* * *

The rifles were a coup for the young Red Guard Yang Wai-kit. Once the student took a weapon in his hand, he was rarely without one. He began to strut around like the revolutionary leader he thought he was.

Let him hog the glory, Mo thought. Let the little Lenin be the big man in the eyes of the troupe. Mo was content to show the 18s how to carry, load, and fire the rifles, how to clean them and store ammunition. He had been a soldier; he didn't need to play one.

After a week, the list of victories of the 18s comprised two sessions of target practice at an old abandoned range outside town and a public denunciation of the No. 114 Metalworks Red Guards as counter-revolutionary. This was getting Mo nowhere.

The last link in the chain that led to Hong Kong was a man as blithe and superficial as Koon was astute and serious. Little Eye was the son of a fortuneteller, one of the professions that the Revolution outlawed. Mao Zedong was busy grinding away at the Four Olds—old customs, culture, habits, and ideas. Family portraits and wedding dresses were tossed on the fire. Churches were boarded up, and temples were used for storing truck parts. Anyone burning incense to their ancestors or telling a fortune was asking for a month or two in the cow shed, that cold, filthy, stinking sty where reactionaries were tossed to contemplate their sins.

Still, Little Eye—so-called because his right eye was noticeably smaller than his left—was known to practice his father's trade on the sly. He loved telling fortunes, because it fed his other hobby: snooping. A friend's sister asks him if she should get married, and now he has a bit of news: so-and-so has a lover. A woman wants to know an auspicious day for a long journey: that could mean a flight to Hong Kong. Little Eye loved collecting all kinds of intelligence. It was the only black market he had any kind of talent for. If something was going on, Little Eye knew about it.

Mo had met Little Eye at the electric factory, where the jovial man did as little work as he could, but loved to regale Mo with tales of which girl in the factory had just had an abortion, which manager had just given his supervisor a fresh-killed goose in an effort to move up the ladder. Once, after a number of beers, he hinted that quite a few families in the area were hoarding illegal riches. That got Mo thinking.

The People's Revolution had brought with it a great surrender of private wealth. Jewelry, valuable artwork, expensive furniture and clothes, and Western-style goods were all carted away to be burned or sold to finance the Revolution. But some people found it very hard to part with wealth. People kept reminders of the capitalist era—very expensive reminders, sometimes— tucked in the back of cabinets, hidden at the bottom of rice barrels, buried under floors.

But the fortune teller was not a complete fool. Over rice at the worker's canteen, Little Eye would drop hints to Mo about what he knew, but he named no names. Once those people were arrested, there was no secret, and knowing secrets was the fun of it all.

* * *

Little Eye was rolling his cart past the assembly line when Mo tapped him on the shoulder.

CHAPTER TWENTY-EIGHT

"I had a dream last night," Mo whispered. "Can you tell me what it means?"

"No one better. But not here. Meet me in the warehouse at your break."

Little Eye's job as a cleaner gave him the run of the place. His responsibility was to push a cart full of brooms, mops, and buckets all over the factory and keep the facility clean. But often he found that doing the first of these was enough. As long as he was in transit, any supervisor watching figured he was going somewhere else to clean. No one kept track of the work he actually did. He could get by rolling his cart around the building half the day, riding the massive freight lift from floor to floor so as not to dwell in one spot too long. In between jaunts, he would curl up among the pallets in the warehouse and have a smoke, or else join whatever group of workers was on a break and shoot the breeze, holding off real work as long as he could. Occasionally he had to swab a floor to keep up the pretense.

When Mo met him at the warehouse, it wasn't to talk about dreams.

"You told me about some people who were hoarding," said Mo. He scanned a couple of corridors of pallets and the catwalks above to ensure they were alone.

"Maybe. What of it?"

"I need to know details."

"Why should I tell you?" said Little Eye.

"There's money in it."

"You're up to something."

"What do you care?"

"What's your birth sign?"

Mo thought a moment. He wasn't much for that nonsense.

"Rat, I think."

"Of course. Rats know how to work for success. You make plans, work until something happens. I'm a Monkey—I work when it interests me, and I lose interest fast. The last job I had that was any fun…"

"Quiet."

"See? You're clever. You think of things. It's not a good idea to complain about work these days." This time it was Little Eye who checked for eavesdroppers. There were none. The factory was idle today; often it was, thanks to industrial planning that would be laughable if it weren't tragic. "You have a point, Mo," Little Eye said. "No sense dwelling on the past, especially since it's a crime."

"So do we have a deal?"

"What? Tell you what I know on the promise of money sometime? What would I buy with it? There's nothing in the stores."

That much was true. If there's one thing that Communism was good at creating, it was shortages. Mo thought for a minute.

"Okay, then," said Mo. "I'll do your work."

"You'll what?"

"I'll mop your floors, or whatever you do. Some of it, anyway. I have to do my shift, but when I'm done, I can make things easy for you."

The words themselves seemed to lift a burden from Little Eye's skinny shoulders. He stood a half inch taller at the thought of beating the system and having more nap time as well.

But it would be dangerous. Everything was dangerous in China. Up to now, he'd found what he believed to be the safest way to live, short of actually doing his job. He looked at Mo for a few seconds, weighed his options.

"There's an official, living south of here, in Fangshan. Back during the Three Antis campaign his job was to stay on the backs of former landlords and Kuomintang officers. You know how rich some of those bastards got. While confiscating their money, this guy skimmed off plenty himself. Now he takes bribes to help get people into Hong Kong and Taiwan."

It all made sense to Mo. The Three Antis campaign was the Chairman's way of purging corruption, waste, and bribery. But corruption is a tenacious weed, and the very act of uprooting it spreads the seeds to new patches of ground.

* * *

From then on, what time he didn't spend working, or attending those deadly political meetings in the Loyalty Room, or mopping Little Eye's stupid floors, Mo spent verifying Little Eye's story. When he was satisfied, he approached

Yang and told him that preparation was over, that it was time to do the work the 18s were founded for. He described the official that Little Eye had told him about, listed his crimes, his reactionary history, his counter-revolutionary crimes.

"Go to his home, shake him up. Let his family know what kind of slime he is."

"You coming along?" asked Yang. His voice trembled—they were approaching a point from which they could not return.

Mo shook his head. "This is a Red Guard operation. I'm just an advisor."

"What if there's trouble?"

"There won't be, once they see your rifles. But this is important—don't use the guns. Once they see them, they'll respect you. Do not use them."

"What if they don't respect us?"

"I showed you how to use the butt of the rifle if someone tries to be a hero. And if the women give you trouble," he added, "humiliate them."

"How?" asked Yang. Was that hope in his eyes?

"You figure out how, that's up to you. One more thing. This cadre's hoarding money. Not sure what form it's in. You need to force him to show you, and bring it to me. I'll know where to take it."

Yang said nothing.

"Next time I'll get you some grenades," Mo added.

* * *

They pulled it off, just as Mo said they would. Yang brought back a small crate packed with American silver dollars, some watches, a few taels of gold. Mo looked it over, shoved it in a sack, and disappeared for the night. But he kept his promise and continued instructing the Guards.

At the factory two days later, after washing a truck bay that hadn't seen soap since Chiang Kai-shek ruled China, Mo extracted the name of a cadre, name of Ping, who was holding back money from the state. Yang marched the 18s to his apartment, beat him, and hurled his furniture through the window onto the street. Yang personally blackened the eyes of Ping's son.

Calling the man a traitor to the revolution, the kids began tearing books from shelves, yanking drawers out of chests, and spilling clothes onto the floor.

"Where's the money? We know you're hiding it!" shouted Yang.

"There's none—I swear." Ping was a short, squat fellow with a plump face now red from exertion and fear. Yang grabbed his teenage daughter, almost tore her arm out of its socket as he pulled her across the floor to the back room.

"I'll be finished with her in ten minutes. Then I'll ask you again."

"No!" he screamed. "Leave her! I'll show you."

He led them to a shack behind their building. In a covered pot underneath a vegetable bin they found some packs of American dollars. Yang himself threw the cadre down and kicked him in the teeth. The students left, pausing only to paint some characters on the outside wall of the house. On the way out, Yang took a last look up at the second-floor window, where the girl was sobbing in her mother's arms.

* * *

Yang had become the leader of his Red Guard chapter by accident—he took charge at the first few meetings and bullied others to get his way. A few of the smarter ones resented Yang's relationship with Mo, and the privilege it implied. But the raid changed that. Now Yang led from power. No one disputed him, and before they made a move, the 18s waited for Yang's word.

Guards from two other groups defected to the 18s. Yang accepted the first few, but on Mo's advice, he began turning them away. You don't want too many people on these raids, he said. You'll get talkers instead of doers. And we don't want talk.

That suited Yang. He lived for the raids. Giving orders, kicking in doors, watching respectable men tremble and weep—that made him feel *alive*. The women, too, were a perk. One of the counter-revolutionary wives was particularly feisty. He had his men hold her down while he made her regret her decision to resist.

Let Mo have his money, Yang thought. *I've got the best job in the world.*

* * *

Gold, silver, and foreign currency were the usual finds, although after Mo trained him to be a bit more observant, Yang produced some very fine jade, several Ming Dynasty scrolls, and a ceramic horse that he had had difficulty concealing on his way back from the raid, but which had to be priceless.

Had the 18s been the only faction of Red Guards around, they could have gone from scheme to scheme, with Mo filling his pockets and Yang drunk on power and lust.

Other Red Guard factions plied the streets, though, and one of them, the Sons of the Long March, was determined to purify socialism in their area. Mo had helped Yang discredit them, even frighten them once by firing over their heads (Mo warned Yang not to kill any students), but the Sons were persistent. They charged that the 18 were counter-revolutionary, corrupt extortionists.

The game was up when one of the 18s squealed. Tied to a stove and flayed with strips of rubber and wooden sticks, the hapless boy told the Sons how Yang took charge of loot when they raided the houses of corrupt cadres, and turned it over to an ex-army man.

The word was out: find Yang and deal with him.

That night Yang, breathless and sweating, sought out Mo. "They're after me," he said, his voice a mix of fright and incomprehension. "The Sons are saying I'm corrupt. What can I do?"

Mo looked at him, nodded as if this were a minor, everyday hitch. "It'll blow over. You just need to hide out for a few days. I'll have a talk with the Sons, make a deal with them. You'll be back in circulation in no time."

"Hide? Where?"

"Give me a couple of hours. I'll find a place."

At ten that night Mo led the boy to a storm cistern in Chongwen. An iron gate prevented anyone from entering the cistern, but the mouth of the tunnel was wide enough for Mo's purpose.

"This is where you want me to…"

Yang barely saw the flash of the bayonet knife before he felt the blade. He clutched the gash in his belly and caught the warm offal as it spilled out. Mo left when his victim's knees hit the ground.

Along with Yang's abdomen, Mo's had severed his own Red Guard affiliation. It was time to cash in. Mo had no interest in emulating the Kuomintang officers and former landlords who stuck around and got massacred. He remembered the zealots of the Three Antis campaign who, having done their duty and their looting, took their turn on the chopping block. The Red Guards might be next, along with anyone who aided them. But not Mo.

Into an army duffel bag went his roll of US silver dollars, a gold bar, the scrolls, a sock containing three gold watches, and some jewelry. He carefully bundled the ceramic horse in an old rice sack. Bicycling through the darkest, narrowest streets he could find, he made his way to a man named Yee, the proprietor of a sundry shop in Daxing.

In the back room of the store, under a naked electric bulb that dangled from a wire, Mo handed his loot to Yee, who scrutinized each item with a merciless eye while his son, another former army man, stood ready to settle any disagreements with the meat chopper tucked in his belt.

"Ten for the watch," Yee said.

"No, twenty," said Mo.

The man shook his head. Denial of the worth of things was his profession. "Ten. And fifty each for the scrolls."

"You're crazy."

"Then take it somewhere else, see if you get a better price."

Yee can sense I have no time to bargain, Mo thought. And Yee was right. The boy's body would eventually be found in the storm cistern. He planned to be far away by then.

When they'd agreed on everything but the ceramic horse, Yee pulled up a floorboard and took out the money. Mo knew U.S. dollars well, but they still looked strange, green, and powerful, like the leaves of some medicinal plant whose essence promised great strength. The man counted out some bills. Mo pocketed the sheaf.

"Last chance for the horse," said Mo. "One hundred."

Yee shook his head. "Pack it up," he said, not looking up from his table filled with booty. "Take it with you as a gift to your family." He laughed, and his son took the cue, bursting into giggles. With a grunt, Mo hurled the statue against the wall. By the time the clay dust had settled he was gone.

* * *

The next day in a garage behind Fengtai District Electronics Factory No. 2 Mo divided up the loot with Koon and Little Eye. Koon understood immediately that it was time to make for Hong Kong.

"I know a way to Hong Kong," Mo said. "You catch a boat down south."

"No, it's okay. I'm going the overland route."

"Boat's faster," said Mo.

"Swimming's involved. Sharks are fast too."

"Suit yourself. What about you?" he said, addressing Little Eye.

"What do you need to know for?" Little Eye seemed to be taking this whole disruption in stride.

"What do you think? I'm risking my ass. Until I'm over the border, whatever happens to you could screw me up."

"I'm staying."

"You don't want to do that," said Koon.

"I'll take my chances here."

"You're crazy," said Mo. "Things are going to get hot." He hadn't told them about killing Yang, but he'd hinted that the party was over, and Koon, at least, seemed to catch on.

Little Eye spat in a corner. "I go to Hong Kong, then what?"

"You work. Get rich. Everyone there is rich."

"But if you don't work, you starve. Right here I've got an iron rice bowl. Why go to a place where you have to sweat to make a living?"

It might have been funny had Mo not known what would happen if the body were found before he escaped and the police or the army got to this stupid little man.

"It's your choice," Mo said. "Koon, I'll find you in Hong Kong. Little Eye, since we won't see each other again, let me take you out for a beer." His finger traced the bayonet knife under his shirt.

"I could use one," said Little Eye.

"I'll take care of Little Eye," said Koon. "You've got a long journey. Best get going."

Mo looked at Koon, nodded, and left.

* * *

An old Red Army colleague had told Mo of a man who lived in the seaside town of Long Fung in Guangdong. It was one of the towns where, if you kept your ear to the ground and met the right people, you could get out of China. Mo made the two-day train journey. After that, it didn't take long to find the man. Strangers only came to Long Fung for one reason. Soon Mo was sitting in a tea house, talking to a boat pilot who was planning a fishing excursion. Yes, I'll take a passenger. Got any money?

Mo showed him some US dollars.

"What are your plans when you get there?" the pilot asked.

A curious question. It took a moment, but he figured out what the pilot was up to.

"I'm going to work for my rich cousin. You need a job? He could always use someone good."

The pilot was no fool. "If you have a rich cousin in Hong Kong, why didn't he buy you out?"

"He's already brought over six of my family. There are eight more. It takes time. I haven't got the patience. Let me go with you, and I'll get you ten thousand a month and a year's bonus for getting me there."

"Two years' bonus."

Mo pretended to think about it. "Eighteen months," he said. Done. Two days later he climbed aboard a fishing junk and, after spending a restless day moored at sea with nets cast, the boat took off on a slow journey toward the most remote of Hong Kong's many islands, a craggy place called East Ping Chau. The island was much closer to Guangdong than Hong Kong—just four kilometers away, or a few minutes' desperate chase by a PLA Navy patrol boat. But East Ping Chau was shielded by British law, and China, for reasons it kept to itself, had not reached out to grab the place.

It was dawn when the pilot pointed out a stub of land.

"There it is," he said. "Get ready to swim."

The pilot made a move to kill the engine the very moment Mo slashed his throat, emptied his pockets, and dumped him overboard. After tying the wheel and shoving down the throttle he jumped overboard himself and swam the last mile. All he brought with him from China was a roll of banknotes and his bayonet knife, now clenched in his teeth in case a shark tried to beat him at his own game.

Mo holed up on East Ping Chau for the day to dry his clothes and get a feel for Cantonese—a messy, ugly language to his ears. Using some Hong Kong dollars that some unfortunate counter-revolutionary had tucked in a tea jar, he made his way to the New Territories, and from there past boundary Street to Kowloon, where the colony's touch-base policy stipulated that he was free and clear. Just to make sure, he went all the way to Hong Kong Island to surrender himself.

It was a boom year in Hong Kong. Buildings were shooting up like corn. Businesses were starving for office space, and people craved housing. With his new Hong Kong ID card, he had no problem getting a job on a construction crew.

He'd arrived in Hong Kong. He could do anything here. Everyone in China knew that this was the place where you could become rich. Where money wasn't hoarded by the government, but was there for anyone to grab, given enough luck and pluck. He'd have plenty of it soon enough.

Chapter Twenty-Nine

Tsim Sha Tsui District, Hong Kong, Wednesday, 1:02 p.m.

"Why did this take so long?" says Lok.

"We had to review a lot of footage, sir. Watch this."

Million Man clicks the remote, and a choppy video image of a Kowloon street appears on the screen. Lok recognizes a storefront on the right as Soddy Leung's knife shop.

"This is the only camera with a view of that side of the street. It's from a jewelry store across and west a few doors. The best we could find. The knife shop had no walk-in customers after one p.m.—I get the impression that the place does most of its business with restaurants and hotels, and that's mostly by phone. But here…we found that twice, around the time of the murder, a van stops in front of the store and blocks the view."

"Two different vans?" says Old Ko.

"Yeah. This one's a snack company van, probably making a delivery, but the other one…" He signals Ears to jam down the fast-forward icon, and the cars and passersby race across the screen.

"…take a look."

A dusty white panel truck noses into the loading space in front of the store.

"No writing on the truck," says Pang. Can you see the driver?

"Not too well. Just bad luck, his head was turned."

"Delivering something?

"Who can tell? The side doors are facing away from us, and there are no windows in back. But if he's delivering something, he's pretty quick. In and out in a few minutes."

"So, how do we find the van?"

"This is what took us so long, sir," says Ears. "We gathered footage in a four-block radius around the store."

"And?" says Lok.

Ears clicks a mouse, and a second video file starts up. "Same street, a block west, sir." He races forward and stops at a picture of the white van. The plate number is clear. About time something was.

* * *

Tsim Sha Tsui District, Hong Kong, Wednesday, 1:42 p.m.

A PC inserts his head and shoulders into the room and informs Lok that he's wanted in the report room.

Lok looks at his watch. Today is Ching Ming, and he was due to take off for a few hours and help the family sweep his ancestor's graves, but it's too late to catch a ferry to Cheung Chau.

* * *

The Report Room is where citizens lament crimes committed against them, witnesses vent their outrage, and lawyers arrive with expensive briefcases and ready answers. The noodle vendor Ding is sitting by a wall, still in his blue work smock, looking as if he'd been pulled bodily from his habitat and placed in a police station against his will. He's seated to the right of a young woman clutching a baby. Probably the wife of a *lan jai*, some habitual offender who has managed to pass down his genes so that the Hong Kong police will have work for generations to come.

Lai-ping's brother died without children. What if Lai-ping has a boy someday? Will he follow his reckless uncle to an early grave? If she bears a child by the man she's seeing now, most likely. But perhaps Lok's influence will balance the weight of a bad ancestry. Perhaps that's his task.

Lok waves Ding over.

"You still want that guy Dollar-ten?" says Ding. He looks relieved to be away from the other citizens with their problems.

"Yes. What have you got?"

"Never mind. What have *you* got?"

"Eh?"

"Seven hundred."

"I said five hundred."

"So give it to me."

"For what? You haven't told me anything."

"Think I'm stupid? I tell you, then you send me home without my money."

Lok smiles. *At least with Ding, I know who I'm dealing with.* "Let's take care of you," he says. He ushers Ding into a conference room and requests a cup of tea for him. Big Pang joins the meeting and draws some papers from a folder.

"Here's how it works, Ding. This man is kindly helping to register you as an informant."

"What? I don't want that."

"It's the way it's done. You'll be given a number. You'll present the number and this form and …"

"Can't you just give me the money?"

"No, I can't. It comes from the Rewards and Special Services Fund. Pang will take you to the person that pays you. That's the system."

It's more than a system, of course. It's a way of keeping his career from being destroyed on a whim. Running informants is about the most dangerous thing a policeman does. Any *jum* who decides he doesn't like the police—and that's most of them—can suddenly claim that the cop is holding out on him, or worse, has been taking kickbacks on the informant fees all along. The Internal Commission Against Corruption will jump on it: after all, it's an easy case that promises headlines. Newspapers love police corruption.

"Will I get paid today?

"I'll see. First, we need to hear what you've got."

"Does he have to hear this?" Ding twitches his head in Big Pang's direction.

"Pang is a witness. We need to make sure that I'm not just writing out vouchers to my nieces and nephews, don't I? We've got rules here."

Ding scrutinizes the two detectives. "Okay. I'm in a *tai chi* group with a lot of northerners. A couple of them know a guy called Dollar-ten. He has one eye larger than the other."

Lok and Pang look at each other. Good nickname. "He shows up at *tai-chi?*" asks Lok.

"Him? No. They tell me he's a cripple. But he works at the jade market. Find him there anytime."

Lok sits back, folds his arms.

"Well? Good enough?"

"Come outside," Lok says. "I'll write you a voucher."

"Told you I'd give you good stuff."

"It'd better be," says Lok. "Or else you'll need that five hundred for a down payment on a new noodle cart."

"You're all a bunch of crooks," Ding mumbles as he stamps through the exit.

* * *

Tsim Sha Tsui District, Hong Kong, Wednesday, 2:19 p.m.

Lok's cell phone rings. Kelvin.

"Hi, *Ba Ba.*"

"Kelvin. What's up?"

"*Ma Ma* said it was okay to call."

"Sure. How was it?"

"Lots of people. The ferry was packed."

Hardly a surprise. In death, as in life, Hong Kong people are jammed together. Cheung Chau Cemetery is prime real estate—with its view of the water, the *feng shui* is perfect.

"Did you do a good job?"

"Yeah. Kitty swept, and I placed the offerings. A plate of chicken, bananas, and two glasses of tea."

Lok conjures an image of his grandparents' resting place. Two gravestones, rather plain, angled toward each other, each displaying a name, a ceramic tile inscribed with a grainy monochrome photo, and a date of death. And, Lok will never forget, a tile bearing the engraver's name and phone number on the back of the stone.

"On the way back, I saw an old man cleaning bones. I was thinking I wouldn't want that job."

Neither would Lok, but Kelvin's reason is more typical—fear of the ghosts that hang around undertakers, morgues, graves, and hospitals. Lok calculates that in two years, it will be time to disinter his grandfather and have his bones cleaned and placed in the columbarium up the road.

Such a temporary place, Hong Kong. People leave to study abroad, to retire in Canada. Its constitution, which guarantees the people's rights and freedoms, has a fifty-year expiration date. Even the graves are rented.

"Hey!" Kelvin says, and Lok hears Kitty commandeer Kelvin's phone. "*Ba Ba*? We passed the coffin maker's shop. He was closing one of them—I had to run to get away."

So that her soul wouldn't be trapped under the closing lid.

Too late, Lok thinks. All our souls are trapped. The lid always closes. It's just a matter of time.

Chapter Thirty

Tsim Sha Tsui District, Hong Kong, Wednesday, 3:44 p.m.

Like everything else, the door to the Great Wall Disco construction site resists Horace. It jams, squeaks, and then finally gives. He clicks on his flashlight—better not to attract attention with room lights. He used up ten minutes of his lunch hour getting here—somehow, he found a taxi—and he's allowing twenty to get back. That leaves him with thirty minutes to scout things out.

No security cameras; they haven't been installed yet. And no watchman, since the door locks are sturdy enough to keep away copper and wood thieves. With his manager's key, filched from the rack at the office, Horace can move undetected and unencumbered, like a ghost.

It's a vast place which, judging from the framing going on, will have a number of separate rooms with floors at different levels. It makes no sense to Horace, but then, he has never been to a nightclub. He steps slowly through the wooden skeleton, a maze that leads to the back of the establishment. Electrical conduit tubing dangles everywhere, the wires hanging out like snakes' tongues.

Through a service window he can see a freezer and a number of refrigerator cases. Further along is a brand-new doorway, freshly hammered out of the cinderblock wall and sealed, for the moment, with plywood. From studying the work orders, he knows that it will be the new emergency exit.

In a while, Horace will make the call. Maybe after work. No sense in giving Mo too much warning. Let him roast.

For a moment the room reels and his knees tremble under the burden of his frame. Hunger, probably. Horace could use some food. And sleep. When did he sleep last? Not since that day—how long ago, now?—that Mo first strode into Great Fortune Property Management.

On that day, Wayne enthusiastically pumped Mo's hand, ushered him into his office, and kissed his ass as only he could. If Mo glanced in Horace's direction that day, he didn't recognize him. Horace, however, would never forget the man who had gutted him and left him to die.

Sleep can wait.

* * *

Beiimg, China 1967

Yang could see nothing: nothing. He could hear only his own breathing, shallow as a bird's. But he could feel. His chest and stomach seemed to be on fire. The floor of the storm drain was wet and rough, and he felt his blood cooling as it seeped onto the concrete. He dug his elbows onto the pitted surface for traction, but as soon as he tensed his body to move, the pain tore him apart, and he splashed back into the puddle. He would never move from that floor again, not under his own power.

Did he have the strength to shout? He gulped some air, coughed, and felt blood-flecked spittle run down his chin. The cough echoed in the tunnel. He inhaled again, this time bracing against the pain, and bellowed at the top of his voice.

* * *

On his way back from his job at the power station, a man named Keng pulled off the road and leaned his bicycle against the iron fence that edged the roadway. He squatted down and stared at the works of his bicycle for a moment, then stood again and drew out a Hongtashan. He lit it and inhaled deeply, a ritual that precedes any new undertaking, even one as simple as tightening the rattle out of a bicycle chain. It was still some miles to Fengtai, and he'd been riding for a while. No harm in resting.

Eventually Keng set about working on his chain, the remaining half of his cigarette clamped in his lips. He'd just about finished when a young man—he looked like a student—rode up to him. "Comrade, can I borrow that wrench when you're done? My pedal's just about fallen off."

Keng nodded, offered him a cigarette, and went on tightening his chain. The student, a slender young man named Lee with well-combed hair and a threadbare shirt, leaned on the iron fence. Bicyclists filed past them, some jingling bells to warn of their approach. A truck carrying metal washtubs nosed through the swarm of bikes, dispersing them like gnats.

"Did you hear that?" said Lee.

"What?"

"Someone called out. From over there." He pointed to a gully some fifteen feet below the road.

"You're making up stories."

"No, listen." They fell silent.

This time Keng heard it. A faint moan, and the words *I'm hurt.*

"We should help him," said the student.

"Forget it. None of our business."

"But he said he's hurt."

"Nothing for you to worry about. Mind your own affairs." He worked a nut back into position with a grunt. "Damn thing's been rattling all day."

Another muffled shout sounded from the drain.

"Shit," said Lee. "Sounds like he's dying. Better call the police."

"Better stay out of it," said Keng.

Lee thought for a minute and said, "I'll go over and see what it is."

Keng shrugged. *Fool,* he thought.

* * *

The young man jogged down into the gully toward the sound, almost tripping once over loose rocks. At the base of the gully he discovered a kid, probably another student, who had been filleted like a perch and left to die in a puddle in a storm drain.

The kid, name of Yang, would have lasted at the most an hour, had the surgeons at the Municipal Hospital not had so much experience basting together workers chewed up daily by the ravenous machinery of China's factories. An intern puffed away at his Zhongnanhai Super Light as he sewed Yang up, filled him with blood, and waited for him to recover or die.

Chapter Thirty-One

Kowloon Tong District, Hong Kong, 2003, Wednesday, 4:55 p.m.

Sylvie is sitting in a soft chair by the window, thumbing an unopened copy of the *European Journal of Obstetrics & Gynecology and Reproductive Biology*. Her eyes follow, but she can't seem to focus on anything, so she stares out the window and follows the lights of the cars that ply the Kowloon streets.

Is Bonitus in one of them?

A key rattles in the lock. In a moment Ivan is by her side, placing a comforting hand on her shoulder. But his silence is no comfort.

"No sign of him yet, is there?"

"*Ba Ba's* working on it. Should know something soon," he says.

"Soon. That's what you said yesterday."

"Sylvie…"

She looks at him. "Ivan, you had me lie to the *police.*"

Ivan walks to the kitchen, retrieves a beer. "Want anything?"

"You know what I want."

"This is a family matter, Sylvie," Ivan says. He sits down and takes a sip of his beer, draws a coaster from a pile on the bookshelf and places it under the glass as he sets it down on the coffee table.

"Family matter…yes, and it's my family. Ivan, this is Bonitus we're talking about."

"Look, I know this sounds crazy, but this kind of thing happens here."

"Really? Because I don't remember that in the marriage ceremony. 'In sickness and in health, murder or kidnapping…'"

Ivan ignores the jab, and speaks slowly, as if he's making the point that will settle things once and for all.

"My father worked his way up from nothing in Hong Kong. Along the way, he had to associate with people who were not exactly clean. That's how you do things. Every business does it. If you build a building, open a store, make a movie, whatever, you're going to have to deal with the triads. No one likes it, but it's what you have to do."

"I know that, but…"

"One of his rivals is making a point. He just wants *Ba Ba* to watch his step. Once we know who it is…"

"You don't even know who it is?" Sylvie feels a shred of hope slipping away.

"*Ba Ba* does, I think. He doesn't want to say. They're not going to hurt Bonitus, I'm sure of that. They just want *Ba Ba* to come to the table and discuss something. Maybe he made them lose face. Remember the Golden Sun Shopping Plaza deal? *Ba Ba* took that away from Crazy Poon. Found out what Poon bid and got in under. Poon had already told friends that he was going to have his girlfriend's group performing in the restaurant there. He lost a lot of face, and he's been pretty furious at us since then."

"I lied to the police, Ivan."

"This isn't America, Sylvie. The police and law don't come first here. Family is what ties it all together."

"But our family is not together. Bonitus is…" She bursts into tears.

"He will be back. I promise. But what I'm saying is that people here settle family matters without the aid of outsiders."

"Outsiders?" she says through the sobs. "Listen to yourself. Like some kind of superstitious peasant. You're a lawyer, Ivan. You need to believe in the law."

"I do, Sylvie. But I also believe that I need to protect my family. If I tell the police, they'll put all kinds of things under the lights, and Crazy Poon or whoever it is will be furious. Right now, he's playing a game we know how to play. Once we bring in the police, he'll feel threatened and betrayed, and there's no telling what he'll do."

"He'll feel betrayed? What about me? What about us? We're the ones who have a missing boy. How is that not betrayal?" The tears have subsided, replaced by the flare of anger in her eyes.

"Look, you still don't understand." He takes another sip of beer.

"I'll say I don't. When I married you, I looked up your father's doings. I saw that his past was, shall we say, colorful. But I thought it was just that, the past. My grandfather made whiskey in a still during Prohibition, and he spent a few weeks in jail once. It makes a good story at parties. But this isn't a story. I'm *living* this … we're living this. And Bonitus, God, what's happening to him? What is our son doing now? Is he suffering?"

"I'm sure he's not…"

"You're sure? You don't even know who's got him. How can you be sure? Ivan, if he doesn't come back to us…"

"He will come back to us. He will…"

"If he doesn't, I don't know how I'll live."

"Sylvie…" He reaches for her hands, but she recoils.

* * *

Kowloon, Hong Kong, 2003, Wednesday, 4:59 p.m.

The wheel is off the cart. At first it was just an amusing little comment, but now Mo wonders. All his projects are sputtering, and the disco, which was supposed to ease his way into a life of legitimate enterprise and wealth, is stalled utterly. His grandson is still being held by someone, and Ivan is preoccupied and not much use.

Mo is in the limo, going nowhere in particular; he thinks better in the car, that's all. He had to lease a new Mercedes, of course; no one would drive a car someone died in. Even then, when he told Hiccups Kwok to take over as his driver, Kwok gulped audibly. Whether it was Goldfish's ghost or the idea that he'd be the next target, Mo didn't know. But having employees' loyalty compromised was not good.

If the wheel wasn't off the cart, it sure seemed that way.

Mo spent hours going over every word Dollar-ten had said, looking for holes in his story, evidence that he lied. But no one that crippled could have pulled off this operation. So he's back where he started, with nothing to go on. No one saw the murderer, no one can find Bonitus, and no one seems to know who's behind it.

The knife seller was on the news. So far the police haven't issued a description of the killer, so perhaps the vendor didn't get a good look at him. Certainly no one's mentioned a man with a limp, so Dollar-ten is out of the picture.

Dollar-ten—what a crazy little bastard. Koon really put one over on Mo back in China, implying that he would take over the task of killing Dollar-ten so Mo could get on his way. The idea was to leave no witnesses in China. Well, Koon did that, after a fashion. Once Mo took off, Koon told Dollar-ten that the police were about to arrest him for hoarding cash and associating with a counter-revolutionary capitalist roader.

Dollar-ten turned white and begged for Koon's help. Later that day the pair were on their way to Hong Kong.

Did Koon ever tell Dollar-ten the truth? That he lied to scare him into fleeing China and keeping them all safe? It doesn't matter to Mo. What matters is getting Bonitus back.

He lights a *Ma Bo Lo* and goes over names in his head, names of men he's cheated, intimidated, or otherwise screwed.

Protection? Nothing there. He's always sent flunkies to collect or, in the event of arrears, to smash windows, kick in display cases, overturn desks. And his clients have been behaving for a long time, he's been told.

Pirated fashion goods from China? Where's the problem? All he does is buy the goods for resale and slip envelopes to some mainland officials. Everyone benefits.

Land auctions? No one would single out him for punishment. Everyone games the system.

He thinks back to more turbulent days.

Then his cell phone rings. It's the idiot.

"Talk," Mo says.

"You want the kid?"

"Fuck you. You know I do. Is he still all right?"

"Perfect. Getting fat on all the rice I'm feeding him. I ought to charge you extra."

"Let's get this done, shall we? I expect him back unharmed."

"Fine. But you'll have to meet me."

"Right."

"Tonight. Two a.m."

"Where?"

"Your place. Your nightclub. Walk in alone, and bring the money. I don't want anyone with you. No bodyguards or gunmen. Just you, unarmed. Walk through the front, into the back room, by the fire exit. Wait for me. I'll bring you the kid."

"Two a.m., got it. And listen, dickhead, if the kid isn't happy and perfectly healthy, I will personally slice you and bleed you out. Do you understand?"

There is a pause on the other end. "I understand extremely well."

The phone clicks off. Mo goes over the instructions in his head. There must be a way to get the upper hand here.

The second time he runs through them, he finds it.

"Great Fortune Property Management," he says to Hiccups. "Do you know where that is? Step on it."

Chapter Thirty-Two

Yau Ma Tei District, Hong Kong, Wednesday, 5:00 p.m.

"Haven't been here in ages," says Ears. From Kansu Street they turn into the Jade Market, which bustles with oversized and overloaded tourists.

"Me neither," says Lok. "Dora doesn't care for jade. She prefers diamonds and pearls."

Ears pauses a second before venturing a joke. "But she married a policeman anyway?"

"You have a point, Ears." They stroll like a couple of tourists through a corridor of stalls, each one stuffed with baubles made from jade and, probably, other jade-like materials. Lok can't tell fake jade from real; he never cared for the stuff himself. Nor does wearing a stone for good luck appeal to him.

Not that Lok isn't superstitious. But it's one thing to refuse a gun that had last been fired by an officer killed in action. And the windows still stay closed in the Hot Room because it seems to help at the station. But luck is too elusive for amulets or incense. He's seen too many dead bodies draped with gold longevity charms, tied with infinity knots that are supposed to bring eternal fortune. Once, in his PC days, he was almost killed while breaking up a marital fight in a room festooned with Double Happiness scrolls.

"Should we ask someone, sir?"

"No need, Ears. Take a look." He points to a booth holding a particularly cheap-looking array of beads, bracelets, and pendants. Dozens of necklaces hang from a bar about head height, above stacks of shiny green bangles.

As they approach, a lean man with salt-and-pepper hair and a poor shave gazes at them with two eyes of distinctly different size. A cane leans against the back of the stall.

"Dollar-ten?"

"That's right."

Lok flashes his warrant card. "I'd like some information about your association with Mo Tun," he says.

They start to talk. Ten minutes of Dollar-ten's story convinces Lok that they need to do this at the station.

* * *

Two hours later, Lok and Ears have put together a story just short of incredible. Mo Tun, a Hong Kong entrepreneur, property man, and occasional figure in the tabloids, got his start from a well-organized looting operation that worked out of a Red Guard group during the Cultural Revolution. An operation that Mo directed.

"And when was the last time you saw the others?"

"Yesterday. Mo and Koon caught up with me at a fortune teller's."

"What did they want?"

"It was crazy. They thought I had something to do with a missing kid. I don't know anything about it."

"Don't you?"

"Now don't you start. I haven't seen those guys in years. They're both successful, and I'm just a jade seller. What do I have to do with them?"

"Then why did they come to you?"

"The guy who took the kid is from Beijing. They said something about it, I don't remember."

"Beijing, you said?"

"Yes, like me, like Mo and Koon."

"So what did you tell them?"

"I told them to find the fourth guy in our…group. Yang. Maybe he was the one who did it."

"Yang—the student who led the raids? What happened to him?" Lok says.

"No idea. He wasn't in on the final split. Don't think he left China."

"Why not? He would have been in as much trouble as anyone if word got out about their looting."

Dollar-ten shrugs.

"Interview concluded." Lok recites the time and date and shuts off the recording device. Dollar-ten makes a motion to get up, but Lok speaks.

"One more thing, and I want you to think about this. Have you had any dealings with this Koon in Hong Kong?"

Dollar-ten shakes his head. "Not since the split. We were nobodies then. Mo hadn't started his business. I don't know what Koon was doing. I still don't."

Lok flips his notebook closed and looks to Ears.

"I was wondering," says Ears. "Mo found you at Wong Tai Sin?"

Dollar-ten nods.

"If you were a fortune teller in China yourself, why do you let someone else tell your fortune now?"

The old man grins, revealing jagged teeth as yellow as some of his jade. "I was never that good at it. A fortune teller has to know people. Back in the village it was easy enough—you know everyone anyway. But strangers? Couldn't read them. Not in Hong Kong. Once I left China, I didn't know the world anymore. Couldn't tell my own future, couldn't tell anyone else's."

* * *

CHAPTER THIRTY-TWO

Tai Po, Hong Kong, 2003, Wednesday, 5:15 p.m.

"Don't even recognize the place," says Old Ko. "Almost missed the turn."

"Must have been different back in the days of the Ten Kingdoms," says Million Man.

"Enough jokes. It's changed even since you were a kid. I remember coming here with friends to hike in the hills. All you had was a small town and Tolo Harbour."

Tai Po is a new town, one of the industrial satellites in the New Territories that feed Hong Kong's insatiable appetite for commerce. In Old Ko's youth it was a dusty market town. But prosperity, the new Tolo highway, and the push for public housing changed Tai Po. *Hong Kong towns have a way of erasing their past,* thinks Old Ko. *Just like its people.*

The two Detective Constables pull up to the nondescript pile of cinderblocks bearing the sign:

Wing Tao Food Distributors.
Frozen Chickens and Ducks

"I'll lead on this one," Old Ko says.

"Frozen chickens? All yours."

Benny Chan, the owner, is fat and cheerful, a short man with a round face echoed by a pair of unfashionable black plastic-framed glasses. Or perhaps they are fashionable. Old Ko can never keep up.

But he doubts Benny Chan cares much for style. Chan wears a plain short-sleeved shirt and faded blue trousers smudged with dust—the type of owner who pitches in and pushes a hand truck once in a while.

"You have a van, license BA 9731," Old Ko says.

"That's right. Is something wrong?"

"No. We're just interested in a stop you made Thursday evening. A shop owned by Soddy Leung?"

The smile freezes on Benny's face. Appropriate, given his business. "Commercial kitchen supplies."

"That's right."

"Uh, yeah. I stopped there. Dropped off some ducks."

As Old Ko notes this, Million Man says, "Why did Soddy need ducks? He isn't a restaurant owner or grocer."

"Not sure. He orders them from time to time." The desk phone burbles, ignored. "I need to sit down—my back." He walks around his desk and lowers himself in a padded chair

The office is as no-nonsense as he is. A file cabinet, desk, and a few photos of farms in Guangdong. A fish tank near one window bubbles away, its inhabitants flitting back and forth in their smaller version of Hong Kong.

"Do you know a man named Goldfish Head Lau?" Old Ko says.

Benny's head jerks forward and his jaw drops. "The guy who was just murdered? Are you serious?"

"Yes. Did you know him?"

"No. Never saw him. Don't know him. I just do frozen food. Chickens and ducks."

Old Ko can sense enthusiasm in his answer, a rush of adrenaline that a rabbit must feel when the eagle swoops and misses. Benny is relieved to talk about Goldfish Head Lau, because whatever he's hiding has nothing to do with him.

"Mind if we look around?"

Benny's smile warms up again. "Sure." He stands up and leads them from the small office into the warehouse, a vast single room into which fans the size of jet engines disgorge chilled air. Men in coveralls and parkas are stacking boxes in one corner. In another, a worker shovels ice into cartons while his partner layers in frozen ducks. Million Man walks over, peeks into the carton, then into the ice trough. "Those will be going to restaurants throughout Hong Kong and Kowloon," Benny says.

Smiling with owner's pride, Benny shows them the operation, tells him how many thousand chickens and ducks come through his place each month. "Just two and a half days from farm to table," he says.

His curiosity about chickens satisfied, Old Ko turns to Benny. "Did you see anyone in the shop that day? Anyone buying something else?"

Benny's eyes look off to one side. Old Ko has heard that the direction they look can reveal a lie, but he never bothered to learn which direction was which. He has his own methods.

"No," Benny says. "It was empty."

"You're sure of that? No one left when you came in, or entered when you were leaving?"

"No. I don't think so. Sorry."

Old Ko makes a couple of notes in his book and flips it closed. "Now, we have one more favor," he says. "While we were talking, your men were piling boxes over there, blocking that aisle on the end. All the other aisles are kept clear. Mind if we take a look?"

"Oh, that's nothing. I don't know…"

"Get your men to remove the boxes, please."

With a vacant stare, Benny Chan signals his men to clear the way, and the two of them walk into the last aisle.

"Just more ducks," Benny says.

The aisle looks like the others, the same metal shelves, the same boxes. Old Ko puts his hand out, and Million Man passes him a box cutter. Ko slices the clear film and straps, and pulls up the lid. A large cat with mottled yellow fur stares at him.

"Civet?"

Benny is silent. Ko opens a second box, and sees a scaly body, like a snake, but with feet and small, sharp claws.

"That's a pangolin," says Million Man.

Old Ko turns to the owner, whose head is withdrawing, turtle-like, into his shoulders. "So what's going on, Benny?"

"I'm not hurting anyone. Just meeting demand. It's a little extra money. I'll stop. You don't really care about this, do you?"

"Were you telling the truth about the shop? Did you see anyone else?"

"No! I swear!" Again that relief at being able to tell the truth about something.

"And Goldfish Head Lau?"

"Nothing! Never saw him. Can you give me a break?"

In answer, Old Ko looks at Million Man. "You need to notify customs," he says.

***

Tai Po, Hong Kong, Wednesday, 7:28 p.m.

On the way back Old Ko drives—he doesn't care for the way the younger officers handle the car. So the idled Million Man taps a number on his phone.

"Hi," he says.

"Hi. Still on for tonight?"

"Sure," says Million Man, but I don't think I'll be up for a big restaurant meal. I had a late lunch."

Old Ko glances at his partner. Neither of them has eaten.

"Hmm, okay. Something small, then."

"How about we grab some *won ton* and watch a movie at your place?"

"Wow, Mister excitement. Okay, if that's your plan."

As soon as he hangs up, Old Ko asks what's going on.

"What do you mean?"

"*Won ton?*"

"I like won ton."

"You running out of money?"

Million Man pauses, decides to tell the truth. More or less.

"I could stand to cut down on spending. Women are expensive."

"That they are, my friend."

Old Ko has never called him that before.

Chapter Thirty-Three

A field near Jinzhou, Manchuria, China, 1968

The first thing Yang noticed about Manchuria was that he hated sorghum porridge. The second thing was that there was nothing to eat but sorghum porridge. In fact, sorghum was everywhere, as if some god had taken a pile of the grain in his giant fist and conjured a private torture chamber for Yang.

Recovery in the Municipal Hospital had been a monotonous pageant of nurses and pain, relieved only by morphine tablets and visits from his mother, who fed him soup and kept asking what he had done to bring this on. He wondered that himself. Indeed, apart from the scar that bisected his torso and a toe fungus from drain water that seeped into his shoe, the only thing of permanence gained from the experience was the decision that he was no longer a Red Guard. The Guards had been reined in, their hold on China weakened along with Mao's. Once on his feet, Yang tried to rejoin the university, but there were no places. Jobs were scant, too: Mao's excesses had succeeded in crippling the country's industry. Yang was beginning to sense the failure that Mo had known all along. The country was in decay.

But if Yang had no more use for the Revolution, the Revolution had a use for him: he was ordered to Manchuria to join the thousands of urban youths who were being educated in the ways of the peasantry.

A few months of toil in a commune fanned Yang's hatred of Mao and the Revolution. Reeducated by peasants? Educated in what? Collecting buckets of shit from the latrine and throwing it on the crops? He arrived during a stifling summer and was put to work growing *kaoling*, the ubiquitous sorghum that the Manchurians grew in their fertile black soil. They ate it in porridge and bread, fed the stalks to pigs, weaved baskets with it, thatched roofs with it, wiped their asses with it. They used everything, used it completely till there was nothing left, the way the Revolution used people.

Manchuria was a procession of heat, horseflies, and mosquitoes. Worse than them was the drudgery: hours of squatting in the sun digging roots or nailing tar paper to roofs, returning to his shack too tired to think, just in time for a political meeting. One time he fell asleep while his comrades were reaffirming their commitment to the class struggle. He was subjected to a struggle session himself. Like hungry jackals, his fellow workers nipped pieces out of him, berating him for his snobbery, his bourgeois tendencies, and his belief that his city origins gave him privilege and status.

"You think because you went to University, you're better than us peasants," said the commune's political officer. "Don't you know what the Chairman said about intellectuals?" Yang did: they were the Stinking Ninth among the Class Enemies. But how was he an intellectual? He never finished university, after all. First they ruined his future; then they damned him for having tried to obtain one.

Repellent as the work and the peasantry were, what pushed him beyond any limit of toleration was the daily meal of sorghum porridge, a tasteless gray muck that entered and exited his body in much the same consistency.

Yang's glorious reeducation consisted in poking holes in the soil, dropping in *kaoling* seeds, and covering them with shit, some from pigs and sheep but most from humans. Sweat and stench were constants in his world, relieved only by the rains that pummeled the shacks while he tried to sleep.

While waiting for the grain to grow, which it did with amazing speed, he spent his days repairing walls in the village, reinforcing them with *kaoling* stalks and mud, all under the contemptuous stares of the locals who chattered away in their filthy-sounding dialect.

The summer had been good for the *kaoling*, just enough rain, so that in the autumn the stalks, half again as tall as Yang, bent under the weight of their bright purple heads. He scythed down the stalks until he could no longer lift his arms, and then hauled a granite millstone over the heads to thrash them. It was donkey's work, but the donkey was too busy, they told him.

One day, as he straggled behind his work group returning from the field, he saw a girl walking in the opposite direction, into the endless corridors of *kaoling* that had not yet been harvested. She carried a bundle of some kind with her.

What was she up to? She had no scythe, and in any case field work was over for the day; it was time for political activity. So he followed her. Whatever she was planning, it was surely counter-revolutionary. Part of him sympathized with her, part of him plotted to turn her in and gain some political credit with the commune bosses.

A full half mile into the field, she sat down and pulled something out of her bundle: a scratched-up violin, muddy brown in color. She tightened the bow and began to play.

The sound, muted by the dry breeze and the acres of *kaoling,* made his knees weaken. He'd attended concerts back in Beijing. But this music sounded different. It was a tender, like a butterfly that one must hold with extreme delicacy so as not to crush it. And in this wilderness, it was out of place to a comical degree, though what he felt was not mirth but anguish: anguish for himself, for China, for a world of despair and debasement.

When he approached the girl she froze and made a grab for the violin bag. "It's okay," he whispered. "I won't tell. Play some more."

She did. Her name was Wai-wai, and she had been sent for reeducation because her father had taught history at a Beijing secondary school and had mentioned Europe favorably in one lecture or another. A bunch of his former students, now Red Guards, made him stand bent over for hours wearing a sign stating that he was a bourgeois reactionary.

As if having a rightist father weren't bad enough, Wai-wai had learned violin and played the music of that bourgeois capitalist Beethoven, and so she was a class enemy. When she was ordered to the commune, she managed to smuggle her instrument out. She found that the fields were the only safe place to play it, lest she end up like the boy who had been telling his comrades a story from a western book called Tarzan. His head had been shaved, and he had spent all day baking in the sun, kow-towing to the entire commune, until he collapsed from sunstroke.

Most evenings after that, Yang went to listen to Wai-wai play, forgetting for a short time his aching muscles, his turbulent gut with its constant diarrhea, his itching skin, blistered hands and fungus-infused toe.

Wai-wai was not pretty, but her playing spoke of a tenderness inexpressible in the harsh air of the commune. It was Bach, she said, banned like all the others for creating beauty outside China.

To Yang, that beauty became her own. As her bow and fingers navigated the path of the old melodies, he found his eyes wandering across her body, hidden though it was in her shapeless uniform. Sex was forbidden, of course. Any bourgeois romantic attachment was counter-revolutionary, just as her sequestered violin practice sessions were surely antisocial. This girl was the opposite of Mo: through her music and courage, she gave strength and asked nothing of him. That bastard Mo had emptied him of everything, starting with his blood.

Wai-wai had made Yang think of something he'd long forgotten: his own future.

Soon it would be too cold to practice outside. What would they do then?

It never came to that. In a few weeks, the harvest wound down and most of the *kaoling* had been cut and thrashed, the seeds placed in earthen jars, and the husks, leaves, stalks, and roots stored for the winter. That was when he got word that his mother had died. No one was sure exactly when; the message came from a telephone kiosk in a nearby town and made its way to the village with the first convenient supply truck. Yang was given time to travel back to Beijing to attend the funeral, if he still could.

That night he told Wai-wai he was leaving for a while. "But I'll be back," he said.

"Just in time for winter," she said.

He'd learned about the Siberian winds, which would soon overrun the vast plain and rattle through the flimsy poplar shack he shared with a dozen newly-minted peasants. Of course, he could always keep warm by burning *kaoling* stalks.

It was hard to imagine that, once the cremation was seen to and the joss sticks lit, he was going to return to Manchuria of his own volition. But there was no way to get exempted from rustication and nothing for him to do back in Beijing. He had no money, no ration coupons, no legal permission to live in the city. So he would return to Manchuria for the one thing that was worth having. Unless...

"Come with me," he said, his own words startling him, but not so much as when she said yes.

In the morning, Wai-wai feigned illness and lay in an infirmary bed until she could sneak away into the fields. There, she retrieved her violin and caught up with Yang. Together they happily walked the eleven miles to the train station, oblivious to the day's mounting heat. But sitting on the hard wooden train benches, fear returned. They had no options, really. True, some of their friends had already fled the commune—it was happening all over China, he heard. Where were they going? What kind of a life were they able to live?

"Maybe you should go back," Yang said. "Tell them you had a fever and wandered off, got lost. I'll be back in a week or two."

"And then what?" she said.

They needed no reminder of what their lives would be. No one had said that rustication was temporary. They might spend the rest of their lives among the *kaoling*, chanting slogans like good communists, collapsing in bed each night from exhaustion, as empty as the seed husks they'd thrashed.

No, Yang decided they were finished with the Revolution. They were finished with China.

The next morning, when they rolled into Beijing, Yang found the ticket seller who looked the most overworked, who would be least likely to have time to argue with him. "Passage to Shenzhen for two," Yang said. "Hurry up. We're meeting down there to struggle against the landlords." Yang had no armband, no school ID card, so he decided to bluster his way through.

"No free passes now," said the man, who looked about sixty and had protruding teeth like a locomotive's cow-catcher. Yang hadn't heard that the order giving free train travel had been rescinded.

"Chairman Mao commanded the people not to repress the Guards. All right, then. I'm coming back with the Dongcheng District Revolutionary Police Corps. We'll take action against you for supporting the landlords. I'm sick of you rightists getting in the way of the Revolution."

The man hesitated. Perhaps his brother or cousin was one of the hundreds who were beaten by Red Guards in the streets of Beijing. In any case, he tossed a couple of tickets at Yang.

On the eternal journey south, the train stopped every mile or so to take on passengers and freight. Yang and Wai-wai had to change trains a number of times and endure long waits in hot, dusty stations. At first they spoke to no one out of fear. Half a day later they couldn't recognize the speech around them anyway. As they approached Guangdong, the people sounded as if they were trying to talk with dirt stuffed in their mouths.

Eventually they arrived in Shenzhen, which resembled every other sleepy mud-hole in Guangdong. Nothing but ignorant fishing people here, squawking in their peculiar dialect. But across the bay was Hong Kong.

From here there were two escape routes—everyone knew that. You could sneak across the border under the barbed wire and risk a quick bullet. Or you could swim. Yang persuaded Wai-wai to go by water.

Along the shore, they found a couple of tires—ones that had no doubt made the journey before and floated back. They huddled on the beach, under some bushes, and waited till dark. Nights were warmer down there.

Small though the town was, the waterfront saw activity at night. Boats were being unloaded, and police were patrolling and shining flashlights here and there. They waited for hours in the dark until things looked quiet enough to make a move.

Yang had no belongings. Wai-wai had only her violin, but no way to keep it dry. "Leave it," he said. "I'll buy you a new one in Hong Kong with my first paycheck." Her face full of her sadness, she pushed her violin under the bushes and they walked to the water's edge, and into the South China Sea.

Within a half hour or so he realized they were not alone; in the black water a few other heads bobbed up and down, part of what Yang now realized was a nightly exodus, a migration like that of geese or heron, bound for the pinpoint of light that he knew was Hong Kong.

Wai-wai was not a strong swimmer, but she kept up, paddling with her spindly legs and holding on to the tire, which floated just below the water's surface. She told him she wondered if it would sink and drag her down.

Yang worried constantly about getting lost. He knew that one could steer by stars, but he didn't know how. Once the beach was lost in the blackness of the moonless light, he relied on his untested sense of direction and followed the sounds of the others who were swimming.

A boat rumbled by, searchlight sweeping the waves. Yang ducked under the water and held his breath until the engine sound faded. As the first glimmer of sun reddened the sky, Yang saw the coast of Hong Kong. He was freezing, his hands and feet numb, but he picked up the pace of his breaststroke.

Wai-wai had fallen back. Yang saw her head and shoulders back with two other swimmers. He was treading water, waiting for her to catch up, when she let out a small shriek of pain and clawed the air.

"Wai-wai!"

"Shark," one of the others shouted. "Keep going! Don't stop!"

But he did stop, just for a moment, and looked at the spot where Wai-wai had last been. Nothing but a few fading ripples.

Then he turned around and swam for his life.

Exhausted, shivering, and alone, he crawled onto a beach in Yuen Long in the Hong Kong New Territories and collapsed by a boat yard. A few locals noted his arrival, but no one came to his aid.

* * *

Tsim Sha Tsui District, Hong Kong, 2003, 4:27 p.m.

A trip to a housewares store is all it takes to set up the room for his meeting with Mo Tun. Horace makes a few preparations, locks the door of the disco, and leaves.

On the street, he glances from side to side, sees no one looking, and pulls the battery out of his disposable phone. He throws the battery in the first trash can he sees and chucks the phone in one a couple of blocks away.

His own cell phone rings not long after that. He doesn't recognize the number.

"Great Fortune Property Management."

"Daisy Wong, at Four Seasons Commercial Centre. We have a very serious problem, and you need to deal with it right now."

Horace steps into the street. A car horn blasts him back onto the curb; he had wandered in front of a Mini Cooper and almost ended his life.

"They keep telling people to watch where they're going," says the driver, loud enough for Horace to hear. "It's like playing the lute for a cow."

"Are you there?" says Daisy Wong.

"Yes. What's the problem?" Horace recoils from the curb and clutches his phone to his ear.

"The garbage wasn't taken out last night. We came in this morning and the wastebaskets hadn't been emptied."

"I see. I'll get back to you…"

"See that you do, please. Also, an electric pencil sharpener went missing a few days ago. I think your janitors are poaching things."

"Really? Uh, I'll have to look into that…"

"I don't see why we should have to lose items just because you can't properly vet your employees."

"I see. Yes. I will discuss this with my superior and get back to you." As much as he hates using the word "superior" he needs to get rid of this woman, and making her believe that her request is going up the line might do it.

"Fine. In fact, why don't you let me talk to your superior now?"

"I, uh, I'm not in the office…"

"What's his name?"

"Her...Petula Hsiao."

"Do you have her number?"

"I think so, yes. He scrolls down his cell phone's directory and reads off The Girl's number. When he's done, he asks her if that is all. No answer. Somehow, he'd managed to cut off Daisy Wong. No doubt she's calling The Girl right now and adding that to her complaints.

Horace grips the cell phone until his hands seize, but the thing won't be crushed.

Chapter Thirty-Four

Kowloon East District, Hong Kong Wednesday, 6:34 p.m.

Mo and Lento arrive at Great Fortune Property Management to find that the boss, Wayne Lai, left at five to play squash with a friend. Mo isn't concerned—the top man rarely knows what's going on anyway. To get answers, find the highest-placed woman working under him. That turns out to be Petula, an efficient creature clothed in name brands from head to toe, with a cool smile and a spiral pad under her arm, turned to a page full of notes and tasks. Her fingernails are trimmed and buffed for serious work.

Mo shakes her hand and lets Lento do the speaking.

"Sorry to keep you tonight," he says. She stands behind an orderly but well-used desk. Stacks of printouts, invoices, and reports rise to either side of her computer screen.

"Not at all," she says. "I don't get out of here before seven, usually. What can I do for you?" She sits down, opens her binder, and begins to twirl a pencil on the ends of her fingers. Energy, some brains, and she's not afraid of work. *Here's the kind of person I should be hiring,* Mo thinks. *With five of her and Lento, I could run a professional operation, slow down a little.*

"We need a list of the construction workers who are on the disco site," Lento says. "We want to talk to whoever's in charge at the site, too."

"The contractor?"

"If that's who it is, yes."

"That's an unusual request. Can you tell me why you need it?"

Lento shakes his head. "It's a confidential matter."

"I'm not sure how…"

Mo speaks up. "Not negotiable. I can't do business with you unless I get this information."

Some of the vigor drains from her face.

"All right. Give me a couple of days…"

"Now," says Lento. "You need to get on the phone now and get that information."

Without another word she goes to her computer and begins to pore through records. *She gets it now.* You need to do that once in a while—let the citizens peek over the wall into the places where things aren't cordial, where the blade is sharp and smells of blood.

"Just the disco? No other properties?" she says.

"For now," says Lento.

The kidnapper made a mistake when he gave his last orders. *Walk through the front, into the back room, by the fire exit.*

The fire exit didn't exist a few days ago. He'd only just had it put in to comply with building codes. Only someone familiar with the job would know of its existence. That means that whoever this very lucky idiot is, he works close to the building site. Maybe when Mo visited to view construction progress, this insane demon caught sight of him, knew he was rich, and chose to take a wild risk.

Whoever he is, he's wrong. Mo's fingers twitch like a crab's legs as they attempt to close on something that isn't there: the ceramic horse the black market man Yee tried to cheat him out of decades ago. Every once in a while, Mo recalls the horse. His hands still feel the weight of it and the release as he catapults the statue into the wall. He remembers the look on Yee's face as the petty crook realized who he was dealing with.

Mo is about to see that look on the face of another man.

Chapter Thirty-Five

Sha Tin District, Hong Kong, Wednesday, 6:32 p.m.

Chief Superintendent Koon wears an impeccably pressed uniform, one obviously tailored to his slim body. Nicely groomed, too. *Here's a man who enjoys his job.* He gives Lok a vigorous handshake and they sit, surrounded by the usual mementos in a District Commander's office: the photos, the soccer ball, the awards.

His prominence made him easy to trace. There were only a few men with his name in Hong Kong—sometimes there are hundreds, which can make a search difficult—and only one that matched the age and birthplace. When he found out that the man was a cop, DC Shatin no less, he checked over the names again, hoping he had made a mistake. This was a career killer.

"So, you're at YauTsim," Koon says. "I spent a few years there before transferring to RCU. How's K.K.?"

"ADC Kwan is fine, sir. Did you work together?"

"Years. And Old Fu?"

"He retired, but he's been brought back on contract. A good station sergeant is hard to find."

"God, that man was tough."

"Still is, even at his age."

The small talk evaporates, leaving behind a distressing silence. Lok decides to jump in without preface. "Sir, the investigation has turned up something I'd like to discuss with you.

Raised eyebrows. "Me? Okay, I'm curious. What's going on?"

"I'm assigned to the Goldfish Head Lau murder. We've been looking into the associates of his employer, Mo Tun. You know him, of course."

"Of course."

"One person of interest is a vendor at the jade market, name of Chan Wei-ping, known as Dollar-ten."

"Good God. Him?"

"You know him, then?"

"How could you forget a name like that? Knew him back on the mainland. We were both born near Beijing."

"When did you see him last, sir?"

"I lost track of him pretty soon after coming here. Life was busy back then. I lived in Wanchai, which was quite a slum in those days. You aren't old enough to remember. I was doing odd jobs for a red pole and might have staked out a career in the triads. But I got cold feet when one of my friends had his initiation ceremony. I guess I wasn't ready for the Death of a Thousand Cuts."

Back then the triad initiations would still have been elaborate affairs, with robes and chants and incense and promises of death to anyone who betrayed the society.

"Anyway, I joined the force instead. Probably for the best, eh?"

"You've done well."

"It's all in knowing whose ass to kiss," Koon says.

Lok lets it drop. No sense in flattery anyway. The camaraderie is about to end.

"You said you lost track of Dollar-ten, but he told us you came to see him the other day."

Koon keeps his cool, just swings thirty degrees in his chair, faces Lok. "I did lose track of him—I hadn't seen him in more than twenty years, but Mo Tun called and asked me to meet up with them."

"So you're in contact with Mo?"

"Before this week, not for years."

"But you went with him anyway."

"I'm answering your questions as a fellow policeman, Inspector Lok. Do not think that this is an interrogation."

"Can you tell me what they spoke about?"

Koon shakes his head. "That's between the two of them. Mo just wanted me along to scare him, let him know that we all…that we were all aware of him."

"I don't understand," says Lok.

"Mo is trying to find out who killed his chauffeur. I told him that you were on the case, and that you'd probably get good results. But if you've met him, you can see how he is. Impatient, bad temper—he's a *lan jai*, after all.

"Was he the friend that got the triad initiation way back when?"

"No, but good guess. Anyway, he had his own ideas about who killed Goldfish Head and wanted to pursue him. I discouraged him, but it didn't help. He insisted we go.

"Why would Dollar-ten have anything to do with the murder?"

"You'd have to ask him that. It turned out to be a dead end anyway."

"Does it have to do with your time in the army together? The looting?"

This time Koon reacts, but not as Lok expects him to. No red face, no shouting. Koon has a right to be indignant. He's broken no Hong Kong law, has no blemish on his official record. In fact, Lok is the one in dangerous waters.

Instead, Superintendent Koon bows his head slightly, a gesture of helplessness, almost surrender.

"Look, Inspector, there are millions here who were born in China. That's a lot of histories. Each one who escaped as I did immediately became a criminal in the eyes of the communists. When I came here, I lived in a squatter hut smaller than this office with nine other people—three triple-tier bunk beds, sawed off to fit them inside so if you sat up, you hit your head on the bed above. I had nothing but my brain and the conviction that I would get out of that hut and never return.

"Now you come here asking about things that happened in another world, when Mao had the country by the throat and we'd all gone mad with fear, or worse, with communist zeal.

"Why bring it up now? It's dead. Yes, we stole some money to bankroll our start in Hong Kong. But none of that is real anymore. It has no bearing on this case."

"Mo seems to think it does, sir."

"I can't help what Mo thinks. As I said, I don't associate with him anymore."

"Did he mention kidnapping?"

Now Koon pauses, turns to stare out the window at the throngs of Sha Tin, the green oval of the racecourse, and the parkland beyond.

"Inspector. Are we clear on the scope of things? I had a short conversation with Mo Tun, in which he gave me no information of any value to the murder investigation, an investigation in which I have no part in any case."

"Nothing we say is on record, sir. I just needed the benefit of your knowledge of Mo Tun from before—from China."

Koon nods, and Lok senses that he's defused the situation. Perhaps, by not threatening Koon's career, he's saved his own.

"Sir… a kidnapping?"

"He mentioned something about it. I advised him to report any information he had. He refused. I really don't know the details. Perhaps it was just a warning snatch, and the grandson is back now."

"Grandson? I didn't mention a grandson, sir."

He turns back to face Lok, makes a brief attempt at a smile. "See yourself out, Inspector."

* * *

Yau Ma Tei, Hong Kong, Wednesday, 6:52 p.m.

Ears and Big Pang are driving to Soddy Leung's knife shop, having heard the tale of Benny Chan, a cheerful Tai Po chickenmonger who deals in frozen cats and bear paws on the side, and who will now be dealing with Hong Kong Customs and the Ag and Fish Department. Soddy will probably be arrested as well. But that will not happen tonight, and perhaps the knife seller will be inclined to tell the truth meanwhile.

"Maybe all that rhino horn will have improved his memory," says Big Pang.

"Think it does?" says Ears.

"No. I suppose I'm the modern type. I go to a Western doctor. You?"

"Both. I take some herbs."

"Which ones?"

"Deerhorn. It's good for the heart."

"How's that?"

"When the deer runs, the blood goes to the horns. Did you know that?"

Big Pang shakes his head and changes the subject, "Where's Ah Lok now?"

The light is green, and the cars, too many for this time of night, begin to roll *en masse* toward the next corner, slowly like a mechanized glacier.

"Not sure where Lok is today," Big Pang says. "Something to do with the old Dollar-ten geezer you spoke to in the Jade Market. Hunting up another China connection. Mo Tun seems to have been up to something strange back on the mainland."

They turn onto Nanking Street.

"There it is," Ears says. "Looks closed."

The shop is indeed shuttered. "I'll let *Ah Lok* know," says Big Pang. "He might want to call him at home. Meanwhile, want to get some dinner?"

"Sure. See anything around here?" They scan the block on both sides. No restaurants.

"Guess not," says Ears. "I was planning on visiting my grandmother anyway. Maybe I'll just pick up a bag of cuttlefish or something."

"Not around here, you won't. Maybe next block."

Ears runs his eyes along the storefronts and doorways on both sides of the street again. "Interesting."

"What? That there's no food here?"

"No food, no food stores, convenience stores, no restaurants."

"So?"

"The other truck on the CCTV was from a snack delivery company. Why did it stop here where no one's selling snacks?"

Chapter Thirty-Six

"Did you bring the phone?"

"I'm not allowed," Doby says. But this time Doby is determined not to let this kid talk him into anything. *Always listen to me, Doby, Ba Ba says. When you do what I say, things go well for you, don't they?*

"My father told me just to feed you and clean out the basket," Doby says. "I'm not even supposed to talk to you." He drops the food bag at his feet and looks for the waste basket. This time it sits in the far corner of the room; he'll have to walk into the room to retrieve it. He catches himself at the door, afraid to move because of something uncomfortable in the air, something he senses even amid the smell of shit and old rice boxes.

But the coast looks clear, so he swallows his doubt and crosses the room. As he reaches the corner, the boy springs up and dashes for the door. He grasps the handle and pulls.

Doby is big, however, and his long arms reach the boy before he can even pull the door open, much less run through it.

"Stop!" Doby yells.

"You stop! I want to go home!"

"*Ba Ba* says no. I can't let you out." Without any visible effort, he pulls the boy from the door and deposits him back against the rear wall. Doby isn't angry, just confused. *Why won't he understand? I have to obey* Ba Ba.

Tears well up behind the boy's spectacles. They run down his cheeks.

"Please," he says. "I need to be home. It's not fair. I hate this place."

Doby doesn't know what to say.

"My *yeh yeh* will be angry."

"My *Ba Ba* gets angry sometimes," Doby says.

"Are you afraid of him?"

"Yes." Crazy question. How can you not be afraid of *Ba Ba* when he's angry? He shouts, his face turns red like the Chinese flag, and his eyes seem to burn like hot coals. If he takes hold of your wrist while he's mad, it hurts for days. And if you say the wrong thing, his hand seems to fly from nowhere to the back of your head, again and again, until …

Until … he can't remember what makes the hand stop. It's been a long while since *Ba Ba* has hit him. Doby figures he's behaving much better. Maybe he won't have to worry about this kid replacing him. *Ba Ba* wouldn't do that to him, would he? But then why does he want him at all?

"I'm afraid of my *yeh yeh,* too," the boy says.

"Does he hit you?"

Bonitus shakes his head. "My *Ma Ma* says no one can hit me. She's a *gweipoh.*"

Doby doesn't know any *gweipohs.* White women make him uncomfortable.

"Is that why you have those spots on your face?" Doby has seen *gweilos* with freckles, especially the red-headed ones that look like monkeys.

"Yeah. They call me *baan mau.*" Spotted cat. His tears are drying now. "What is your dad going to do with me?"

"I don't know."

"Why does he want me?"

"I don't know. Your *Ma Ma* really says no one can hit you?"

The boy nods.

"And your *Ba Ba* obeys her?"

The boy shrugs. They remain silent for a while, the boy sitting against the wall, Doby leaning against his. Then Doby walks over to grab the wastebasket, keeping his eyes on the boy the whole time.

When he returns with a clean basket, the kid is still sitting, knees up, chin resting on his crossed arms.

Put down the food. Empty the wastebasket in the toilet and rinse it out. That's all.

"Did you read the second book?" the kid says.

Doby nods.

"Good stuff, right?

"Right."

"Want the last part?"

Doby nods again.

"I don't have it here. But I can get it."

"Where?"

"I can't tell you. I can't describe the place. But I know how to get there. Bring me there, and I'll get it. Then you can bring me back."

It makes sense. There are a lot of places that Doby knows about that he can't describe.

But something else does not seem right. He has to think about this. He wishes *Ba Ba* were here.

He draws out his cell phone. "Let me call *Ba Ba*," he says.

"No!" says the kid. "He'll say no. But you know it's okay. The comic book is for you, not for him. It's our secret. You need to take me to get it and not tell anyone, okay?"

Doby thinks again. What could go wrong?

"The third part is the best," the kid says. "They're painted green now, right? In the last part they escape, and Horse gets his sword back, and..."

Doby's cell phone rings. It's *Ba Ba*.

Chapter Thirty-Seven

Kowloon District, Hong Kong, 7:37 p.m.

"Here are the ID photos of the workers—that should be all of them." Petula is smart, obliging, somewhat humorless, qualities that Mo is fine with right now. Mo recognizes none of the faces, so he has her sort out the ones with the X under the birth date, the symbol for residents born on the mainland.

"Call the foreman. Ask if any of these are from Beijing."

"Now?"

"Of course now, you stupid bitch. Do you think I have all night?"

Petula's cheeks redden, but she clicks through to the contact files and locates the foreman's cell number. She has a difficult time keeping a calm demeanor, but she sounds businesslike enough, if not very chatty, as she determines that no, he didn't hear any Beijing or northern accents on the job. They're all from Guangdong.

"What about other contractors, not construction? Who did you contact when you set up this job?"

"Who? Dozens… lots of people. Government agencies, contractors. Water, electricity, gas, fire safety, crowd safety, environmental, taxes, health, commercial permits…"

Mo sweeps his hand across her desk and sends a pile of papers flying. "Get me the list!"

"It's not one list; it's all in the project binder in separate sections. I can compile…"

"Do it! Now!"

Mo stomps off into the main office as Petula clicks away at double speed, breathing at double speed as well. Mo paces the aisle, past empty desks and dark windows. What do these people do, anyway? The cubicles are adorned with statues of Snoopy and *anime* characters, family photos, little amusements that have nothing to do with the job. Do these people even work? It's Jelly Pong all over again. You labor to get to the top, you slice your way through obstacles, only to place your trust in…

He pauses at a photo on the wall. The face of a man in middle age, a portrait of distracted confusion. But the face is familiar. He knows that face.

"Who the fuck is that?" he yells. Petula looks up.

"Who, Mo *sin-sahng?*

"That man," he says, pointing to the Employee of the Month.

"No one, sir. Horace Yang, an employee."

"Yang! Get me his address, now. And where is his desk?"

Petula walks into the main room and gestures to a nondescript metal desk. Just a computer and a pad of paper, no anime figures or photos.

Mo yanks open some drawers to find photocopies of spreadsheets and company data. The bottom drawer is locked, however. Mo circles the office, ransacks some drawers, finds a knife, a bigger knife, and then a screwdriver. Back at the desk of Horace Yang he pries open the bottom drawer. The gym bag is there. He pulls it out and opens the zipper.

Seven million dollars.

Jelly's gun is not there, however.

"Mo *sin-sahng*, is everything all right?" Petula is shaking now.

Did she see the money? He's not sure, but he'll make sure she doesn't talk about this. "Just get me his address," he says.

Chapter Thirty-Eight

Kowloon, Hong Kong, Wednesday, 9:03 pm

"Yang Kwok-wai, English name Doby Yang, 22 years of age, driving a red Mitsubishi van license AB 5661. Last seen wearing…"

The Mercedes-Benz Sprinter glides along the West Kowloon Corridor. Lok is on the driver's left, keeping tabs on the Uniform Branch and its search for the snack van and the driver, one Doby Yang.

Lok has just been to Soddy Leung's flat for a short talk, during which both men suppressed their amazement at the volume of facts that the knife merchant was suddenly able to recall. After explaining that he never, ever traded in illegal species and vowed never to do it again, Soddy remembered that he did indeed sell the knife to a middle-aged man, short, nervous-looking with a scant crop of wispy hair and skin the color of dried cow intestine. The sale was between five and six that evening. Video footage put the snack van at the shop at five-thirty-five, and the company gave them Doby Yang's name.

The van deposits Lok at Tsuen King Garden, one of the innumerable tower blocks that exist to stack Hong Kong lives as tall as is practical. Doby's mother, one Winnie Chan, answers the door of the second-floor flat. The furniture is worn and sparse, the rug under the dining table faded. Some soup is on the boil in the kitchen, a yellow, grease-stained nook lit by a fluorescent lamp that casts a bluish glow on the rising steam. A television, the most garrulous member of every Hong Kong family, chatters in a corner.

"

The weight of the other thirty or so floors above them seems to aggravate the stress of a bleak and pressured household.

Winnie seems to feel the pressure too. A frail thing, she looks up at Lok in a manner of one expecting nothing good.

"Chan *tai tai*, we'd like to ask you some questions about your son, Doby Yang."

"Why?"

"He stopped his van at Leong Tai Commercial Kitchen Supply on Thursday. Any idea why?"

"No, why would I?"

"Do you know where he is now?"

"At work, I think."

"At work they said he finished his deliveries."

"What are you saying?" Winnie Chan offers no welcome, no formalities of greeting; for her, Lok's arrival has suspended time and place.

"Do you know who might have been with your son in the van last Thursday night?"

She thinks for a moment. "Just my husband. Doby picks him up after work sometimes."

"When did they get home Thursday night?"

"I don't remember. Thursday. What's that, the one with pilots and the airline people? I watched that and went to bed. They must have come in late."

Lok knows the show *Triumph in the Skies*, though he doesn't watch it. "Do you have a picture of your husband?"

"Picture? I don't know. Let me see. Why do you need this? Is he in some kind of trouble?"

Lok says nothing.

"Did he have an accident?" She's asked more questions than he has so far, and beneath them he feels the chill of dread.

"We're just trying to locate him."

She walks off, returns with a four-by-six snapshot taken years ago on a gray day at the Lantau Buddha. The photo shows Horace and Doby in the foreground. Doby is tall, with an open, delighted face and a marvelously thick mat of hair, standing a full inch to the vertical and fanning out at the ends like the spines of a sea urchin. His father is a good deal shorter and less pleased with the outing. Contrasting with Doby's smile, Horace is casting a baleful eye at whoever is taking the photo—Winnie, presumably. *Hurry up and get on with it, woman.* Lok can almost hear his impatience.

Horace has a prominent forehead, gleaming with oily perspiration. On his head a few filaments testify to a history of hair, not recent. His eyes are clouded and distracted. There's a mole on his left cheek, not much smaller than his tiny, lipless mouth, that retreats along with his chin. The man does not inspire confidence; Lok will say that much. But he matches Soddy's description. Short, nervous, almost bald, skin like cooked tripe.

Behind them, the Buddha stares at the camera, the embodiment of patience. *I'd be patient if I had the time,* Lok thinks.

"Where was your husband born?"

"Beijing. We met here after he came over."

"What does he do?"

"Great Fortune Property Management. East Kowloon."

"Chan *tai-tai*, does your husband know Goldfish Head Lau?"

She shakes her head in confusion.

"How about Mo Tun?"

She remains still.

"Does your husband know Mo Tun, Chan *tai tai*?

"I… I don't know."

"I don't understand. Has he ever mentioned him?"

"Yes."

"When? In what context?"

She bites her lip and clasps her hands together, elbows close to her body. Lok knows the gesture. She wants to be held but is so used to being denied another's embrace that she cannot ask.

"Chan tai-tai? When did he mention Mo Tun?"

"In his sleep."

Chapter Thirty-Nine

Horace dials Winnie at home, having prepared a story that a large crisis has arisen at work, and he is vital to its resolution. He'll be working very late.

It's not Winnie who answers, though; it's a man.

"Horace Yang?"

"Who is this?"

"PC 58993 Keung Man-ho. If you would be so kind as to go to the Yau Ma Tei Police Station at 627 Canton Road, we would like to speak with you urgently. Can you go there right now?"

Horace hangs up and calls Doby. After too many rings his son picks up.

"Why didn't you answer? Where are you?"

"Sorry, I…"

"Never mind. I want you to do something for me. Do not answer any calls from anyone but me."

"There are some messages…"

"Don't listen to them. Don't…"

"Someone's calling now…"

"Do not answer! Do what I say. When your phone rings, look at who is calling. If it's me, answer. Otherwise, do not pick up. I will call you soon and tell you what to do."

Outside, a light sprinkle has wet the pavement and thickened the city's air.

Horace walks along Jordan Road, oblivious to the shop windows and office complexes, heedless of the couples returning home after dinner dates. A tingling begins in his right toe, a sign that the alien spores under his toenail are communing with the moisture. Horace has learned to ignore the itch until it goes.

Eventually he ends up back in Mongkok, and it is there his mind begins to focus.

Outside an old building on Sai Yeung Choi Street a simple sign, cut from the flap of a cardboard box and inked with a marker, sits in a window. *Room for Rent*. He rings the bell and asks the woman who answers to see the room.

"Now? It's late."

"I need to do this. I'm expecting guests from the mainland, and I want it set up for them."

The woman, fifty-something and businesslike, ushers him into her flat. The room is a bedroom down the hall from her own. Horace thanks her and leaves. It won't do.

Many rooms are for rent along the streets. He looks at four more, and it is the fourth that he takes, paying a thousand dollars up front for five days to a man of about thirty dressed in sweatpants and smelling of sweat and Tsing Tao. Of all the available flats, only this one is separate from the landlord's home. There are three small bedrooms, each with its own lock and key. So there is no one to snoop but other guests—and there are no other guests at the moment.

This is where it will happen, he thinks. *This is where I will restore my life*. He dials Doby's number.

"*Wai?*"

"Doby, can you bring the boy to me?"

"Yes."

"Now?"

"Yes."

There follow instructions, as always. This time the litany is long, but necessary. *Bring the van around to the delivery exit. Don't let go of the kid. Tell him you're bringing him back to his parents…*"

When Doby has repeated the instructions, Horace disconnects and lowers himself slowly onto the coarsely blanketed bed. A half-open window sucks in traffic noise and sticky, polluted air, as well as chatter from the sidewalk.

I'll have money. Seven million plus seven more. I'll take Doby to Canada. With Mo dead and the boy dead, it will be better than before. A rebirth. Mo was keeping me here, Mo and The Girl, and Winnie, that stupid woman, and that idiot Wayne. It's all because of Mo Tun. He tried to kill me, but I stayed strong and kept going, and now it's my turn to be on top of him. I'll kill the boy in front of him—no, that's too much risk, taking the boy over to the disco. I'll throw the kid's body at Mo's feet, then I'll kill Mo. And then Canada. If I could only take Mo to Canada to watch me spend his money and build my own disco and be the one that... the one that... Mo will be rotting away, and I will be far away in Canada. Doby will help me make a start... I can go back to being an accountant... The Girl can't reach me there. Wayne can't tell me not to be an accountant...

* * *

Wan Chai, Hong Kong, Wednesday, 9:44

Doby hangs up, closes his eyes, and mentally goes over the instructions. The boy eyes him anxiously.

"We need to go," says Doby.

"Where?" The boy eases along the wall away from him.

Doby pauses, wishing the instructions were more detailed. But then, he'd have trouble remembering more things. "To … to your parents."

"Why not just let me go, then? I can get home. I have an MTR pass."

Doby has no answer.

"Do you want the comic?"

"Yes, sure. You can get it for me?"

"I can show you the store. But you need to take me there. It'll be easy for you to find. And then I can go in and get you the comic."

"I'm supposed to…"

"Then I'll go wherever you want. But let's get the comic first."

"Can we get it after?"

The boy thinks for a minute. "Maybe the place will be closed. They could sell out, too. We'd better go there."

"But my *Ba Ba* wants me to take you to him."

"What? I thought you were going to take me to my parents! You liar. Fuck you!"

"I will...I mean, I can take you..."

"I don't want to see your father again. He's a bastard. I hate him. If I ever see him when I'm bigger, I'll kill him. I hate your fucking bastard father. His mother fucks monkeys. He can go home, eat shit and die!"

The words hit Doby like flaming coals. He grabs the boy on the arm and pulls him to the door. In his mind he's banished thoughts of the third volume of the tale. He's rehearsing *Ba Ba's* instructions. *Don't let go of the kid. Lock the van from the outside using the extra padlocks. When you arrive, park right in front of the address I gave you and call me...*

Chapter Forty

Tsuen Wan, Hong Kong, Wednesday, 9:22 p.m

"So he's alive," Mo says to Lento, who is guiding the limo along Tsuen Wan Road. It's been years since he has spent time in Tsuen Wan. Just as well Lento is around to drive—Mo would get lost with all this new construction.

"Who is he?" Lento says.

"Nobody. A student back in Beijing. I was ex-PLA. I figured he was dead."

"Why is that?"

Mo doesn't answer. Not that he is ashamed of what he did to Yang. The kid needed killing. The great revolutionary depended for his face on what Mo could give him. When that dried up, Yang would have turned on Mo. It was dicey enough making an unauthorized trip to the Guangdong coast; a manhunt would have made his escape much rougher.

"It's through here, I think." They both purged their cell phone batteries before driving to Horace's flat. It's probably just cop show stuff, all that tracing of cell phones, but Lento suggested they take no chances.

Mo had left Petula weeping and shivering at her desk. "Go home," he had said to her, squeezing her slim fingers until she caught her breath. "Forget tonight. Forget the work you did for me. That's the smart thing to do. If you ever tell your boss, or your family, or anyone else what you did here..."

"I won't!" Petula said. She cut him off, as he expected, to spare herself the specifics of death. "I'll say nothing! I swear! I don't care what you do!

Please…"

They leave, satisfied that fear would always be the uppermost thing in her mind when the name Mo Tun was spoken to her.

* * *

Horace lives in a tower block on a byway called Tsuen King Circuit. A police van is parked on the curb in front of Horace's building, red lights ablaze.

"Too late," Mo says. They drive on.

"What now?" says Lento.

"You need to get on the last ferry to Shenzhen," Mo says.

"Can it wait till tomorrow night? I think I found a buyer for the limousine. A car with ghosts is hard to unload."

"Forget it for now. Go to Shenzhen. You'll need an alibi."

"What about you?"

"I'll arrange one later. It'll be better if we're not each other's alibis. Get out of Hong Kong, and don't come back for a week or two, when this is all done with."

"Why Shenzhen? I could just go somewhere with security cameras and have a drink."

"Provided the cameras are working, and the cops are smart enough to look at the footage, and they believe the time stamp. Plus they'll keep you in a room asking you questions. No, it's too risky. Going through immigration is positive proof, and you'll be out of the way. Less chance of interrogation till everything has died down."

Lento checks his watch. "If we're going to make the last ferry…"

"Step on it," says Mo. "But don't get stopped by a cop."

* * *

Kowloon Tong, Hong Kong, Wednesday, 9: 40 p.m.

"Ivan," says Sylvie, "I'm going to tell Inspector Lok about Bonitus.

"Sylvie, *Ba Ba* says that it'll be over tonight. We'll get him back. Please…"

Never did she conceive that things would come to this—that she would be fighting her husband to save her son.

"Is this why we live here? To pay money to criminals and put our son in harm's way?"

"He's not in harm's way. I told you…"

"Is that why you studied law? Look at your classmates. Ben works for the UN, Jared for the ACLU. And you're making it easy for your father to break the law."

"He's a businessman, Sylvie. That's what Hong Kong business is."

"Is it? I read the papers, Ivan. I pretend that it's all nonsense and gossip, that it's dark stuff from the past, but now I know it isn't. I think maybe he's evil. And this is our punishment."

"No one's punishing us, Sylvie."

"What do you call this if not punishment?"

"Just give him till tomorrow. *Ba Ba* says it'll be over after tonight."

"And what about the next time some rival decides to make a point?"

"Sylvie, I love you."

Never had the words sounded so useless. Just a statement of feeling, a mere description of what's going on in Ivan's head.

All at once Ivan, the flat, and Hong Kong seems to recede into the distance, losing color and shape. She is alone.

If a husband's love is meaningless, what has meaning?

Chapter Forty-One

Tsim Sha Tsui, Hong Kong, Wednesday, 10:20 p.m

"Doby Yang, CCC 2799, twenty-two, driver for Pao's Snack Food Distribution. His boss says he's not very bright, but a good worker." Lok reads from his notebook; his team are back at the station, pursuing the case into the night, so he's had no time to update the computer log.

"What do we mean by 'not very bright,' sir?" says Million Man. He copies out the Chinese Commercial Code for "Yang," which gives him the correct character for the name. Lots of Yangs, Youngs, Yeungs in Hong Kong, sounding alike, written differently.

"Not sure. He can drive, but he left school as soon as it was legal. His boss says he reads slowly and doesn't write much but is otherwise pretty normal. It was his van that stopped in front of the knife shop, but he stayed in the van when someone else went in, so there's a good chance he's not the killer. We'll know when we bring him in.

"Next, Horace Yang, father of Doby, fifty-eight. Works at Great Fortune Property Management, which handles a new nightclub that Mo Tun is opening. We're thinking he was riding in the van with his son, and probably also the one who bought the knife and killed Goldfish Head Lau. There's an order to pick him up too."

"Motive, sir?" asks Old Ko.

"We'll get to that. Now the third corner of the triangle: Mo Tun, sixty-four, president of Diamond Rich Enterprises, and a *lan jai* from day one. About to open a disco, probably to launder money from other operations like extortion, protection, pirated DVDs. Never really got anything good on him, apart from his associations with other known criminals and undesirables. If nothing else, he's guilty of knowing more than he told the police."

"We could arrest half of Hong Kong for that," says Big Pang.

"All right," says Lok. "What do these three have in common?"

"None of them are answering their cell phones," says Ears.

"Right. So they're into something that they want to keep us out of. For the record, I don't think Doby Yang is smart enough to be working anything on his own. He's being led along by his father."

"The Yangs don't have any connection to Goldfish Head," says Ears.

"Mo is from Beijing, just like Horace Yang. They had some kind of association back in China, during the Cultural Revolution. Horace was a Red Guard back then, Mo Tun ex-PLA. Yang's group denounced people they knew were hoarding money, and then looted their homes. The money got Mo started in Hong Kong. We learned this from a former cohort, a man known as Dollar-ten, not a suspect."

"Mo got rich, but the other two didn't do so well," says Ears.

"That's right. Dollar-ten seems to have come to terms with it, but Horace…"

Lok understands Horace, a man who spoils everything. Egotistical and short-tempered, powered by a furnace of self-hate, he steps on weaker people like ants, ruins love, brings only bile and despair into the world.

"All right," Lok continues. "Now, the boy. Bonitus Mo was last known to be riding with his grandfather before Goldfish Head's murder. Where did he go? Why won't they say where he is? Possibility: he was taken by Horace, who is still holding him, or who has killed him. Possibility: it was an attempted kidnapping, and Mo or Lento interrupted it. Now Mo Tun is hiding the boy just to be safe. In either case it's likely that Mo is looking for Horace, same as us."

"So, what's our next step?"

"Lento," says Old Ko. "If we can find him, we can put some pressure there.

He must know what his boss is doing."

"Go do it. Wake him up if he's asleep. What else?"

"The wife?" says Ears.

"Winnie? Don't think there's much there. She's pretty much a zero, but she might know something more about her son, like where he hangs out. That's yours."

"Now, sir?"

"Wake her up. Anything else?"

Million Man and Big Pang page through their notes. Million Man shakes his head.

"How about the company Horace works for?"

"Great Fortune?" says Big Pang.

"Yes. Maybe someone there has heard from Mo. And don't worry…"

"I know, sir," says Big Pang. "Wake them up."

Chapter Forty-Two

Mong Kok, Hong Kong, Wednesday, 10:25 p.m.

They wait until the street is deserted, and Horace hauls the boy across the pavement and into the apartment building like a mannequin, limp feet hovering a few inches from the floor.

There's no lobby as such, just a just a corridor with a stairwell and a single flat to the rear of the stairs. Easy access from the street is why Horace chose it. Doby wrestles the boy into the room, Horace's hand clamped over the boy's mouth the entire time. A clumsy dance through the corridor and he's in the room, another and he's tied to the bed with clothesline Horace bought for the purpose.

When Horace removes his palm, the boy starts to yell. Horace slaps his cheek soundly and the boy stiffens, his eyes welling with tears.

"If you shout, I'll do it again."

The boy turns toward Doby, his eyes making a silent but very obvious plea.

Horace watches them stare at each other. Infuriated, he grabs the boy by the collar.

"Pay attention to me, not him," says Horace.

"My *yeh yeh* will kill you," says the boy.

"Nothing your *yeh yeh* can do anymore."

"Your mother fucks monkeys."

"That's a pretty dirty mouth for such a young boy. Didn't you ever learn to respect your elders?" He seizes the boy's throat and squeezes. "Didn't you learn the proper way to speak to me?"

Horace studies the little half-Chinese boy, measures his mounting discomfort, his pain, and then his panic. When the boy's face is red as a New Year's lantern he releases him and stamps to the bathroom.

"Please," the boy says to Doby in a half-whisper, half whine. "Help me. I'll tell you where to get the comic."

"Where?" Doby says.

"What's this nonsense?" Horace thunders, charging back in. "Don't speak to him!" He looks down at his hands, then at the boy.

"Get me a knife," Horace says. He fishes a key ring from his pocket and works one of two identical keys off the loop to hand to Doby. "Use this to get in if I'm not here."

"Where should I get the knife?"

"I don't care, just buy me one!"

Doby moves to the door.

"Yan Tai, it's a shop on Tung Choi Street by Mongkok Road. They have the comic. Please help me."

"Go!" says Horace.

* * *

Mong Kok, Hong Kong, Wednesday, 10:48 p.m.

Knife, knife ... where do I go to find a knife? Doby climbs in the van and shoves the key in the ignition, but he doesn't start the engine. Instead, he closes his eyes and tries to make a picture in his head. Knives ... he once saw knives at the Wing On Department Store, but that's far away, on Des Voeux Road in Central. Was there someplace in Tsim Sha Tsui? It's hard to think straight. Maybe it'll be better to drive a while and look around.

He fires up the van and sets off down the street. Despite the late hour, restaurants and gift shops are still open. So are food stores and sundry shops.

Gradually the words of his father subside in his head, and those of the boy replace them. *Yan Tai, it's a shop on Tung Choi Street by Mongkok Road.* Could they still be open? Would they have knives too?

He arrives at Yan Tai to find it is a little sundry shop offering candy, soda, newspapers, a jumble of housewares, and toys. Doby's spirits drop to the pavement as he realizes they are closed. There's a light inside, however.

He parks a half block down the street, jogs back to the store, and peeks through the window. In the back, a family is having dinner.

He taps on the door. Nothing. He taps again, and inside a chair scrapes on a bare floor. Seconds later the door opens a crack.

"Come back tomorrow. Closed," says a man with a hoarse voice. He smacks his lips as he speaks, then daubs them with a paper napkin crumpled in his fingers.

"Do you have Green Warriors 3?"

"What?"

"The Legend of the Green Warriors, third part."

"What's that, a comic?"

Doby nods.

"Come back tomorrow; you can look."

"Can I buy it now?"

"Come back tomorrow. Are you deaf?"

"No. But I need to read it. Do you have it?"

The man thinks.

"If you want it now, it'll cost double."

Doby nods eagerly. The man opens the door and gestures to a rack in front of the counter. He flips a light switch, and the shop wakes up as if it's a new morning. Doby runs over and scans the pictures on the covers. In thirty seconds he's holding the final volume of the series.

"Five dollars, so that's ten," says the man. Doby fumbles in his pocket and hands the man his ten. In a moment he's out the door.

It's all Doby can do not to open the book and start reading. But he has a job to do. *Get me a knife.*

Then an idea comes upon Doby, a rare thing, especially an idea this good, an idea that seems to make real sense. He'll go back to the shop where *Ba Ba* bought a knife the other day, before they picked up that boy. Doby is not sure what *Ba Ba* did with that knife, or why he needs another, but the shop is certain to have one.

Ba Ba will be proud of him.

Chapter Forty-Three

Underneath Hong Kong Harbor, Wednesday, 11:10 p.m.

Lok, Ears, and Million man are in a blue and white, speeding through the Cross Harbour Tunnel toward Central. The Duty Controller called nine minutes ago with the news: the UB spotted the son's delivery van near the knife shop. According to the report, the son panicked and ran. He was fast, ducked down into the MTR and got lucky—managed to catch the Wan Chai line. Lok notified the Uniform Branch at all stations to watch out for him.

"What if he gets off at TST, sir?" says Ears.

"My guess is the boy will go Hong Kong side. He's trying to put real estate between himself and the cops chasing him. But notify Big Pang and Old Ko to meet the UB at Tsim Sha Tsui, just in case."

Million Man makes the call. No matter where the young man ends up, someone from Lok's team will be there. All they know is that Doby Yang is not too bright; whether that means trouble is not known.

They're shooting down Connaught Road when the District Console Supervisor's voice crackles on the radio.

"Suspect Doby Yang has been spotted in Central."

"Where? We're heading there now," says Lok.

"Two PCs gave chase on Man Po Street near the Finance Center Mall. He's running toward the Outlying Island Ferry Terminal."

Strange choice, Lok thinks. In less than two minutes they pull into the

Terminal. The last ferries have just docked and disgorged cataracts of day trippers.

"There, sir!" Ears shouts. He points to a head bobbing through the crowd, swimming against the tide. Doby has hopped the turnstile and is running towards the emptying ferry. The fool doesn't realize the ferry is moored for the night.

"Doby Yang!" Lok shouts. "Stop where you are!"

Doby looks back, his face contorted with fear, but he keeps running, bumping into startled people laden with backpacks and coolers.

"Stay here, in case he doubles back," Lok says to Million Man. "Ears, over there!" he shouts, pointing to the catwalk, a ledge jutting over the water, just wide enough for one ferryman to stand and tie up the boats.

Doby charges onto the boat, past a confounded old man in a blue sailor suit who is picking up trash from the tables. Lok follows, flashing his warrant card at the gawping ferryman. Doby bounds up the stairs to the top level of the ferry and bursts through the double glass doors to the outer deck.

Lok dashes after him. When he arrives at the outer deck, Doby is attempting to climb the outer railing back down to the lower level. *The kid doesn't know what he's doing,* Lok thinks.

"Stop, Yang *sin-sahng,*" Lok shouts. "We just want to talk to you. No need to run!"

Doby takes one look at Lok and jumps from the railing. His arm is outstretched to grab one of the steel braces between the decks. But his hand slips, and he plunges into the oily water between the ferry and the dock.

On the dock, Ears starts to remove his jacket and shoes.

"Don't jump in!" Lok shouts. He snatches a life preserver from the railing bracket and tosses it over.

"Grab this! Swim that way," Lok shouts, pointing into the harbor. "You need to get away from the boat!"

But Doby ignores the preserver, tries instead to scramble up the side of the ferry to the railing.

"Get out of there!" shouts Lok, but too late. A swell of the tide pushes the ferry toward the dock, slamming it into the piling once, twice, again, as it does hundreds of times each day. This time, Doby is between the boat and the piling. When the ferry floats free, Doby is limp and quiet, the fear in his face replaced with a look something like surprise.

"I couldn't do anything," says Ears. His voice cracks.

The ferrymen steady the boat and haul Doby out.

Chapter Forty-Four

Mong Kok, Hong Kong, Thursday, 12:16 a.m.

Doby has not returned from his errand. It's been an hour, spent unpleasantly staring at the dark, furious eyes of the boy and the dusty corners of the bedroom. Clothesline binds the boy's hands and feet, and a gag torn from the gray-white bedsheet keeps him silent. He lies on the bed, breathing, taking up space, reminding Horace that there remains something precious to Mo Tun that has not yet been taken from him.

Why not just strangle the little bastard? Horace itches to feel his fingers around that little throat again, but the knife will be…symbolic. It was a knife that Mo used on Horace. To see his own grandson gutted in the same manner will bring into Horace's life a kind of perfection. So rare, perfection, satisfaction, justice.

Where is Doby? Traffic? Not at this hour. Trouble finding a knife? More likely. Perhaps it was too much for the boy. At this hour, finding a knife might be hard.

Or he could have lost his way, forgotten where the flat was. Of course! Horace draws his cell phone from his pocket, dials Doby. It goes straight to voice mail.

"Doby. Don't worry if you can't find what I sent you for. Just listen to me. Don't go home. Don't come back to the where I am, or anywhere else. Just park somewhere and rest until 3 a.m. Then meet me in front of the building where you've been bringing the food. I'll see you there. Play back this message so that you remember it all. See you at three."

He glances once more at the phone log; the police have called again. His reply is to drop the device to the floor and bring his heel down onto it, once, twice, again, and again, until the screen is a crystalline powder. The boy looks on in terror.

Time to go. The boy can wait. Mo Tun can't. Horace tears some more strips from the bedsheet, ties the boy's hands to the headboard, his feet to the frame. He leaves, barely aware of the boy's eyes following him to the door.

Chapter Forty-Five

Tsim Sha Tsui, Hong Kong, Thursday, 1:29 a.m.

Mo steps out of the taxi at Star Ferry, about as unremarkable a destination as one can give a driver on Kowloon side. He half expects the driver to remind him that the ferry has shut down for the night, but the man says nothing; people use the ferry terminal as a rendezvous long past sailing hours. Another cab swings by the curb and disgorges three women in impossibly short skirts. To Mo they appear loud and empty-headed, with their spangles and cell phones and giggles, but they don't interest him.

From Star Ferry, Mo walks along Canton Road. The air is still warm and humid from the spring rain that washed over the city a few hours ago. The shops are closed here—all expensive fashion stores with European names like Chanel and Vuitton. It takes five minutes to reach the building that will house The Great Wall Disco. He passes the overpriced restaurant on the bottom floor—*eighty dollars for a plate of spring rolls, and they call me a crook?*—and enters the lobby, where four banks of elevators span the building's thirty floors, mostly offices. Under his arm, he clutches a flight bag full of money, the bag that sat on Horace Yang's desk a few hours ago. Yang won't know he's being paid the same money twice—the idiot won't have been back to his office now that the police are on to him.

What worries him is Jelly Pong. How did this character Yang manage to overpower Jelly and kill him? Jelly was no brain, to be sure, but he was younger than Horace by thirty years or so, and fit.

And where is Jelly's gun? Mo pondered bringing one himself but decided against it. *Horace Yang is an amateur, and an idiot as well. Best to fool him. Act sincere, offer payment in good faith, and wait until he's off guard. No telling what would happen with two men pointing guns at one another, one of them a madman.*

The elevator opens upon a dark corridor stripped of tile and paint and finished surfaces. A few safety lamps cast a harsh light upon the torn-up landscape of the room. He starts to thread his way through a maze of bare wood frames that await sheetrock. Not too much progress since his last inspection, he notes. *This thing is taking longer to build than the original Great Wall.*

"Where are you, Yang?' he shouts into the darkness. "I know who you are."

No answer.

"Horace Yang! I remember you. You thought you ruled your own little part of China. But you were a stupid bastard then, and you're one now." His words echo off the harsh concrete floor.

Mo walks through the room, past stacks of wood and boxes of hardware: bolts, screws, brackets, electrical conduit, bags of construction debris. Slowly he makes his way to the rear fire exit.

"Why don't you show yourself? I've got your money. Got my grandson? Let's hope he's all right, for your sa—"

A hissing sound emanates from behind an unfinished wall. The sound deepens, and then a rock smacks him in the face. He's on the ground, being pounded by *… what? Rocks... no... water... a spray... a fire hose, that's it. The prick is hosing me.*

He brings up his forearms to shield his face from the torrent and keep from drowning, but the pressure throws him off balance. A sharp whack in the buttocks tells him he's been knocked down. The money bag tumbles away. Disoriented, soaked, weakened, he feels the water pummeling him, pushing him along the floor. The jet smacks into his head and drives it into something hard. A flash of light explodes on his eyelids, and then nothing.

* * *

Mo awakens shackled to a pillar, a painted steel girder bolted securely to the floor and ceiling. The chain looped around his ankle is small enough to bind it snugly, strong enough to give him no hope of breaking it without a cutter. Padlocks secure it to his ankle and the pillar. Mo yanks the chain a couple of times, examines the locks, fingers the immense bolts that hold the pillar fast. *No way out here.*

Mo's suit is still dripping, so he can't have been unconscious long. The pain in his temple is still fresh, a raw throbbing that reaches into his head and behind his right eye.

The room, apart from him, is empty. One fluorescent bulb on a cord hangs from a ladder, casting into the room an austere light which fails toward the corners. Still, it's bright enough to reveal that the bag of money is gone. He feels for his cell phone; gone. He's checking to see what else is missing when a man walks through the shadows and into the edge of the dimness.

Horace Yang. The first name is new to him—he'd first heard it from Petula's trembling lips. It must have been a Hong Kong acquisition. Mo takes pride in having no English name. *I am Chinese,* he tells his men. *Let them learn my Chinese name.*

"Where's my grandson?" says Mo.

"Where do you think? He's dead." Yang is speaking Mandarin, and the words sound too familiar, almost invasive, as if the man is probing some private region of his mind.

"He's not dead. I don't believe you."

"I cut him open, the same way you cut me open."

"You don't have the balls. You're a coward. You always were—you need a mob to give you courage. Come out here into the light."

Horace Yang steps forward. He was never much to look at, and age has pulled some nasty tricks. Yang is shorter than Mo, with a flabby, pressed-in chin and dull eyes. Perspiration has soaked into his sparse hair and flattened it to his gleaming head. He wears a pale blue short-sleeve shirt and off-the-rack trousers from one of the Chinese department stores. *This is a dumb little bureaucrat, an office worker, an ant. How did I let this happen?*

"Why did you do it?" Horace says. Yes, that's the voice he heard on the phone. The idiot.

"What do you mean?"

"Don't pretend you don't know. Why did you attack me, leave me to die? You could have just gone away and let me continue."

"Continue? People like you can't continue on their own. You would have been caught within a day or two. And you would have given us up before you were shot."

"You would have been safe in Hong Kong."

"Maybe. Who knows?"

Mo gently tests the length of his chain: just a couple of feet. Horace hasn't left anything nearby for him to grab. He's an idiot, but he's crafty.

"Do you know why you're here?" Horace says.

"I suppose because I cut you with a knife, what, thirty years ago? Now you're the big man, is that right? Now you're on top, giving the orders. Congratulations."

Horace shakes his head. "I recovered from the cut. Somehow. But nothing was the same after that. No more school, no chance of anything in China."

"You came here, same as me. You had the same chance I did."

"*Hu shuo ba dao!*" Bullshit. "I had no chance. My chance was in Beijing, and you took it away from me."

"I gave it to you in the first place. You were a kid, a stupid kid who liked power and playing general and having girls held down while you did them. You wouldn't have had anything without me."

"I'd have been a university student in China."

Mo laughs. "Where are those university students now, Yang? How are they doing in China? I never had any university. But I knew how to work."

Yang stares at Mo, his jaw twitching.

"I worked all my life."

"You showed up at a job. That's not the same as working."

"What makes you think you can insult me now? You're chained to the floor."

Mo glances at the chain around his ankle, then looks up at Horace. "I gave you your money, Yang. What more do you want? Do you want my grandson for yourself? I'll bet he's told you what you're made of."

"I'm going to show you the body of your grandson."

"You know, Yang, you remind me a little of a guy I know, the one who got me the names of the people who were hoarding. They call him Dollar-ten. He's like you. He pissed away everything he had when he came to Hong Kong."

"I never had anything."

"You had two arms, a brain, a pair of balls. Too bad they were all too small to do you any good. Look at the people at the top here. Look how many of them started with nothing. And then you get a chance, and what do you do? You piss it away. Dollar-ten did that—he bet his money on horses. In a few weeks, everything he came with was owned by the Jockey Club.

"I told you, I had no money when I came. I had to wait tables."

Mo nods his head, as if he's had his conclusions confirmed. "So that's your complaint. You had to wait tables. Let me tell you a story. I once had to slice up a man who owed more than a hundred thousand to a loan shark. He was a teacher, of all things. Quiet man, a skinny little piece of shit like you, but decent enough. He just started losing too much at mahjong on weekends. He thought he was getting better at it, that he could win his money back. So naturally he gets in deeper than his teacher's salary can ever dig him out from.

"When I showed up, I thought he'd run, beg, hide under the kitchen table, that kind of thing. But you know what he did? He sat down, told me to have a seat, and said to do whatever I had to do.

"That was a new one for me. I asked him why he was so calm. And he asked me if I'd heard of Nasrdin Avanti. Know who that is?"

Horace stares for a few seconds, shakes his head.

"He's a character in some old stories from Yunnan. Clever bastard, this Avanti. One time, he borrows a big clay pot from a rich man. This man's a miser, always holds on to his stuff, but Avanti manages to borrow the big pot. He comes back the next day with two pots, the big one and a smaller one, and says, 'Congratulations! Your big pot had a baby!' And he gives the old miser both pots. The old bastard is happy, of course. He gets a free pot, right?

"Well, Avanti borrows the big pot again. The next day, he comes back with a sad look on his face, tells him that the big pot has died. The rich man says, 'What the hell are you talking about? A pot can't die.' Avanti laughs and says that if a pot can have a baby, it can die too."

"So what's that supposed to mean?" Horace says.

Mo leans back against the pillar. A cigarette would be good now. "It means that if you lead a certain kind of life, you've got to take what comes with it, good or bad. The teacher realized that he had become a gambler, in debt to a loan shark, and he had to take what went with the life."

"What did you do to him?"

"Cut off his ear, a couple of his fingers. He stuck them in a box with some ice and took a taxi to Queen Elizabeth hospital. But what I'm saying is, that teacher accepted what went with his life. The same with Dollar-ten—he realized he was a loser, that he'd never be rich, and he accepted that. But you won't accept the life you chose. You just blame me instead."

"Chose? You think I chose this life? My job, my wife, my children?"

"Do you ever go to a fortune teller, Yang?"

"No. Don't believe in them."

Mo nods. "All right, we've got that in common, at least. But I saw one the other day, and he did *chien tung*. You know what number came up? 53. *Ng sam*. Not born. Like they say, 5354. *Ng sam ng se*. Not living, not dead. The fortune teller was telling your fortune, not mine."

"Bullshit!"

"Oh, yes, Horace Yang. You were never born. You tried once, but you never got out of the womb. Instead, I aborted you. I cut your life short, just as if I'd killed you. You can murder me, take all the millions, and you'll still be dead. Because you don't have the courage to live. You never did. You were afraid every moment of your life. You were afraid to live your own life under the communists, so you signed up to be a Red Guard and kiss the ass of the Party. You were afraid to approach a woman unless your lieutenants tied her down for you. You were afraid to risk anything in Hong Kong—you just took a tiny little job, and the money they paid you like the sucker you are, year after year doing the same work.

"A wife, you say? Who did you marry? Some little nothing, some mouse who does whatever you say? You were the first man who asked her, and she was the first woman who said yes. And then you beat your kids, I'll bet. Oh, you're king in your little flat, because you're a dog everywhere else. And now you come to me wearing a cheap quartz watch and discount clothes and a peasant haircut and you want to blame me.

"Did you figure it out yet, Yang? You can't kill me—I already killed you. *Ng sam ng se!* You're a dead man, and your whole life has been —"

Horace lunges at Mo, seizes his throat, presses his neck into the pillar, and watches Mo's face turn red, then purple. Then he drops away, collapsing on his back at Mo's feet. Horace's shirt is a glistening pool of crimson. Mo grips his army knife, the one Yang didn't think to search for, concealed as it was in a tailored pocket by his ribs.

Horace gurgles a few words, then lies still.

"What's that you said, Yang? 'It was not supposed to be like this?'" Mo examines his own suit, drenched in blood. He reaches over and pats Horace's body; no cell phone, no padlock key. Not even a pack of cigarettes. Then he leans back against the pillar.

Not even a pack of cigarettes.

"You got that right."

Chapter Forty-Six

Central District, Hong Kong, Thursday, 1:18 a.m.

No crime scene people have been called to the pier; it was an accidental death, after all. The young, broken body is stretched out on the catwalk, awaiting the ambulance that Lok hears keening in the distance. The medical technicians will have no luck with this one, he thinks. Neither will Doctor Lee, because this time Lok knows more about how the victim died than the good doctor.

Lok kneels by the dead young man and goes through his pockets. A thin wallet, no credit cards, just some cash. A few coins, a ring of keys, and last, another key, this one shiny and new.

Million Man jogs onto the catwalk.

"Careful," Lok says. "We don't need two men in the harbor tonight."

"No, sir. I just heard from Old Ko. He checked Yang's phone records. His phone's not signaling now—the last calls we have are a few hours ago, from Mongkok."

It would have to be Mongkok, most populous district on earth.

"Here you go," says Lok. He hands Million Man the key.

"What's this, sir?"

"A key, Million Man."

The Detective Constable reddens slightly.

"Sir?"

"First thing tomorrow—I mean first thing, six a.m.—take this to every key maker in Mongkok. Find out if anyone remembers making it."

"Not too likely, sir."

"I know. But it's all we've got right now. I'm thinking Horace Yang rented an unregistered apartment."

"What do we do if we find the key maker?"

"That will give us an idea of where the flat is."

"And? We make copies and try every lock in Mongkok?"

Lok looks wearily into Million Man's young, uncomprehending face.

Chapter Forty-Seven

Mong Kok, Hong Kong, Thursday, 6:14 a.m.

Awakened by the dawn light, Bonitus blinks, then seizes in fright as he realizes that the nightmare is not over. He is still tied up like a hairy crab at market, muzzled like a dog.

The terrible man is gone. So is Doby.

He tries again to twist out of his bonds, but he tried for an hour last night and only succeeded in making his wrists and shoulders ache. The knots are just as tight now. And his arms still hurt, his hands are numb.

He's hungry. No one's fed him since they brought him to this room yesterday. And, with renewed anguish, he realizes he has to pee. Surely they'll come soon and let him go to the bathroom, or at least give him a wastebasket.

For a while he holds it in, thinking about his empty stomach, and the four walls of the room. It looks a bit less gloomy in the morning light, but just as shabby as when he first saw it last night. Not like his own flat, with its gleaming wood floors and vast windows.

The minutes pass, and then an hour, then two, and finally, desperate and ashamed, he releases a flood of urine and tears.

Chapter Forty-Eight

Kowloon, Hong Kong, Thursday, 8:18 a.m.

What surprises Million Man is that none of the men and women are surprised. Each time he hands over Doby's key, the key maker examines it, shrugs, gives a noncommittal answer, but doesn't think it strange that a policeman would be asking if he could recognize a key as one of his.

The fifth place Million Man visits is Fook Lee Shoes and Keys on Argyle Street. The proprietor is one Leung Tai-kok, a hawklike fiftyish man with shoulders bent by work and fingers stained by nicotine. Leung takes the key and places it under a desk lamp on his tool bench. He pulls down the eyeglasses that had been perched on his forehead and studies the key, first one side, then the other.

"Yes, it's mine," he says.

"You're serious? You know it's yours?"

"It's mine."

"How can you tell?"

Leung removes his glasses and looks at Million Man. "What do you mean? How can I tell? Do you know your job? I know mine. I make keys every day and have for thirty years. See this spine of mine?" He reaches over his shoulder and pats his own back for emphasis. "I'm bent like a willow from leaning over the grinder every day, year after year." He holds up the key and points to what looks to Million Man like nothing at all.

"These two diagonal file marks? Theyr'e my signature. I do that on every key I make. Also, see how clean it is, how all the flash is filed smooth." He runs his hands along the blade of the key, from bow to tip. "You see? No resistance when the key enters the lock." He mimes the insertion and removal of a key. "Only someone who really knows keys would do that. You have to be the best, and that's me. Those kids at the shop across the street don't know the first thing about craftsmanship. If it's in Mongkok and it's made well, it's my key. Never forget that."

Million man doubts he will. He produces the photos of Doby and Horace.

"Do you recognize either of these people?"

Leung takes a quick glance, shakes his head. "I don't notice people much. I'm concentrating on my keys…"

Million man steps outside, calls Lok and reports. Lok listens, then gives Million Man his next order.

Million Man walks back into Fook Lee Shoes and Keys and tosses Doby's key on the counter.

"A hundred copies, please. Right away."

* * *

Two hundred men from the Uniform Branch, YauTsim District, began searching before noon. They go in pairs, armed, since there is a chance that Horace Yang will be with the child and he could be violent.

A circle has been drawn that encompasses most of Mongkok. The PCs work their way along each street, entering each residential building and trying each lock with their key. They have been told to average one lock per minute, which means the entire available force will try six thousand doors per hour, or sixty thousand at the end of a ten-hour day. After ten hours they will be relieved, handing their keys to another two hundred men who will take up the search.

The second shift is not needed. At three thirty-five p.m., two PCs find that the key fits a lock—something that happens about one out of four times, and turns—something that has never yet happened. Following instructions, they enter the flat, guns drawn, to find a boy, tied and gagged, almost unconscious from hunger and fatigue and despair, but alive.

* * *

Tsim Sha Tsui, Hong Kong, Thursday, 5:09 p.m.

Once Bonitus Mo is reunited with his parents and placed safely in the hospital for observation, Lok meets with his team to step up the search for Mo Tun.

"Lento is in China," says Old Ko. "Here is the info from Immigration. Mo wasn't with him."

"Why would Mo want to hide from us?" asks Ears.

"He put a child in danger by not reporting a kidnapping," says Million Man.

"Don't think he's worried about any charges coming from that," says Lok. He'll just claim that he'd been threatened by the kidnapper and was too frightened to report it."

"Mo, scared?" says Big Pang.

"Ridiculous, I know, but it's not likely that a magistrate will pursue charges. Prosecuting families of kidnapped kids isn't high on our list."

"Sir, I spoke with Petula Hsiao, the woman at Great Fortune Property Management," says Big Pang. "This might or might not be of interest. She says that construction has been halted on the disco. The site was shut down yesterday, due to non-payment of fees. Nothing will happen there until the construction people get paid."

Lok ponders this. "Not sure what it has to do with us. Mo must be lying low with his lawyers, cooking up some alibis. Now where are we with Horace Yang?"

"We've posted a couple of men from UB at his flat, in case he turns up there."

"Don't think he will," says Lok, "unless he breaks down completely and gives up. But we'll find him."

Lok is keen to capture Horace Yang alive; he wants to know why an accountant became a murderer and a kidnapper. If they find Horace, he'll tell them. If they find his body, then that will be Mo Tun's doing, and they will lean on Mo until they get an answer.

Million Man says, "We've circulated his photo and description to the UB, taxi drivers, Traffic, MTR and ferry personnel, airport. He's not getting out. Hey, did you see this in the description? 'Vertical scar running from neck to navel.' Wonder where that came from?"

Lok shrugs. "We've all got scars, Million Man."

* * *

Tsim Sha Tsui, Hong Kong, Thursday, 6:26 p.m.

Million Man is alone in the meeting room when a woman opens the door and leans in. She's well-dressed, middle-aged, slightly plump, but nicely put together. She's carrying a small attache case and a shopping bag from Wing On. Her hair is bobbed and shiny, the tips curling inward on her rounded face, two inverted commas setting off her smile. A businesswoman, Million Man guesses, or a city official meeting with one of the Big Balls.

"Is Ko Man-man here?" she says.

"Old Ko?"

"Yes." She stifles a small giggle. "That's what they call him. I'm Cherry Chang, his wife."

Not bad, Million Man thinks. This lady was a beauty in her day. The thought of Old Ko married to someone this alluring upsets his estimate of his colleague. Perhaps his own affair with Icy, who's got a good ten years on him, has awakened him to the charms of older women.

"Should be back pretty soon," he says. "Have a seat." He ushers her into the meeting room.

"Thank you. I've been on my feet all day. Are you on my husband's team?"

Million Man nods, introduces himself. Cherry's smile turns slightly sly. "Is he giving you a hard time?"

He laughs. "I suppose so. But I give as good as I get."

They talk for a few minutes about her job with the Hong Kong Government, about policemen's wives, the horse racing that Old Ko loves so much. They talk about Inspector Lok, of course. In minutes they're laughing and she brings up the idea of going out to dinner some time.

"Not sure that your husband would be in favor of that."

"Leave him to me. He does what I tell him."

"And here I thought you had an unusual marriage."

"We do."

"How so?"

Cherry glances at the door, as if wary of interruptions. "Can you keep a secret?"

He nods.

"I'm serious. This can't go beyond us."

"I can keep it to myself, whatever it is."

She leans back in her chair, folds her hands in front of her. "I worked in a bar, the Lucky Man, in Tsim Sha Tsui. That was a long time ago, believe me."

Million Man does his best to show no reaction. Lucky Man is an infamous topless bar, one of the oldest in town. His eyes move inadvertently to her chest for a moment. He hopes she didn't catch that.

"Back then, I was going out with—forget that—I belonged to a Sun Yee On Red Pole, Freddie Mok. A really nasty character. Man-man walked in one day, on his rounds, and caught my eye. He showed up again when a drunk Australian got mad about being overcharged and started knocking over stools and tables. I was just coming off shift, and he caught up with me outside, asked me out. It was a crazy thing for a cop to do. I was up to my neck in gangsters, and the bar was into money laundering, drugs, everything. In those days I was chasing the dragon, too."

Million Man is taken aback by that. This vivacious older woman smoking heroin? Can't be.

She reads his thoughts. "I know, I don't look the type now. But I was a different woman then, believe me. I tried to get rid of Man-man, told him I was on drugs, told him I was no good, but he wouldn't listen. Every night he met me after work, a few blocks away from the bar. In no time we fell in love.

"I was scared of what Freddie Mok would do. He was violent, with no conscience whatever. If he found out about us, he'd go crazy. And Man-man knew this, so he walked into the bar one night and told Freddie he wanted to buy me out. That's the only way to get a triad's girl, so that he doesn't lose face. It cost him fifty thousand. Back then, that must have been eight years' pay. He'd been saving up for a flat, and he gave him all that and borrowed more. Then he got me off drugs and married me."

Million Man struggles for words and gives up. Anything he can say will render him a fool for everything he's said up to now.

"Eventually, he paid everything off, and I went to school and got a job. But someone had noticed him hanging out at the Lucky Man, which was an unapproved place of business, off limits to policemen. A notice went in his file, and that's all it took. It didn't matter how he did on his promotion exams. He was going to stay a PC."

"Doesn't sound fair. Couldn't he explain to the brass?"

"You know what it's like. Why promote someone with anything at all on his record when there are nice clean boys they can move up?"

He gets the implication—nice clean boys like Million Man.

He's about to thank her for telling him when the door clicks open, and Old Ko strides in.

"So there you are," Ko says.

"That's right. I've been chatting with Million Man here."

"That must have been informative. Did he tell you he knows everything?"

Her smile brightens a few degrees.

* * *

Tsim Sha Tsui, Hong Kong, Thursday, 9:41 p.m.

While the team waits for the check at Harbour Palace Seafood Restaurant, Old Ko and Million Man argue about how far Flying Hawk had pulled away from the field in the 1200 at Happy Valley.

"He's always bad on that track," says Old Ko. "He needs at least 1400 meters to perform at his best."

"You're crazy. You could give him twice that, and he'd still be running now."

A waiter places the bill on the table. Lok calls him aside and says, "Get me Ocean Yeh." The waiter, a teenage boy, doesn't seem to understand the order, so Lok repeats it slowly and dismisses him. A few minutes later the man he'd seen in front of Lai-ping's flat appears. Again, it's a t-shirt under a jacket, a look he obviously considers flattering.

"Meet me outside," Lok says to the team. They remove themselves, and Lok gestures to a seat. Ocean is a couple of inches shorter than Lok, but he has a barrel chest and powerful shoulders. A gold Rolex peeks out from underneath his jacket cuff.

"You know who I am?"

Ocean shakes his head.

"My name is Herman Lok. CID, YauTsim."

"How can I help you? I'd..."

"Don't bother acting friendly. Lai-ping must have told you about me."

"Sorry, no."

He lets that sink in.

"Lai-ping is a good woman."

"Sure. What's your interest in her?"

"Just that I don't want her hurt. I know you were mixed up with her brother, probably got him killed. Lai-ping's had enough pain for one lifetime. I don't want you causing her anymore."

"Now wait, you can't..."

"I can. But I'm willing to deal. Name the fee."

Ocean Yeh sits back in his chair, now at ease. "Forget it," he says.

"Name the fee."

He shakes his head. "She doesn't want to leave me. No sale."

Lok nods. "Listen to me," he says, leaning forward to cast his shadow in Ocean's face. "Lai-ping is grown up, and she can do what she wants. But if you ever hurt her in any way, I will come for you. I will tear your business down brick by brick and throw it into the harbor. I will arrest everyone you ever knew. I will tell your superiors that you're putting their operations in danger by being an asshole. And I'll be telling the truth."

"What are you saying, Lok? You want me to be scared, is that it?"

"No, Ocean, I want you to be smart. I'll be checking on Lai-ping from time to time. If I ever hear that she's unhappy, that you've treated her like shit the way you people usually treat your women, then you're finished. If you shame her, or endanger her in any way, then you are beyond help. God help you if you raise a hand to her. No one saves a mad dog. They just put it out of its misery."

Ocean springs to his feet, sending the chair clattering to the floor, and storms out of the restaurant.

* * *

Mongkok District, Hong Kong, Sunday, 1:04 a.m.

"One a.m....this always happens around one," Icy says, her eyes drifting across his lean, naked body to the nightstand clock.

"What?"

She draws a slow, deep breath. "What I'm going to say." She turns onto her elbows and draws the sheet over her body. Million Man senses that she's covering herself to keep from distracting him. Good move.

"Million Man, I haven't told you much about me."

"What do I need to know? Want a beer?" He starts to get up.

"No. Stay here." She gathers her thoughts in silence. "My life is ... complicated."

"I know you're busy. Your job must be really …"

"It's more than a job."

"Sure. I understand."

"No you don't—LF Industries? That's Lung Fong. My family is Fong."

"What?"

"It's my company, Million Man. When my father died, it went to me."

"You're an heiress?"

"I'm not an heiress. I'm an owner. I run it."

"That must be…interesting."

"Million Man, it's the ninth largest company in Hong Kong."

"So what are you saying?"

"I can't really get attached to a man. There's too much going on. It's been hard enough getting to see you these few times. There's no possibility of a real relationship when I'm so busy."

"We have a real relationship."

She ponders this. "Yes, in a way. But it's not going anywhere. I chose you because I knew it wouldn't go anywhere."

His mouth drops open, but words are slow to come. "I don't believe you said that."

"Don't take it wrong. You're a lovely man and I enjoy being with you. But you're not the man you're going to be in a few years. You still have a lot to learn. You make everything a show—the car, the clothes, the restaurants. That never lasts. I've seen older men put on the same show, and it's pathetic. If you put all that energy into being the real Million Man, you could do anything."

"But we're so happy. This is going so well."

"Things will change, I guarantee it. You'll start to feel neglected, resentful. There's no way I can build anything worthwhile with a guy like you—the timing isn't right."

"But…" His voice cracks, and he stays silent.

"Oh, I've hurt you. I didn't want to do that. You're so wonderful. And we had so much fun."

She kisses him on the lips, and he feels the warmth once again, and he wonders what that warmth really is. She stands up and begins to dress.

"You don't have to go," he says.

"I'd rather. But I have a gift for you."

"That's okay." The words sound lame and a little disagreeable. He feels as if he's been drenched with water.

"I made a few payments for you," she says.

"You what?"

"I paid off your car, and I paid your rent for a year. That should help you get settled."

Again his jaw opens. When he gains control, he sputters something about not needing it. Now fully dressed, she leans over him and clasps his hands in hers.

"Look, Million Man, I could spend money like other people. One woman I know has ceramic dogs—hundreds of them. Do I look like the kind of person who'd collect ceramic dogs? I could collect great art, but the people I'm surrounded by don't care about art, and frankly, I don't either. So what do I spend my money on? Men. Good looking, smart, sexy men.

She leans closer and kisses him one last time, then embraces him in a manner suggesting a shared triumph. The way his mother embraced him when he got good marks on a test.

"Remember me," she says.

* * *

Kowloon District, Hong Kong, Sunday, 11:57 a.m.

The three warriors await execution in the dungeon of the Old King, while the song and laughter of the victory celebration fills the castle.

The Old King's daughters, angry that their father is about to kill their brave and handsome husbands-to-be, decide to rescue the men. Disguising themselves as servants, they descend into the dungeon and concoct a scheme.

Lanterns are everywhere during the festival. Musicians are playing, guests are feasting, and at the height of the evening, a troupe of actors appear to thank the Old King for conquering the Western kingdom.

"Things were very difficult before, under the last king," said the actor who plays the red-faced demon. "Thank you for banishing him. We would like to perform in your honor tonight."

Pleased and flattered, the Old King agrees.

While the actors set up their stage in the palace, the three daughters tell their brother, the prince, to announce that this is a very special performance, celebrating a great victory, and everyone should attend.

In a short while, the room is crammed with people, and the rest of the palace is deserted.

The three women sneak away during the play and release the three warriors. They ride all night and all the next day to reach the western kingdom, one swordsman and one daughter to each horse. They arrive to find the monarch of the western kingdom imprisoned in his own palace. In one quick and fierce battle, they fight off the Old King's guards and free the prisoner.

The next day the western kingdom's armies mount an attack, and this time they are the ones who are prepared. In the fierce battle they free their kingdom and conquer the Old King's lands as well. Out of thanks to the Old King's daughters, they let the old king live.

The ruler of the Western Kingdom is grateful to the trio. He gives each of them land and gold. They marry the daughters of the Old King and continue to fight for the just.

The End

Lok closes the comic and lays it on the table, taking a last look at the three warriors on the cover. He hadn't read a comic book since he was a kid, but this one had fallen out of Doby Yang's jacket during the chase. The young man was clearly attached to it; he'd cast a panicked glance at the book when it fell, and even seemed to consider interrupting his flight to pick it up.

"Dora," Lok says.

"Mmm." Dora is at the computer in Edna's room, Edna being out late as always. Studying at the university, Lok hopes.

"Come in here for a second?"

She does. Lok rarely asks her to drop what she's doing. "What's going on?" she says. "How's the comic book?"

He smiles and makes an indifferent gesture. "I didn't catch the first episodes, so I didn't know what was going on. But I want to ask you…"

"What?"

"Ah…do you…"

She tilts her head to get a new angle of vision on her husband.

"You look nice," he says.

"Thank you. You didn't call me out for that."

He takes a few seconds to think, and she waits. One of Dora's good instincts, when to talk and when not to. If Lok could only find the gene for that trait and clone it.

"I've been gone a lot lately," he says finally.

"Right. The Mo Tun case. You haven't caught the murderer yet, have you?"

"No, but this isn't about that. I'm usually working when I stay out late, but sometimes…"

"Oh, is this about the woman you're seeing? The young one who doesn't have a lot of money?"

Lok feels blood rush to his head, as if he'd been picked up and held by his feet like a chicken. "How did you…"

Dora sits on the edge of the chair opposite him. "You go to her flat about twice a week."

"Yes, but…" It sounds like a surveillance report.

"And you're not sleeping with her," she says.

"Of course not, but how did you…"

"Herman, you have long days and short days. On the long days, if I can't reach you, you come home with your hands smelling of a different soap—sandalwood and lavender. Only a woman would buy soap like that. The soap at the station is just some industrial stuff."

Soap, Lok thinks, but he's not really thinking yet.

"And the money?"

She lowers her head in the tiniest gesture of disappointment at her husband the detective. "That soap was on sale at Watson's a couple of months ago. I took a sniff. Not great stuff, but cheap."

Lai-ping's soap. Something so simple.

"And how did you know I'm not sleeping with her?"

She smiles. "Really, Herman. The soap smell is only on your hands. I'm not stupid, you know."

No, Dora is not. Relief floods into his body as if a dam had burst. He tells the whole story to her, of a girl left alone after brother was killed in a shootout. How he was worried that Lai-ping would go the way of so many gangster's women, and how he might have failed, now that Ocean Wong has his hooks into her. He explains that the dance lessons were a way of getting her to meet people, seeing a side of Hong Kong life that she wouldn't see in her little Wah Fu estate flat. He leaves out his one night of temptation, but wonders if she can guess that too.

"Herman, it's so obvious that you were trying to be a father to her. Why do you get so nervous?"

"She's young." He turns away in embarrassment. "I think she had feelings for me ..."

"...and that's why you suggested dancing lessons—lots of people around, so you'd be safe."

Another revelation. "Yes, I suppose so..."

"Herman, you have a lot to learn about women. But I'm not mad at Lai-ping. I have those feelings for you, too, you know." She kisses him on the ear.

Lok turns to Dora and studies her face. *Do not forget this, Lok. Whatever happens, do not forget the kind of woman you married.* He takes a breath and picks up a sheaf of papers he's been meaning to get to—a guide to properly formatting crime statistics for submission to the Service Quality Wing for their latest initiative.

With a gentle tug, Dora removes it from his hand and settles on his lap.

"Do you think your dance class would be shocked," she says, "if you showed up with a new partner?" Their lips meet.

Chapter Forty-Nine

Happy Valley, Hong Kong, Monday, 9:08 a.m.

Eunice arrives in her office to find Sylvie in her chair, hands cradling her head.

"Are you all right, Sylvie?"

"Hello Aunt Eunice," says Bonitus, from the corner of the room. Eunice sees the boy and runs to him, hugs him. "Bonitus! Wonderful to see you!"

"I'm all right," says Sylvie.

She turns to Sylvie. "Yes you are. How are you managing all this?"

"Bonitus," Sylvie says, "Go to the second-floor lounge. There's a TV there. I'll come for you later." Her son obeys.

"Oh, sorry," says Sylvie. "Want your chair?"

"Later. What's up? Why isn't Bonitus in school?"

Sylvie seems preoccupied. "What? Oh, there were too many reporters. They said to give him a day off."

"Maybe you should take a day off too, be with Ivan."

Her head jerks as if she's just awakened, and she turns to face Eunice. "He was just some madman, Eunice. A madman who knew Ivan's father in China. It wasn't business; it wasn't under my father-in-law's control for one minute. I was lied to. Bonitus might have been killed. He was probably going to be killed." Tears fill her eyes.

Eunice sits across from Sylvie and grasps her hands. "Sylvie, sweetheart, it's all right. You're still suffering the trauma of all this. It must have been terrible."

"I can't take this," she says through the tears.

"It's over. It's okay."

"It's not over! I'm furious at him! He chose his father over Bonitus. Over me. And I was stupid beyond belief. I let them cow me into keeping quiet. It was a kidnapping, for God's sake. No worse crime on the books, and I sat there and let Ivan convince me that his father knew what was best."

"I understand. But Ivan really believed his father was doing the right thing." She grips Sylvie's hand a little tighter.

"They held my son prisoner for days. Should I just forgive them for that? If it weren't for the police, who knows if he'd even be alive?"

"You're right." Eunice releases her hands and sits back. "I'm trying to be the cool-headed one here, but…"

"I've had it up to here with filial piety," Sylvie says. "I thought I could do this. Do you know what Ivan's family says? That I'm a good wife, even for a Chinese."

"You are."

"Is that what being a good wife is? Obeying your husband even when your child's life is at stake? Trusting that your husband's criminal father knows how to deal with his criminal friends? I can't do this, Eunice."

"Maybe you just need some time…"

"I was typing up my notice. On the way out, I'll retrieve it from the printer, sign it, and leave it at the desk for you. I made reservations for Bonitus and me. We're on a plane tomorrow."

Eunice withdraws from the embrace and looks at her. "Are you sure about this, Sylvie?"

A man's voice interrupts. "Sure about what? Oh, hi, Eunice."

Ivan is in the doorway, dressed for business, briefcase in hand. "I didn't see you this morning, so I thought I'd check in on you. Did Bonitus get off to school?"

Sylvie stares at Ivan. Then she stands and walks out. Ivan turns to the empty doorway, then to Eunice.

"Is she okay?" he says.

Eunice shakes her head.

Chapter Fifty

Tsim Sha Tsui, Hong Kong, Monday, 10:44 a.m.

Something taints the air now, a close, fetid smell. Mo has seen a few corpses in his time, but he's never been close to one for this long. Horace Yang is lying on his back at arm's length—the distance Mo could kick the body. The blood no longer catches the gleam of the light, having faded by the hour and caked dry into a rivulet that runs from Yang's belly to the center of the room.

Mo spent the first day getting explanations ready. If a security guard turns up, he'll bribe him within an inch of his life. *Just let me go and forget what you saw.* Same if it's one or two construction workers. If the whole crew shows up at once, he'll have to give them a story about how Yang chained him and attacked him—not too far from the truth, in fact. The best lies are never too far from the truth.

If the police come first, he'll try the same story. They'll see the money, the chains, and figure that Yang had gone nuts during the payoff and tried to kill Mo. Not far from the truth either.

Mo spent the second day thinking about a drink. Food, too, but mostly drink. Beer, tea, even water wouldn't be bad at this point. It might ease his pounding temples, moisten his arid throat and tongue. He's weakening, no doubt about that. How long has it been since he's had food and water? Did he eat at all the day before he was chained up? Too far back to remember.

But someone will come soon.

* * *

Item 41

A LARGE SANCAI-GLAZED BUFF POTTERY FIGURE OF A CAPARISONED HORSE
Tang Dynasty

The powerfully and naturalistically modeled horse stands foursquare on a rectangular base with ears pricked forward, harnessed with brown-glazed straps. It has a green-glazed saddle over a pleated saddle cloth decorated with green, amber, and straw glazes. The mane is cropped, the tail bound, and the body straw glazed.

16in. (40.6cm.) long

One of two matched horses which decorated the tomb of Tang Dynasty general Po Wen-yu (C.E. 582- 649). The other is believed to have been destroyed during the Cultural Revolution.

Acknowledgements

My thanks to those kind souls who read my manuscript early on and offered priceless aid: Lincoln Potter, Ron McMillan, Kathleen Hall, Cecily Patton, Colette Martin, Susanna Martin, Mary-Anne Martin, and Lynn Bump.

In Hong Kong, I owe a lot to my friends in the Hong Kong Police Force. Carol Leung is my adviser on Cantonese, Hong Kong, and Chinese culture. My gratitude is as boundless as her knowledge and patience.

Many, many thanks to Gerald Elias, creator of violinist-detective Daniel Jacobus, for dispensing his knowledge generously and opening some vital doors so I could waltz on through.

I thank Deb Well, Shawn Reilly Simmons, and the marvelous people at Level Best Books for taking me on and dedicating their precious time to bringing my book up to their standards.

I'm also indebted to Eric Shalit for the eye-popping cover, as well as years of friendship and invigorating repartee.

My wife Catherine has been a wellspring of love, encouragement, and tolerance. As Inspector Lok said: *Whatever happens, do not forget the kind of woman you married.* My son Toby is no slouch in the LET department either. Consider this a bear hug in print.

Finally, a hat tip to my writer's group, for all the advice and inspiration they've offered me over the years: Arthur Conan Doyle, Anton Chekhov, Elmore Leonard, Edgar Allan Poe, Cornell Woolrich, Donald E. Westlake, Mark Twain, Dorothy B. Hughes, James Crumley, John Ball, William McIlvanney, Richard Neely, Agatha Christie, Martin Amis, James McClure, Charles Williams, Jack O'Connell, George Orwell, Charles Dickens, John D. Macdonald, Daphne DuMaurier, Shirley Jackson, Joseph Conrad, Frederic Brown, Vera Caspary, Iain Banks, Ray Bradbury, P.D. James, Chester Himes,

Ross Macdonald, and Roald Dahl. Let me know if we're still on for Thursday night, okay, guys?

255

About the Author

Charles Philipp Martin, author of two Inspector Lok novels, has been an orchestral bass player, jazz musician, broadcaster, and newspaper columnist in Hong Kong. His short stories have appeared in the anthologies *Hong Kong Noir* and *The Killing Rain*. Born in New York, he now lives in Seattle with his wife Catherine.

SOCIAL MEDIA HANDLES:
  Twitter (x.com): NeonPanicHK
  Facebook: Neon Panic on Facebook
  (https://www.facebook.com/HongKongSuspense)

AUTHOR WEBSITE:
  neonpanic.com
  rentedgrave.com

Also by Charles Philipp Martin

Novels:

Neon Panic, Vantage Point Books, 2011

Short stories:

"Smash & Grab" in *The Killing Rain* (Down & Out Books 2024)

"Ticket Home" in *Hong Kong Noir* (Akashic Books 2018)

"Lau the Tailor" in *Manoa, Vol. 10, The Zigzag Way* (University of Hawai'i Press 1998)